The Museum of Doubt

JAMES MEEK was born in London in 1962 and grew up in Dundee. He has published three novels, *Mcfarlane Boils The Sea* (1989), *Drivetime* (1995) and *The People's Act of Love* (2005), and one other collection of short stories, *Last Orders* (1992). *The Museum Of Doubt* (2000) was shortlisted for a Macmillan Silver Pen award. Meek also contributed to the acclaimed Rebel Inc. anthologies *Children Of Albion Rovers* (1996) and *Rovers Return* (2001).

He has worked as a newspaper reporter since 1985. He lived in the former Soviet Union from 1991 to 1999. He now lives in London, where he writes for the *Guardian*, and contributes to the *London Review of Books* and *Granta*. In 2004 his reporting from Iraq and about Guantanamo Bay won a number of British and international awards. *The People's Act of Love* has been translated into twenty languages.

The
Museum
of Doubt

James Meek

F/ 2063829

CANONGATE
Edinburgh · New York · Melbourne

First published in Great Britain in 2000 by
Rebel Inc, an imprint of
Canongate Books Ltd, 14 High Street,
Edinburgh EH1 1TE

This edition published by Canongate in 2006

1

Stories in this collection have previously appeared
in *Ahead of It's Time*, *Billy Liar* and *Rovers Return*

Permission has been sought for the use of lyrics from
I Won't Love You Anymore by Lesley Gore

British Library Cataloguing-in-Publication Data
A catalogue record for this book is available on
request from the British Library

1 84195 808 5 (10-Digit ISBN)
978 184195 808 8 (13-Digit ISBN)

Typeset by Palimpsest Book Production Ltd,
Polmont, Stirlingshire
Printed and bound by Clays Ltd, St Ives plc

CONTENTS

The Museum of Doubt

I want to give you a demon. I want to give you a demonstration of something unlike anything you've ever seen before.

I beg your pardon? she said, Bettina Dron, bed and breakfast proprietor.

I want to give you a demonstration.

He was white tinged with yellow, like splatters of curdled milk, and hair black as a rook in a birdbath. It sizzled up thick and sleek from his scalp, went frying down his chops in whirling vortextual sideburns that ended suddenly, not cut, not shaved, it went from thick to nothing, from jungle to wax. There were moles on his cheeks with the hair pouring in a spout from them like from guttering after a downpour. It was dark and fine. Without touching him she knew his flesh was hot. A thick car crouched behind him on the drive.

Jack Your Firm's Name Here, he said, sitting next to her on the sofa, their knees almost touching. He smiled. Bettina put one hand to her mouth and another to her heart, it'd doubled its speed. His teeth were so beautiful.

Call me Jack. That's my Christian name.

Bettina. Her fingers turned her wedding ring.

Why not rent my name? said Jack. I travel the length of the

land. I'd be Jack Pinetops-Guesthouse. I was Jack Microsoft for a while but after six months they wanted to upgrade me to a new version and I couldn't afford the facial surgery.

Bettina was tempted even though her B&B wasn't called Pinetops. It was called Dron's B&B. In the furthest synapses of her brain Pinetops had crackled unrecognised, unspoken, till now. There was a regiment of pine trees on Hill of Eye, and from the upstairs window you could see the tops of them. She asked Jack for a price.

A price? said Jack. He smiled, his eyes widened half an inch and his eyebrows seesawed queasily up and down. Surely you can't mean money? Do they still use money in these parts?

I've got a Mastercard.

Mastercard! My dear Bettina, Jack Transaction Pending hasn't been Jack Mastercard for many a midsummer moon. Do you have any water? I'm thirsty. Can it really be true that you haven't heard of the Friedrich Nietszche Marketingschule? Every morning we chanted in unison: Does a mother expect to be paid for loving her child? Prices! Bettina, I'm touched.

Tears shone in Jack's eyes. He took a glass thimble and a packet of peanuts out of his pocket. He scooped the tears into the thimble, ripped the packet open with his teeth, downed the liquid and emptied the nuts in after them. With his mouth full, shaking his head, he went on: To think I would have come here to sell you something. To think I would have come all this way in order to exchange some – some good, some item, some simple service for a unit of currency. Oh, Bettina! For you – do you know, I almost would. But there's no need. I may appear to you to be a salesman. I have things to give, things to show and much to explain. I have nothing to sell. You may ask: But is there a product? A product, dear Bettina. There are many products. You might as well enter a forest glade on a sunny spring day and ask, but is there a leaf? You might as well look down on the city and ask, but is there a window? Excuse me for one moment.

Jack got up and ran to the kitchen. He stood with his back to the sink and bent backwards till his spine was u-shaped. He slid his mouth underneath the tap and reached out to switch it on. The water gushed in a smooth stream down his throat, which had no Adam's apple.

Would you like a glass? said Bettina, standing in the doorway, stroking her fingers.

Jack shook his head. Steam wisped from his mouth around the silver tube of water.

Would you not rather use the cold tap? said Bettina.

Jack switched the tap off and sprang up straight. He shook his head and gestured her back to the lounge. She sat down and he squatted on the rug between her and the fire, where pinelogs were burning. The hot water had put colour in his cheeks. His face had turned a chilly pink, like frozen cooked prawns.

Bettina, we've moved beyond money, he said. The forces that summon objects to you must be more powerful, more real than money. The force of time, the force of life, the force – dearest Bettina – of love. Tell me this. Have you worked your whole life to earn enough money to get the things you want for yourself and the people you love? Have you?

Yes I have, said Bettina.

Of course you have! cried Jack. Now, let's sweat the fat off that proposition. First you want to take away the earning and the money. That's just a mechanism. Do you have to see your heart beating to know that you're alive? We need to see the big picture. So what do we do, we climb onto the roof and go up the ladder and get into the basket of the balloon and fly up ever so high, ever so high, till we look down on the world below, and everything looks so very different, so much simpler than it did from down on the ground, doesn't it. Doesn't it, Bettina? What do we see from way up there when we look down? Mm? D'you know? Mm? Of course you do. We can see the truth! We can see the big, plain truth. And you know what that truth is, don't you. Yes. The plain truth is that you've worked your whole life to get the things you want.

But just tell me one thing, Bettina. Just one little thing, mm? Not a big thing, a tiny little thing, but ever so important. Here's the thing: what's work? Mm? What's work? Hard labour? Climbing the stairs, gardening, is that work? Is it? Breathing, is that work? It can be difficult sometimes, we all know that. Or cooking, frying eggs, making a sandwich, is that work? Can be, may be, might be. Maybe it's leisure. Maybe you like it. Maybe you don't. Or breaking rocks. Ever tried breaking rocks? No? More enjoyable than you could possibly imagine. Or strangling chickens. Could be work – could be leisure. For me, leisure, but who knows? Each to their own. Sex. For me, work, but again, some people like to relax like that. You see which way we're moving here, little Bettina? Work is another one of these primitive ideas. People used to think everything was made up of earth, air, fire and water, and now we know everything is made up of little atoms too tiny to worry about. Everything is smooth. People used to think life was made up of work and leisure but now we know there's only life. So what do we have now? You've lived your whole life to get the things you want. This is like x equals x equals y, right, so let's strip it down to this: your whole life for the things you want. Are you following me?

I think so, said Bettina.

X equals y, so y equals x, so what do we end up with?

The things I want for my whole life, said Bettina.

Excellent! said Jack. And now, with your permission, sweet Bettster, the Demon-O-Stration.

The salesman reached inside his jacket and pulled out a small box. He opened it and took out a porcelain ornament, a grey and white gull with a yellow beak. He held it up and stared at it. A screen of tiredness dimmed his face, as if he had lent his own sleep and peace to generations against his will and had been reminded he would never get them back.

That comes later, he said sadly, and put the box away. His face filled with energy. He took out a black notebook computer two inches thick and a foot square. He flipped it open, flung out three spindly legs, unfolded the screen till it was a yard across and unhooked speakers which inflated with a spurt of gas to the size of cupboards. Digging in his trouser pocket, he produced a handful of black spheres like squash balls which he tossed in the air so that they hit the ceiling cornice, where they stuck and split open to shine bright spotlights onto Bettina. The theme from Chariots of Fire began to play. Jack took Polaroid pictures of Bettina and fed them into a slot in the computer while the music got louder and the spotlights spun. The lights roamed over her. The lights were bright and warm, almost material, almost moist, as if she was being licked by the tip of an enormous tongue. She closed her eyes.

Jack started to speak but she couldn't make out what he was saying over the sound of the music, or so it seemed to begin with, until she realised that she'd heard what he was saying a few minutes earlier. After a while, she could remember his words a few hours earlier, and so it went on, his words soaking deeper into the sponge of her memory until she was sodden with reminiscences of his advice and wisdom from her earliest years; advice on fashion, on savings and investments, on home improvements, on what to do with her pocket money, on food and wines, on holidays. She opened her eyes and saw her face reflected in the computer screen as if in a mirror. Her face and the reflected face moved towards each other, swivelled and merged, and Bettina's mind expanded and stretched thin and taut like the skin of a balloon, so immense that it seemed perfectly flat. Pasted on the inner surface was her life, visible all at once, the baby Bettina waving her fat lacy forearms and fingers across the reaches of the inner space to the wedded Bettina, and the first period Bettina running to the bathroom with her heart beating so strong and hot and indestructible and opposite her on the far side of the sphere the old Bettina yet to come with cold dry soft skin and a stick, and all the Bettinas in between, sleeping, running, crying, laughing, eating, kissing, talking, moment by moment – eight billion Bettinas, one for every quarter-second. The Bettinas were naked and alone with each other. They filled the vault with a sound like starlings in the trees at evening.

The space dimmed and flickered and the starlingsong became an anxious murmur speckled with screams. Something dark and huge moved softly, powerfully across the Bettinas, like a velvet-sleeved roadroller crushing a sea of bubblewrap. In the wake of the strokes the crusher painted through the billions, the Bettinas became fewer and larger and more distinct. Gold, silver and diamonds flashed from their wrists, their necks, their arms and their fingers. They gained tights, panties, bras, blouses, skirts, jeans and sweaters. There were ankle boots, knee boots, fur-lined boots, trainers, stilettos, Chinese slippers, brogues, hiking boots, wellies. The Bettinas were fewer and fewer and wearing coats, fake fur, wool, a broad-shouldered belted raincoat. Rugs unfurled, a dozen televisions, two dozen radios, three cars, four suites, beds, curtains, Hoovers, washing machines, a stack of books and a mountain of glossy magazines. A rattle of pans piling up against the cookers and a river of wine, gin, Martini, cider, Perrier, milk and fruit juice burst from the ovens. There was an avalanche of potatoes, spaghetti, tomatoes, bread, cabbage and a mudslide of chocolate and cheese. Then silence and stillness. Bettina was singular, and alone with her goods in a tightening, darkening inner cosmos. She sat down in an armchair, put her arms out around two of the five washing machines she would possess in her life and drew them close to her.

And just in case you're still not sure you've made the right choice, said Jack, here's a little something to put your mind at rest: a brand new Samsung microwave, absolutely free*.

Bettina looked up at the ceiling. The lights had gone and the sun of a December afternoon came through the windows. The carriage clock on the mantelpiece chimed 3.15. A dove strummed its crop in the eaves. Jack was tucking the computer away in his pocket. The new microwave waited on the coffee table. Jack stood at the door. He handed her a series of pastel-coloured folders.

All the information you need is in here, he said, opening one of the folders and flicking through the pages, each of which was signed by Bettina. You've got Life, our Retrospective-Perspective Material-Amatory All-Activity-Inclusive Time Endowment Plan, with the optional SuperLife Bonus, and the Post-Life Redemption Unit Lump Annuity.

Explain the last part again, said Bettina.

Bettina, said Jack, cocking his head slightly to one side, slanting his eyebrows and putting his hand on his stomach, then his shoulder, then the right side of his chest, then the left side: Hand on my heart. I'll spend as long as it takes with you. Once more: with Life, you build up units backdated to the beginning of the scheme which after a certain time you begin exchanging for food, goods, property, pleasure, ornaments and accessories – don't forget the accessories! – until you're ready to acquire the Post-Life Annuity. The beauty of the Plan is that

* Subject to availability

however much or little you've got in the way of goods when the time comes for the Post-Life Redemption, it doesn't matter – you just hand it all over, pick up your Annuity and go on your merry way.

Where? said Bettina.

Oh, Bettina, said Jack, smiling. He reached out to her, snapped a loose thread from her dress, knelt down, picked an earwig up off the floor, swiftly wove the thread into a harness for the insect and began swinging it from his forefinger. Bettina! Where? I'm sure you began planning that a long, long time ago. There can only be one place, can't there.

The south of Spain, said Bettina.

Yes! said Jack, laughing loudly. That's it. The south of Spain! The deep, deep south! He sighed, wiped tears from his eyes and hiccuped. Must be gone, Bettina. I've seen the Tullimandies and the Foredeans. No-one else in this neck of the pinetops, is there? He laughed again and went out the door, trapezing the earwig into his mouth.

Bettina heard the salesman's engine belch and roar and the car take off. She walked to the kitchen.

He must have missed the Museum of Doubt, she said, hoisting the rubbish bag out of the pedal bin. She opened the back door.

The Museum of what? said Jack. His face had reddened, darker than the crimson of the sun going down behind Hill of Eye, and his hair had thickened – not the amount of hair, but the glossy black hairs themselves had fattened out.

Of Doubt, said Bettina. It's up the road, beyond Mains of Steel. The lassie put the sign up a few years ago after she moved in. You see her coming down with her rucksack to catch the bus for her messages. She bids you the time of day and that's it.

Jack hunched into his suit. His shoulderblades rose up and his neck telescoped in, his chin tucked into his collar. He looked around, sniffing the air. Dark, he said. Mains of Steel. There'll be snow. The deer'll come down to feed. I can't call by night. Do you have a room?

Of course.

Bless you, Bettling. I'll get my things.

Jack went through the house, marched out the front door, whistled and clapped his hands. The boot of the car sighed open and Jack moved his luggage upstairs. He had twelve trunks of canvas-covered steel, bound with bamboo. When Bettina knocked later to bring him a towel, she went in and found him in a leather armchair by the fire, dressed in a green velvet dressing gown, typing out a letter with a triple carbon copy on a Cambodian typewriter balanced on his lap. Some of the trunks sat half-open, upended on the floor, exposing bookshelves stacked with scrolls in tasselled leather cases and the scored, mutilated spines of handcopied books. Over the fireplace there were stuffed trophy heads of beasts: a two-headed Friesian calf, a poodle with a forked tongue and a fox which had suffered from Proteus Syndrome.

You've made yourself cosy, I see, said Bettina. Would you like some dinner?

I'll step out for something to eat later, thank you, said Jack.

You won't find much within ten miles of here.

I'll find what I need, said Jack.

Later Bettina woke up in darkness. She heard a snap, like a stick being broken, the sound of something heavy being dragged, and the squeak of shoes in snow. The alarm said five am. She went back to sleep. At seven she went downstairs. Jack was already at the breakfast table, picking his teeth with a horn toothpick. He picked up a purse from a pile at his elbow and handed it to her. It was soft deerskin, roughly but well-stitched, branded with the legend A Present From Pinetops.

Thank you very much, she said. Did you cut yourself shaving?

Oh dear, said Jack, burnishing a steel teapot with the sleeve of his blazer and examining his face in it. There is a little blood.

It's all round your mouth, said Bettina.

Don't worry, said Jack. It's not my own. I'm a messy eater. He took out a white handkerchief embroidered with the family tree of the Hohenzollerns, spat on it, dabbed the blood off, stuffed the handkerchief into the teapot and poured himself a cup.

Bettina offered him bacon and eggs and porridge. He shook his head and pulled a sheaf of laminated menus from inside his jacket. Breakfast at Pinetops, they said on the front. Bettina skimmed through.

Consumer Confidence Breakfast – £4.99 Ten Thick Rashers Of Prime Smoked Elgin Bacon Cooked To Your Order On A Sesame Seed Bun With Five Norfolk Turkey Eggs, Hash Browns, Onion Rings, Jumbo Aberdeen Angus Fried Slice, Traditional Scotch Donut Scones, Mashed Cyprus Tatties And A Choice Of Relishes – Finish One Adult Serving, Get Another One Free!

Protestant Work Ethic Breakfast – £4.99 Sixteen Hand-Picked Ocean Fresh Atlantic Kippers In An Orgy Of Pre-Softened Irish Dairy Butter, Tormented By A Treble Serving Of Farm Pure Whipped Cream, On A Bed Of Two Toasted Whole French-Style Loaves, Garnished With Watercress, In A Crispy Deep Fried Eagle-Size Potato Nest – Too Much To Eat, Or Your Money Back!

Wealth Of Nations Breakfast – £4.99 American Style Waffles With Maple Syrup, One Pound Prime Cut Alice Springs

Kangaroo Steak, Airline Fresh Oriental Style Fruit Plate With Guava, Pineapple And Passion Fruit, Pinetops Special Chocolate Filled Croissants In Rich Orange Sauce, Whole Boiled Ostrich Egg With Whole Baguette Soldiers, Plus Your Choice Of Celebrity Malt Whisky Flavoured Porridges. Includes Vomitarium Voucher, Redeemable For Second Serving Once Stamped.

I don't have these things, said Bettina.
Look in your chest freezers, said Jack.
I don't have a chest freezer, said Bettina.
Look in your kitchen, said Jack.
Bettina went into the kitchen. It had been rearranged to incorporate several chest freezers with transparent lids, piled with frozen pre-prepared breakfasts, shrinkwrapped on trays, complete with disposable plates, cups, napkins and cutlery. In one of the freezers Bettina found a severed deer's head, complete with antlers. She took it out and dropped it into the pedal bin. The antlers stuck out and stopped the lid from closing. She went back into the breakfast room. Jack was gone.

The snow, a couple of inches, was melting on the road as it got light and the car left sharp black tracks. The branches of the sycamores lining the road were outlined in sticky snow, notched with the thaw. Beyond the farm buildings at Mains of Steel there were no more trees. After the sign reading Museum of Doubt the road climbed into the hills, the temperature dropped and there were heavy drifts. Old Tullimandy came out of the farmhouse when Jack drove past. He shouted and waved his arms. Jack drove on. Tullimandy trotted across the yard to where there was a view of the road and saw a black square, the roof of Jack's car, speeding through the four foot drifts. It reminded him of the doctor's computer cartoon of how his blocked artery would be cleared and he felt a pain in his chest. He walked carefully back to the house. Just as well he'd signed up for Life.

The Museum of Doubt was a low whitewashed cottage on the bare hillside with two sash windows and a slate roof. The roof was the same colour as the rocks and scree that stuck out of the snow further up the hill. There were no trees, no walls and no fences. The house had no television aerial. Coal smoke came from the chimney and one of the windows shone with electric light. Jack stopped the car so that the bonnet and the windscreen poked out of the last big snowdrift at the top of the road. He opened the sunroof and climbed out of it. The sun came round the ridge and Jack put on a pair of sunglasses. He went up and knocked on the blue-painted wooden door, under a plastic nameplate which said: The Museum Of Doubt.

She was built like a boy who grows up by the river and has nothing else to do except swim in it. She was thin and fit without being powerful or muscular. Her white face and neck came up out of a Prussian blue sweater thick as a rug and she wore black jeans and old brown moccasins. She had straight copper-coloured hair, cut short neatly. Her eyes listened to what he said but her mouth was blind.

I want to give you a demonstration, he said, sliding his foot over the threshold, stroking the bottom of the door with the tip of his shoe.

Of what? she said, opening the door wide and standing with her hands resting on the doorframe.

Of what you need, he said.

I don't know what I need.

Then I've come to the right place.

No no no, said the woman, shaking her head, keeping her hands against the doorframe, shifting her weight. I don't mean:

I know I need something but I don't know what it is. I mean: I don't know what I need, all the time. I'm incapable of knowing what I need, or whether I need anything. I'm not sure I do. It's my condition.

Eh? said Jack.

My husband used to say that when I tried to explain. I used to ask him why he needed things. He'd say it wasn't always a question of needing. He'd say, supposing the folk at the British Museum started saying Do we really need all these Egyptian mummies? And they'd say We may want them but I doubt we need them. So they'd throw them out. And then it'd be What do we want with these duelling pistols and snuffboxes and Etruscan vases? What's the point? You could never be sure you needed any of it. And all you'd be left with would be empty galleries and you'd have to call it the Museum of Doubt.

Jack stared at her for a while, took off his glasses and showed his teeth in a smile. Jack, he said. I'm Jack.

You're a salesman, said the woman.

That's an ugly word, said Jack. Let's forget about selling for a while. I'll tell you what I've come about. Here's what troubles me. The world is out of harmony. The equilibrium of the cosmos is disturbed. Look at this, now.

He took a set of bronze jeweller's scales out of his jacket and dangled them in the air in front of the woman.

This is the universe, he said.

He burrowed in his trouser pocket. His fingers dropped two pieces of lead shot onto one scale and four pieces onto the other. The scales dipped.

You see, one side has more than it needs. It's burdened down with possessions. The spirit is heavy. It's falling. But the other side has a lack of material things, the possessions it needs to embrace the world. It's flying away. It's vanishing. It's hardly there at all, there's so little to it. There's something missing, something it needs. Now watch carefully.

Jack lifted one of the pieces of shot and dropped it in the other pan. The snow deadened the chime. The scales teetered and levelled.

There, said Jack. Harmony. Is that not good? Is that not desirable? There should always be harmony. The side that has too much should always be giving to the side that has too little. Is that not right? The harmony is for ever. And this – he quickly swapped pieces of shot between the pans and waggled his fingers – this is a detail, a process. It could be a revolution. It could be a gift. It could be a sale. It's over quickly.

I told you already, said the woman. I don't need anything.

I can show you what you need, said Jack. I can see it. What we have here, between your house and the boot of my car, is a classic disbalance. You don't have enough, and I've got so much. You wouldn't want to be reponsible for violating cosmic harmony, would you?

No, said the woman. Here's what I mean. She took the scales from him and tilted them so the shot fell into the snow at their feet. She held the scales up in front of his eyes. Look, she said. No goods. Perfect harmony. She handed the scales back, went inside and closed the door.

Jack laughed, turned and walked a few feet away from the house. He knelt to scoop up a handful of snow and kneaded it in his hand. It fizzed, crackled and steamed. He smeared it over his face and shook his head violently from side to side like a dog which has come out of the sea. He ran back to the house and rapped on the window with his knuckles.

Adela! he shouted. Let me see the museum! I want to buy a ticket!

The door opened and the woman stood in the doorway as before. Jack stepped away from the window.

How did you know my name? said Adela.

It was written on your genes, said Jack, unsteadily. He sounded drunk.

Adela looked down at her trousers.

In invisible . . . ink. Jack's eyeballs had turned almost white and he was swaying.

Are you OK? said Adela, moving a pace towards him. His face had turned the same colour as the snow-covered hills behind his head.

Help me, said Jack, sinking to his knees. His body convulsed with coughing and drops of blood sprayed from his mouth. He fell forward onto the ground and twisted onto his back.

Adela went over and knelt beside him, chewing her lip. She pressed her head between her hands.

Cold, whispered Jack. Help me.

Adela took the shoulders of his jacket in her fists and dragged his body over the threshold of her house into the hall. She closed the door. Jack began to cough again. A spurt of blood came out of one corner of his mouth. His lips parted and what appeared to be a tonguetip made of horn appeared.

Huming imma hroat, said Jack. Pu-i-ou. He dry-retched and the horn jerked a little further out. Adela saw his tongue flapping hopelessly against it.

Adela reached down and tugged the piece of horn gently. It yielded. She pulled harder and the antler slid out of Jack's mouth like the drumstick of an overcooked chicken, along with the attached deer's head. Adela flinched and she dropped the head onto the floor. She took a step back, swung her leg and delivered all her force to the head through the toe of her moccasin. The head leaped from the hall, out through the doorway and into the sky, spinning into a mighty curve, the antlers humming as they scratched the air. She never heard it fall. She slammed the door shut and turned round. Jack was gone.

She found him standing in the kitchen holding a cardboard box. He wasn't coughing any more and there was no more blood around his mouth. His face was dead of movement. He didn't blink. His eyes were big, black and blank, liquid, without subtlety, like the deer's.

You're better, she said.

This is for you, he said, holding the box out towards her.

We've been there already, said Adela. There's no need here.

I see need. I don't see anything here except need, said Jack. Deep within his still face an expression stirred, like a big fish far below the surface of an old lake. He began to fold the box in on itself, punching in the lid, folding down the sides until it was flat, then folding it in half over and over again until it was small enough to put in his pocket. He smiled and spread his arms out wide. His fingers fluttered in space. Adela, you're lovely, but somewhere along the way you've forgotten what life is about. An empty house like this one means an empty life.

No, said Adela. You have to leave.

Adela, said Jack. Listen to me, Adela. Maybe if I say it out loud it'll start to sink in: you haven't got a fridge.

The house had a kitchen, a bedroom and a bathroom. It had five pieces of furniture: a sofabed, a chair, a cupboard, a kitchen table and a stool. There was one cup, one plate, one bowl, one knife, one fork, one spoon, and one pan. There was a two-ring gas cooker. There was a drawer of clothes, another of bedding, and five books. The walls and ceilings were bare white and the floor was covered in linoleum which'd been supposed to look like varnished wood when it was new.

There aren't any prizes for living like this, said Jack.

Living like what?

A failure. You're suffering from PRAS. Post-religious asceticism syndrome. You think that by not having any possessions your soul becomes purified and you become a saintly being, superior to people who buy glossy magazines and furniture and collect records. That's great. That's what Pol Pot thought. The truth is the consumers are the virtuous ones. They express their love for life and for each other and for humanity by buying. That's how the world becomes a richer place, full of colours. The ones who go out and shop, they're the real noble spirits of the universe. They understand how ugly their lives would be if they didn't buy homes and fill them with wonderful goods. You've got to own things, Adela, as many things as possible. It's not a question of being poor. The fewer things you own, the less human you are, and the harder it is for you or anyone else to understand whether you've got a life at all.

I wish you'd leave, said Adela.

Jack's head lolled. He lurched forward and sideways, found the stool and sat down on it. He put his elbows on the table and rested his head in his hands.

I'm still not a hundred per cent, he said. Can you get me some tea?

I haven't much tea left, said Adela.

Jack pushed the heels of his hands up into his cheekbones, looked at her from under his eyebrows and laughed, a tiny, wriggling, greedy laugh, like the body of a worm kinking through a salad. Then he sat up straight, folded his hands pentitently on his lap, found the laugh and killed it. He blinked, sniffed and pinched his nose.

I see, he said.

I've got enough for myself. I didn't ask you to come in.

Yes, of course, said Jack. I'm sorry. It was selfish of me to ask.

I've behaved badly today. You can't forgive me, of course, I don't expect you to. Please – give me a moment, and I'll leave.

I didn't—

Please. Don't speak: it's my fault: I provoked you. A minute to collect my thoughts.

They remained like that in the kitchen for a long time, Jack sitting upright on the stool with his hands on his lap, head inclined slightly, gazing at the skirting board, Adela standing watching him in the kitchen doorway, resting her weight on one leg, gently rubbing the tips of her thumbs and index fingers together. There was no sound: no birdsong, no music, no engine, no clockwork, no running water, no wind. When Jack began to cry, Adela heard the tears moving, a noise like dust slipping down a shallow slope of brass. Jack's back bent and his shoulders shook and he clenched his praying hands between his thighs.

Don't do this, said Adela softly.

Tears dripped from Jack's jaw and he rocked to and fro. His voice came lost from a roofed-in maze inside him. All the years, it said. All the days. All the hours. When Adela heard the words a memory of a dream she had never had came into her mind. There was a statue of Jack in the desert, up to his calves in blowing sand. The statue was made of soft, porous stone, deeply scored by the wind and the rain. Jack's face was slashed with parallel diagonal lines and pocked with air bubbles. His hands were outstretched, perhaps offering some gift, but the gift had long since worn away and he looked like a leper appealing for help. Around him millions of figures wrapped from head to foot in twisted black rags were hurrying across the dunes, the cloths streaming in the wind. They carried smoking buckets of fine sand which they would dip into the ground to replenish, without stopping. Every so often one of the figures would fall and not get up, the drifting sand covering them.

Adela went to the clothes drawer, fetched a white cotton handkerchief and offered it to Jack, who took it and pressed it to his face with both hands. Adela sat on the edge of the table, looking out through the window.

My husband was in sales, she said. That was what he said to other people about what he did. It was what he told me the first time we met but he was looking at me in such a way that I thought about sailing ships. I'm in sales, he said, and I thought of him standing up in the rigging of a sailing ship with three masts and a hundred white sails, all hoisted and full in the wind, and all because of me. It was like Are you happy? Happy? I'm in sails! What he meant was he sold car components. He never said that. He said I'm in sales. Like trouble. Or debt. Or love.

I was waitressing in the daytime and clubbing at night. I had friends, good people. I was dead happy half the time. The only thing was I could never take the happiness home with me and enjoy it later, by myself, whenever I felt like it. It seemed simple enough when you had it but it wasn't, it was complicated happiness, it had too many ingredients, the people I needed, the places I went, the right sounds, the right drugs. I did a little dealing myself and I met some people who helped me out, I turned into a restaurant manager, and I got a mortgage on a basement flat with a garden in a city. That was a change. It was painted and varnished and all the rooms were empty. I walked in the first day with an ornament I'd just bought and put it on the mantelpiece. It made the place look even emptier and I took a couple of days off work and broke the limit on all the plastic I could get. I got furniture, rugs, candlesticks, scatter cushions, little boxes. I had a passion for the little boxes. I had brass ones, teak ones, birch bark ones, laquered Japanese ones. None of them had anything in them. I wanted all the empty space I had hidden in pretty enclosures. And there were so many candlesticks. Of course I had to get matching candles to go with them.

One time I realised I hadn't seen one of my best friends for a long time. We'd known each other for years, slept together a few times. I thought about it and decided I hadn't seen him since I bought this monster bronze coffee table with a verdegris effect. I hadn't missed him, either.

I was in a big pileup on the motorway in the fog. You couldn't see the bonnet of your own car in front of you and we were all tanking along at fifty. There were three dozen cars and trucks went into each other. The cars at the front caught fire but I was close to the back and I stayed in my seat, hands on the wheel, watching the lights flashing at me on the dashboard with that ticking sound they make, listening to the screams and shouts from the fires up ahead. I turned the volume control on the radio to try to make them quieter. A man with a bare chest knocked at my window. He was covered in blood and oil and dirt and he was carrying a handful of cotton strips he'd torn from his shirt to make bandages. He asked if I was OK. He was going to be my husband.

He drove me home later in my car. I asked him to. I liked him. I could see he liked me. He told me he was in sales. I didn't say much. I was in shock because my car was damaged and when it happened I realised that since I'd bought it, I hadn't once gone clubbing, and it didn't hurt.

I loved him. I loved him much too much. I loved him like dying of cancer. He didn't feel the same. He was a good man and he loved me like a favourite dog. I mean he was really fond of dogs. But he never had one while we were together. For him it would have been like polygamy.

He was a collector, he was an enthusiast, he hoarded facts and gadgets. He collected Marvel comics, Motown records and

Laurel and Hardy films on video. He had to have them all. Carpentry was another thing. He got very good at that though he never made anything we needed. He kept adding extensions to the bird table. He called it the bird table of Babel. One day, he said, the god of birds would get angry with his work and destroy it.

There was this time I tried to sit down with him and explain the way things were. I told him about how I'd replaced one of my best friends with a coffee table and swapped going out clubbing for a car. I told him how all the nice things we had in the kitchen, the copper pans and the sky blue crockery, how they were taking up space where other things used to be, a walk, a date, a sky. And he said he knew what I meant, you change as you get older, your possessions get a hold on you, and you need to own more things to be satisfied. And I said well that wasn't exactly what I was meaning, I meant that love and owning things and having a good time were all spaced out along the same spectrum and you couldn't take it all in at once so you tuned in to different parts and right now I was just tuned in to him. He was like a radio station that played one song and all I wanted to do was listen to it over and over again.

And he said I know what you mean.

And I said Do you?

And he said Yes, even though it's irritating for other people and they can't stand it, all you want is the same thing over and over again. I've got all the Laurel & Hardy films on video but the only one I watch is *Sons of the Desert*.

And I said So what's the point of having all the others.

And he said It's the complete set.

And I said But you don't need the others if you only watch one.

And he said I like having the collection. I like having it there. It makes me feel complete.

And I said So you don't know what I mean.

I came back from the restaurant without a job after I tore up the menus and started asking the customers why they ate so much when they weren't hungry. I began taking things to charity shops. First the candles, then the candlesticks, the boxes and the scatter cushions. It was a while before my husband noticed and when he did I said we don't need them. I decided we didn't need the pictures, the plants, most of the kitchen equipment and the gardening stuff. It was only when I took the TV and video away that he got angry. When I told him we didn't need them he said there was more to life than need. He was a salesman, of course, like you. He said I was ill. That was a bad day. It wasn't as if I gave the electrical stuff away for nothing. It got easier after that. I managed to get rid of his records and his comics. I thought he was going to kill me then, although there wasn't much left in the house to do it with. What are you so upset for? I said to him. You didn't need any of that stuff. You've still got me.

He left that night, after calling me a Jesuit, communist, Big Brother, fanatic, hermit, freak, nun, prude, evangelist, sanctimonious killjoy, Calvinist and bore. I said I loved him and asked if he really needed that other wristwatch? He said is there anything you need? I said I need you, and I took his hand and put it down inside my pants. He said I was a sex-mad Puritan who ought to be put away. He took what he could load into his car and left. It took me weeks to empty the house and sell up to get enough to buy this place and live on. The last thing I got rid of was that ornament I put on the mantelpiece. Then I was ready to open the Museum of Doubt.

Jack had stopped crying. He was sitting with his shoulders still bowed, looking up at her, listening. He looked younger.

His eyes were full of wonder and attention, like a child at the theatre, and his face had a cast of wisdom without experience. You're right, he said.

Adela smiled out of one corner of her mouth. I've convinced you, have I, she said, looking out of the window.

I was always convinced, said Jack. It only needed someone to say it. I don't have to ask how you live without music. You listen to yourself instead. You read the same five books over and over again. The world in daylight is your television.

You're making me sound like a mad hermit. I am a hermit. I'm not mad, though.

Jack frowned and stood up. I'm wondering whether we really need this stool, he said. He sat on the floor with his back against the wall.

The floor's cold, said Adela. I don't like to be uncomfortable. I thought you were a salesman?

I was until today.

What happened?

I met you.

Adela sat down on the stool, leaned her elbow on the table and looked down at Jack. Not so funny, she said.

When I began to sell, it was good. It was paradise. It was my calling. I never thought of it as making money. The money thing was an obstacle in the way of me handing out gifts to people. I've walked and ridden and driven the roads for a time. For a long time. I've seen the clients' homes get bigger to make space for the things I gave them. The homes are brighter now, especially the kitchens. I brought those small, dark homes so much light, space and music. I brought them so many cameras, so many motors, so much food. Why did it take so long for me to understand they didn't really need it? Nobody turned me away before you did.

First you make me out to be a hermit, now you're turning me

into some kind of preacher, said Adela. I just live this way. I don't care who else does.

A second sun put its head above the ground and ducked back. Yellow light splashed Adela's skin, cycling to orange and red. A hammer of air cracked the glass of the window in half with a single vertical line and the Museum of Doubt trembled.

You car's just exploded, said Adela.

They went to the doorway. There wasn't much left. There were no flames. The frame smoked for a few moments and then the smoke blew away, like a blown-out candle. The frame and the wheels collapsed inwards into a neat pile.

Propane gas canisters and that line of self-igniting chemical heaters, said Jack, shaking his head.

It began to snow, rubbing white into the black star burned in the night's fall. Jack walked to the nest of entwined metal, reached his hand into its oil-roasted depths and pulled out a new toothbrush in a cardboard and cellophane box. It was all he could save. By the time they went back inside, there was a snowstorm.

Adela lit the fire in the bedroom and they sat on the sofabed, watching it.

I could walk down the hill tonight, said Jack.

Best not to, said Adela.

I was wondering what I'd need to open a branch of your museum.

What you wouldn't need.

Yes. But after I got rid of everything I wasn't sure I needed, what would be left.

Adela looked away from the fire and turned to him. What would be?

Jack reached into his pocket and held out the toothbrush.

Adela smiled. Is that it? I think maybe you must be planning to stop in someone else's museum.

Jack raised his eyebrows. Look, he said, beckoning Adela to move closer and examine the toothbrush. It had a blue plastic handle and white plastic filaments. The word Colgate was written on it.

Look, he said again, when she was next to him, looking down at the toothbrush, held in his two outspread hands like an offering. When you eat, you use the brush to spear the food – he gripped it brush-end up and made a downward stabbing motion – spindle it, or brush it towards your mouth. When you sit down, you use it to brush the ground clean. When you want something to read, you use the word Colgate as an index for the things you know by heart. C is the Code Napoleon, O is Orlando Furioso, L is for Little Lord Fauntleroy. That's the way it goes.

You can't sleep under your toothbrush when it's snowing, said Adela. What do you do then?

You hold it up in front of you like this, said Jack, go and knock on the door of somebody you know, and ask for help.

Adela laughed, looked away and looked back into his face, still smiling. She stayed where she was, close to him.

You didn't have to call it a museum, said Jack. You must have been wanting people to come. You don't doubt you need visitors, do you?

No, said Adela, shaking her head. Her eyes were deep and bright and looking into his, where she was falling from altitude towards an unlit continent, self-eclipsed, falling and knowing nothing of the forest canopy about to catch her, only certain it was warm and filled with prey.

D'you know what I need?

Maybe I do. I don't know what I need but I know what I feel like.

Jack reached out an index finger and placed it between her

lips. Adela opened her mouth a little and stroked the finger moist in a pout. A message of salt travelled into her and the answer was raw hunger. She closed her eyes, the moon rose and she was high with longing to wound a creature. She opened and closed her jaws and pressed her teeth into the finger, wanting to meet bone, wanting the knuckle to break. She felt blood run down her chin and the hunger stopped. She opened her eyes and saw Jack's head hung back, his finger unharmed and unmarked. There was no blood.

Oh, your finger, she said. She took it in one warm fist and squeezed it, kissed the tip. I didn't mean to hurt you. I wanted to bite your finger off but I didn't want to hurt you.

Jack raised his head. You didn't hurt me any more than I wanted to be hurt, he said. Stand up.

Adela got up and Jack unfastened her jeans and took them down. He touched her vagina with his lips and looked up at her. I'd like to fuck you with my tongue, he said.

Yeah, go ahead, said Adela.

When they were tired they lay overlapped on the sofa facing each other, boy-thigh girl-thigh boy-thigh girl-thigh, elbows propping them up at either end.

I'm in sails, said Jack. With an 'i'.

What is it you sell? said Adela.

I sell as much as anyone can ever get.

And how much does that cost?

It doesn't cost anything. It's just Life.

I don't get it.

Life. Guaranteed to last a lifetime. All you can eat, all you can drink and all you can wear before you die.

But you'd get that anyway.

Would you? You haven't.

I haven't got life? Do I not seem alive to you? You thought I was alive enough when you cried my name a minute ago.

Jack looked away. His body slackened and tensed and his face closed, as if he was preparing to reshoulder an intolerable load after a moment's rest. He said: You are alive. You'll die one day like all the rest but you never got what they call a life. That's what they've got, life. But you'll live till you die. It's not the same. You're alive.

Adela shook her head. D'you want something to eat?

Jack shook his head. You can't spare it.

There's soup. You'll have to have some.

Only if you let me pay.

Don't be stupid.

Here, said Jack. He reached into his jacket and took out a small box. He held it out to Adela. This survived. Take it. For the soup.

Adela looked at the box for a while. OK, she said. She got up, put on her jeans and sweater, took the box and walked towards the kitchen.

Adela, said Jack. What was that last ornament you got rid of when you left your old place?

A gull. A grey and white porcelain gull with a yellow beak.

Some time later Adela went to call Jack through for the soup. He was gone. She looked in the morning for his tracks in the snow, but they had been covered up by the freshly fallen.

She opened the box and took out a grey and white porcelain gull with a yellow beak. She went up behind the house to the tall rocks, laid the gull on a flat place, took a heavy stone and pounded it to powder. By evening the weather turned and rainclouds crossed the ridge. Rain fell and washed the powdered porcelain off the rock, where it mixed with the melting snow and was carried away to the river on the floor of the glen.

Bonny Boat Speed

When I see Arnold I remember the woman who could walk. I think about Jenny too of course, not that she looked anything like her dad. I haven't seen her for a long time now. That was why I stopped the woman who could walk, to find out when the healing would be over and Jenny would come out. I didn't go inside. I had nothing that needed healing then. Nothing that you would stand up and say you believed in Jesus for, or that you'd know if you'd been healed of. Praise the Lord! I can love the ones I didn't love before, and stop loving the ones that didn't love me! Hallelulia! I walked up to the hall entrance slowly, early, and I was reading the curved red letters on freshpasted white paper about Pastor Samuel's Ark of Salvation when the woman who could walk walked out. I knew she could walk because she told me. She was big and mobile in skirt and sweater and her hands stuck in the pockets of her open raincoat which was flying behind her in the warm wind over the car park, her face was white and her mouth slightly open and she was staring straight ahead. She had a crutch tucked under her right arm. I had to catch her by the elbow to stop her.

Excuse me, d'you know how much longer it's going on? I said.

She stopped, one foot lifted, balanced by my hand resting on her elbow — it was a soft, round elbow — and looked at me long enough to say: I can walk! before she walked, then ran, to her car and drove away. It was a straight slip road to the M8, a busy enough evening with no roadworks, and as far as I could understand from the paper next morning it happened within a couple of minutes of her merging with the flow that the juggernaut swung easily through the barriers and hit her car head on, with a combined speed of 150 miles per hour. I suppose Pastor Samuel might have said Well, I healed her, so the least she could've done was to have stayed to the end of the meeting. Now she walks, nay drives, with the Lord.

I was concerned for myself. I kept her back for half a second and the juggernaut hit her. In half a second a truck moving at 70 miles an hour travels its own length twice — that's what Arnold told me when I shared this with him, a free sample. From her side she could have avoided the truck by being more polite. We were both in the wrong. I suffered by not knowing I'd have to wait quarter of an hour for Jenny to come out. The woman who could walk suffered by being conscious for at least 30 seconds of the sensation of the destruction of her body by an oncoming lorry (spontaneous Arnoldism.) Usually when I think about the woman who walked the thought is: I didn't summon up the juggernaut, did I. You don't guess the instant when northbound and southbound collide, like a single bolt of lightning. Only when I see Arnold I think about how maybe everything is equalled out in the end, not in a good way, and how easy it is to summon up an irresistible opposing force, after all.

What Siobhan said this one time, and the tenner pointing at my empty tumbler was sharp and fresh as a new razor, was even more ominous than Arnold lurking round the pub as he was: Same one again? she said. Not Same again? but Same one again?

Ah, better not, last ferry and all. I looked down into the glass and dodgemed the sleek humps of ice around the bottom. The unnecessary One hung in the air.

Go on, said Siobhan. You sold a house today, didn't you? Take a cab.

I sell a house most days. I sold one yesterday.

It was a big one, you said.

It was a big one. I felt like rewarding myself with a third g & t. But the taxis skin you for a ferry trip and it's no better picking up a second one on the other side.

I can't drive after three, I said.

Take a cab. Two gin and tonics please, she said. She'd seen the weakness in my face and got the order out the way so we could argue about it over a drink.

I don't want to take a cab, I said, looking over at Arnold sitting by himself at the table by the cigarette machine. He was working, he had the yellow pad out in front of him. He turned and smiled at me. I looked at Siobhan.

It's not the money, I said. I don't like being screwed. I've got to take the car across. I've got a season ticket.

Well drive then, she said, holding the two glasses out in front of her.

But I can't if I have a third drink, I said. I took one of the glasses from her.

Don't drink it, she said.

I won't, I said, and took a mouthful of the stuff and swallowed it down.

You're so weak, she said, smiling and touching her earring.

You make it sound as if that's good.

Oh, I love weak men.

So how do I get home?

I'll give you a lift back.

I was very happy. It was easy to make me happy. Maybe I'd have four drinks and all in Siobhan's company, and a free ride all the way to Kirkcaldy on the big white ship. There'd be time for one on the moon deck bar on the way over and we could sit there studying the constellations, talking. I was grinning too much too close into Siobhan's heroic delighted face and turned again to Arnold. We smiled at each other and waved. I raised my glass to him. He raised his. It looked like water.

Great, I said to Siobhan. In the rush of it I almost said I love you, not meaning it like that, but instead said: Why did you say Same one again?

Confusion sluiced darkly into her face.

You said Same one again instead of Same again.

Did I?

Yes.

She looked into the middle distance, frowning, quiet for a while. So what? she said eventually.

I took a deep drink and went under, groping for something good.

We're like sister and brother, you and me, I said.

She looked at me without saying anything for a few seconds, then put her drink in my free hand. Arnold'll give you a lift, she said, and walked out the door.

I finished my gin, sat on a bar stool and started in on hers, raising the side without lipstick to my mouth, turning it to the side with lipstick. It tasted pretty much the same. I was watching Arnold. He was scribbling away with a pencil. The bar was full but the only person I knew was Arnold, sober as an ayatollah and his car parked outside.

Once there was a group of merchants who returned to the

borders of the empire after months spent crossing the great wilderness. Everyone wanted to know what it had been like. Och, it was all right, the merchants said. Hot deserts of course, cold mountains, wet jungle – still, we made it.

Folk listened to them politely, clapped them on the back and drifted back to their affairs. Some time later another group of merchants arrived. The locals gathered round – what was it like? Incredible, the merchants answered. Absolutely unbelievable. It was so hot that the beaks of the vultures would soften and fuse together and they would die of starvation if they were careless enough to close them. It was so cold that we had to breathe on each other's eyes every five minutes to stop our eyeballs freezing solid. It was so wet that a cup held out would fill with rain faster than a man could drink it.

A huge crowd gathered round the second group of merchants, stood them drinks for a year, offered them their daughters in marriage and secured them pensions for life.

Arnold was making a good living on the discovery that folk hungered after apocryphal facts like drinkers hunger after salty snacks. He had a name. The editors would ring him up: Death Valley, Arn, they'd say, give me ten by six. And he'd sit around and write: In Death Valley in August, you can toss an ice cube in the air and it will have melted before you can catch it. Nine more like that. Or: Dead composers this week mate, say a dozen. And he'd write: If the Italian composer Vivaldi was alive, he would be the richest man on the planet, earning an estimated £1 million a minute from royalties on the use of *The Four Seasons* on telephone switchboards. The secret lay in the utter lack of research and confidence that anyone who could be bothered to challenge his published facts would be rejected as a nitpicking wanker. Besides, whenever one of his jobs appeared, it was so quickly plagiarised that it immediately took on the veracity of gospel – more so, in fact, since every second of every day somewhere in the world an average of 6.5 people challenges the authenticity of the New Testament (6.5 – what Arnold calls the precision principle in successful apocrypha) whereas no-one, not even the Vatican, had ever taken the trouble to complain about Arnold's assertion that, for liturgical reasons, the Pope never flies in aircraft that can land on water.

He never said but I reckon it was something about the six months he did for dangerous driving that got him on the apocrypha thing. He'd been terrified of getting beaten up or abused or whatever in jail and tried to keep in with the authorities on both sides by writing pornographic stories to order. And maybe after a while the sex fantasies began to fray and it began to show that there was a hunger for something else, tiny legends of a world outside, and he began to slip them in: that it wasn't just the smooth slender bodies twining over the sheet which got the screws and lifers going but the insistence in parenthesis that the ancient Egyptians had abandoned goat-hair duvets for duck-down ones when they discovered the aphrodisiac qualities of the now extinct Nilotic eider.

Almost everyone had been amazed he got sent down, he was so middle class, even the advocate was embarrassed, he hurried away afterwards and didn't speak to anyone. I wasn't surprised, though. Arnold was a dangerous driver. He's a dangerous driver now. Whatever they did to him in prison, it didn't change his overtaking habits. It was a gamble on a blind summit and he lost, collided with a car full of students from England. He killed two of them. Arnold went into an airbag but his wife in the passenger seat didn't have one. She wasn't wearing a seatbelt. Perhaps she'd been as unhappy as that. I don't know. Anyway she went through the windscreen head-first. Straight away you imagine it happening in slow motion but it doesn't, of course, you don't see it like that any more than you see the flight of a shell from a gun. There's a loud noise and in an instant, like a badly edited film, it jumps, it's all arranged across the road, perfectly, peacefully, the broken cars, the glass, the bodies and the wheels spinning slowly.

Arnold was 36, same as me. His wife died about the time my divorce came through. Since the trial he'd seen even less of Jenny than I had. She didn't think he'd killed her deliberately, no-one did. Before the accident Jenny said she liked the way he drove. Afterwards she didn't hate her father: nothing so passionate. She went off him. She'd just started at art college and got a flat and never went round to see him any more, in jail or out. When they paroled him I expected him to take to drink, I don't know why. He went teetotal and as soon as he got his licence back he was driving worse than before. That's to say he was a good driver, very skillful, but always found a way to drive that was out beyond the edges of his skill and relied on luck to fill the space between.

I'd left my watch at home. The clock above the bar said 10.25 and the last boat was at 11. Someone told me that the landlord always set the clock ten minutes fast, so that left a good three quarters of an hour to get to Queensferry. You couldn't rely on Arnold to use that time well, though. Of course everyone ran the risk that they might die on their way home from the pub. A loose slate might fall on their heads, or they might have a heart attack, get stabbed. What else could happen? There could be an earthquake. A predator could escape from the zoo. A predator could escape from his mates. But the chances were infinitessimal. It wasn't something you thought about: Better watch on my way home from the pub in case I get killed. Driving with Arnold it was. Even if the chances of death doubled at the third decimal place, you wouldn't put money on it, there was only one life.

To have four gin and tonics and then go out the door thinking and now, perhaps, the afterlife, now, even before morning.

Arnold was coming over. Need a lift? he said.

No thanks.

He nodded at the door. I don't think Siobhan's coming back. Did you say something?

Yes.

Arnold jiggled his car keys. Last boat at 11, he said.

I'll get a cab.

Come on.

No really Arnie, it's great of you, I appreciate it, but I'm fine, I'm doing all right, taxis are good, they're cheap, they're reliable, they're fast. Fast enough, I mean. Not too – yeah, fast enough. Don't want to have you going out of your way.

He looked hurt. He fidgeted with his keys and looked around. He did seem astoundingly calm and sober for an Edinburgh pub on a Friday night. Con, he said, I don't understand you. We've been drinking in this place for the past two years and we both know where we go at closing time. It's not like we're strangers. What is the deal with these taxis? D'you not get embarrassed when you're getting out of the cab on the quayside and you see me driving up the ramp? D'you think I avoid the moon deck bar on a Friday night cause I like the Stoker's Lounge better?

I had wondered about that. My face went the colour of the carpet in the Stoker's Lounge. It'd been stupid to think he hadn't noticed me trying to avoid him on the boat all this time.

I'm sorry, Arnie, I said. I don't like the way you drive.

I hadn't meant to say that. Anyway, he was alive, was he not?

I know, said Arnold. But I'm more careful now.

No you're not. I've seen the way you go down the Queensferry Road.

That's just the way it looks. That is me being careful. I don't hit anything. I never hit anything. I make sure now. I've made sure ever since that time. It's a science, it's dynamics. Anyway, there's plenty of time, there's no need to hurry.

The clock said 10.35, i.e. 10.25, so he was right, there was plenty of time. And even though I'd seen him shoot past and slot his car at 60 through a space you wouldn't try to park in, I'd never actually driven with him.

If you're so worried about the taxi, said Arnold, you can give me a fiver if you like. He grinned.

A fiver? To Queensferry? I could get to Inverness on a fiver. And still have money left over for a deep-fried Brie supper and a chilled Vimto.

Make it ten then.

We went out to the car. We hadn't got there before he'd hit me with some new apocrypha which might've made me change my mind if I hadn't been thinking along the same lines, so much that I was hardly aware he'd said it.

The dice you'd need to roll to reflect the chances of your being involved in a car accident on any one trip, he said, would have so many faces that without a powerful microscope it would be indistinguishable from a perfect sphere.

What was that? I said, fastening the seatbelt. He repeated it while he started the car.

Bet you didn't sell that to News International, I said.

No. I just thought of that one. It's not for sale.

Private apocrypha, eh.

He didn't say anything. That didn't bother me because I was looking at the digital clock on his dashboard. We were out on the road and moving. Arnold was driving at just under the speed limit in built-up areas. Cars were passing us. The clock said 10.35.

Your clock's wrong, I said.

I know, he said.

Right.

They were going to change the name to Kingsferry, said Arnold. In honour of the king who died falling off the cliff, you know, trying to catch the boat late at night.

That's not such a good one, Arnie. Don't think you'd get far with that.

It's true! I'm off work now. No apocrypha in my free time. It's true.

Why would they call it Kingsferry? They didn't start calling Dallas Dead Presidentville after Kennedy got shot there.

Because that's what it's about. It's not about folk crossing the river.

It is as far as I'm concerned. They could call them South Ferry Ferry and North Ferry Ferry and that'd make sense to me.

No, Con, said Arnold, turning to look at me, and even though we were still trundling along at 30, I wanted him to turn back and keep his eyes on the road. He looked worried for me, as if I was about to go out alone into the world without the things I needed to know to survive. If it was about folk crossing the river there'd be a bridge. A Forth road bridge. They could easily build one. It'd be open round the clock and no-one would ever have to be racing to get the last boat again.

We're not racing, though, 'cause we've got plenty of time.

OK, but folk do. And they're supposed to be all into public safety. I tell you what it is, it's put there deliberately. It's a deliberate exception. Because they know you can't resist it. You want it. You want a place in the country where you can be provoked into taking a risk without going out and looking for it too hard.

No you don't.

You do Con. You know you do. There just aren't enough real

risks on the go, and you don't want to go rock climbing or bungee jumping or kayaking, cause you're getting on, and it's too much trouble, and they take all the risk out of it anyway, it's like a fairground ride, and you don't want to go out looking for a fight, and violence in the pictures is just a wank . . . so you sit in the pub and you wait until you're about to miss the ferry.

Don't talk this way, Arnie, it's not good.

It's not that you want to die. You want to live. More than anything, you want to live, you want to have even just the next five minutes of your life, never mind seeing the sun come up again. Only there's something that comes in between wanting one and wanting the other, it's like a separation, you start believing two different things at the same time, that if you die, it'd be the end, and that you can die without actually dying. That you can watch it. That you can do it again. That it'd be interesting. You really believe that. It's strange. I don't understand it. D'you understand it?

A horn opened up behind us and headlights flared through the rear windscreen. The car behind pulled out sharply and overtook with a roar of contempt. Our speed had dropped to 25. So far the only way we were going to die tonight was getting spannered by a fellow motorist. I wanted to talk about going faster. I wanted to talk about what happened to Arnold's wife. I didn't want to upset him.

I'm not into the risk, I said. I was really wanting to get a lift with Siobhan and sit with her in the moon deck bar in the big white ship and go home.

Arnold didn't say anything. I hadn't thought it was possible to drive any slower in high gear but it seemed we were slipping back to about bicycle pace. I remembered he'd been after Siobhan just after he'd got out, and I remembered he'd been sitting down there in the yeasty fug of the Stoker's Lounge for two years while we'd been up there watching the lights of passing ships through the rain on the glass roof and the moon wax and wane over the flint-coloured water of the firth.

We passed the Kwik-Fit garage. I turned round to check the time on the digital clock they had.

Arnie, I said. Let's talk about time.

Despite his mastery of the laws of space and time, said Arnold, Albert Einstein never owned a watch and relied on friends to tell him what year it was.

When we left the pub it was 10.25 by the clock, I said, which was ten minutes fast, so it was 10.15. Your clock said 10.35, but you agreed that was wrong.

Stonehenge tells the time more accurately than the most sophisticated atomic clock.

The Kwik-Fit clock we've just passed says 10.50.

The landlord of the Faulkner Arms always sets his clock 10 minutes fast to make sure none of his customers misses the last boat to Fife.

Christ, was it you told me that?

I didn't think you'd believe that one, said Arnold. He's a landlord, isn't he? His clock's slow. So's mine.

I looked around. Accurate timekeeping by: Kwik-Fit. Arnold's car had central locking, controlled from the driver's seat. Traffic was shooting past. I had the impression we were standing still. But we must have been going at least as fast as a strong freestyle swimmer. Ten minutes to cover seven miles. Not at this rate. Siobhan would be on board already. She was great but it upset her that all I wanted to do was talk to her and loiter in her presence for as long as she happened to be around. She wanted love, or sex, or both, I wasn't sure, which made it strange she'd put up with me for so long. One time we did come across Arnold on the big white ship, just when Siobhan was crying over something I'd said. There are people who treat crying as like sighing or yawning but I hate it, it's a catastrophe. Once when I was wee there was a primary school trip to the city reservoir and we were walking along the foot of the dam wall and I saw some drops of water dribbling down the concrete by my head and I screamed to the teacher that the dam was about to burst. Everyone laughed and the teacher, who never missed an opportunity for a bit of child-battering, gave me a thump on the back of the head. I was relieved. I really had thought the dam was going to burst. What got me wasn't so much the thought of all of us and Mrs Swynton getting swept away by a wall of water but the chest-hollowing innocence of the first little driblets, the inadequacy of the warning they were of the thousands of tons of dark, cold, merciless water pressing against the concrete. They did warn you, but they told you nothing of how deep and overwhelming their source was. I hadn't cried since I was a boy. That was something I could have asked Pastor Samuel about.

Arnold had tried to comfort her. It'd been terrible. She kept coming up against not liking him as much as she felt she should and he kept coming up against the fucking apocrypha every time something more than inane pleasantries were called for. He hadn't been like that before. When I heard him telling her, instead of not to pay any attention to the crap I'd said, that 60 per cent of single women in their thirties were in stable relationships by the time they were forty, the thought of him scribbling away about fantasy women in his cell, struggling to meet some deadline for fear he'd get his head kicked in, and getting infected with the spores of instant harmless wee fictions for instant meaningless wee rewards, almost set me going without the pastor's help.

We were quiet up to the city boundary, him crawling along,

leaning back in the seat, one hand on the wheel, ignoring the cars overtaking us, staring ahead, placid and blinking, and me trying to work out how to open the door, the effect on the fabric of the jacket of rolling and skidding for a few yards, the effect on the fabric of me, the result of grabbing the handbrake and pulling it sharply upwards, calculations of time, distance and speed, and what about going by Kincardine, a place of great and famous beauty by night.

The moment the dual carriageway came in sight Arnold stamped on the accelerator and we were away. We had five minutes to get to the terminal. Once we were up to 90, I started to think we'd make it. By the time the needle shook on 110, I was thinking we wouldn't.

We'll just fly across, then, I said.

Arnold didn't say anything. We came up behind a Mercedes dawdling along in the fast lane at 80 or so. With two sharp movements of the wheel, we slid into the slow lane and back again in front of the Merc, missing a rusting hatchback by the thickness of paintwork.

Don't do this, Arnie, I said. It's not important. Slow down. We'll get there.

I thought you liked it, said Arnold. Just to see what happens.

I never did anything to give you that idea.

You fucked my daughter without wearing a condom, said Arnold.

People get older suddenly. It builds up and comes breaking through. One instant the age you've been for years, the next, the age you'll be for years to come. A dream one night, a drink, a cloud crossing the sun, a word, a thought, and you lurch backward into the next age like a drunk going over the balcony. I felt as if I'd been seized by eight relentless hands and had clingfilm pressed down over my face and body and I couldn't fight it, it was becoming part of me and that was me for the rest of my life with this extra, unwanted, itching skin.

As things stood the rest of my life was being measured out in red cat's eyes beaded along the A90, and the vision of the long cat of after dark expired at the water's edge, if not sooner. Arnold, I said, Arnie, wait, OK. Whatever you think, let's talk. Let's take time to talk. We'll go down the waterfront and get a carryout and sit up all night and talk it over. All weekend if you want. I can't talk when you're driving like this. It's putting the wind up me.

Arnold laughed. Putting the wind up you! he said. Good. Scientists say thirty per cent of the human brain is set aside exclusively to react to fear.

Bollocks, I said. Sixty.

The laugh went out of Arnold's face. He was leaning forward, his chin almost over the wheel, staring ahead. I don't know I want you to talk, he said.

Come on Arnie. She was 17, she knew what she was doing. She was 16.

OK, she was 16 at the beginning, but she was very self-possessed.

It's interesting you talk about possession, said Arnold.

Christ, you're the one who was doing the my daughter my daughter bit! I was working up an anger because I could see we were going to make it to the terminal and up the ramp no bother. She was old enough to be living by herself. It's not like I was the first.

Arnold's left hand came swinging off the wheel and I flinched. But he was just changing down from fifth to fourth.

What are you doing? I said. We swung off the dual carriageway onto the back road into Queensferry, the long way round to the terminal, narrower, slower, and with great opportunities for head-on collisions.

You're such a bastard, Con, said Arnold, and you never bother to remind yourself of it.

I had a tight hold of the door-grip with one hand and my seatbelt with the other. We came up behind a Capri tanking along at 70 and Arnie took it on a blind bend just as something bright and screaming came round in the other direction. I closed my eyes, bent down and wrapped my arms around my head. There was a shrieking sound and horns, the Capri must have melted its brake pads to let us in, and we lived to fight another second.

Whatever it is I've done to upset you, Arnold, I'm sorry, I shouted.

No need to shout, said Arnold, frowning.

Slow down. There's a bend – Jesus.

How d'you think it feels when you're wife's just died and they put you in jail for it and the daughter you raised for sixteen years stops seeing you 'cause she's getting screwed by a man the same age as you are?

Not good. Bad. There's a fffffff . . . there was no connection! She didn't want to see you any more. Nothing to do with me. We were in love for a while, it was good for both of us, and then we drifted apart.

We were accelerating into absolute darkness on the wrong side of the road. There was nothing to overtake any more. Like the wrong side was smoother. I could see the orange glow of Queensferry ahead and a pale scimitar of headlights rising and falling through the trees before we got there, the car we were about to go head to head with, though we knew it, and they didn't, they'd dip their headlights and slow down a little, voodoo steps to safety, they would never know. Apart from the apocryphal 30 seconds. He'd almost convinced me with that one.

There's a car coming, I said.

It's OK. We won't hit it. You know, Con, 95 per cent of teenage girls who have relationships with men twice their age or more say love was never a factor.

I remembered reading that in *Marie Claire* when I was still seeing Jenny and worrying about it.

You're talking shite, Arnold, I said. You're starting to believe your own apocrypha. There aren't any facts about love. Would you move to the right side of the fucking road?

It was over before I had time to wet myself, and when we'd swung round the bend into the blaring glaring squealing ton of glass and metal and flesh hurtling towards us, and there'd been no contact, I realised he'd done this before. Everyone else would swerve at the last moment, at exactly the same time as the other car, but he kept on on the wrong side, letting the other car swerve, so we missed.

Stop, I said. I'm sorry. You're right and I'm wrong. I repent. Could you stop the car? I meant it. I would have stood in the Stoker's Lounge all the way across with my lips pressed to his ringpiece just to be out in the open and not moving. It was 10.59 by his clock, we were just coming down the hill to Queensferry, and I knew he'd try to clear the High Street narrows and all the rest in 59 seconds.

You're not making any sense, Con, said Arnie. You know better than I do what incidental risk's all about, the danger that comes with getting where you want to go when you can't wait. When you were screwing Jenny it was the hell with the crash, maybe you will, maybe you won't. What's the difference? You know you crashed. You do know, don't you? You couldn't stop yourself. You knew you might, and you did. You knew a kid would only be trouble for her and she didn't want one.

I'm not with you. Just stop, eh. Stop. Stop.

I'm not intending to stop. It's hard to stop when you're almost there. You didn't stop. And there are some accidents Pastor Samuel couldn't help her with. He threw up his healing hands and said: If you don't want his child, girl, cast it out.

STOP!

And she did cast it out. Six weeks gone. She really didn't tell you, did she?

I pulled hard on the handbrake. We both went quiet for what seemed like a long time, watching the masts of the yachts fly past, it seems to me with our hands folded across our laps, but I suppose not. For a certain time, memory, the present and apocrypha became the same thing, a trinity, like the Father, the Son and the Holy Ghost. I remembered the car flying off the end of the pier before it actually happened, and I felt it skim three times across the waves like a stone as if it really did, though I knew I was feeling, with every bone and muscle, the apocryphal version of what truly took place, and the vague, imaginary sense of hitting the water once and going down was what was real.

Arnie had the sunroof open and was out of it before the top of the car sank below the water. He braced his legs on the roof and plunged his arms down for me through the flood that was beating me down into the seat and tied to pull me out, forgetting about the seatbelt. We went down into the black firth together, me struggling with the belt and gulping down a gallon of salt water before I shut my mouth, him clinging on to the edges of the sunroof with one hand and tugging on my jacket shoulder with the other. I got free just as a part of me I never knew I had started to try to rationalise the death experience into something negotiable but only making it worse. We were trying to kick off our shoes and jackets and our faces were in the air. We were treading water. The ferry was steaming out of harbour a few hundred yards away. It whistled. Arnold was swimming away from me towards the pier with strong breast strokes. I paddled my feet and coughed. I hate it when folk cry. It's never good, and when it's someone you thought you were fond of, like yourself, it's a disaster. It was too late anyway. There was too much water all around. There was so much of it.

The Very Love There Was

Adam on the floor opened the parcel without tearing the paper, labouring at the tape with the bitten-down pithy remnants of his fingernails to pick it off the gloss of the wrapping. Cate watched him from the settee, lying on her front, feet treading air. Soon they would need to start filling another drawer with old wrapping paper that never got reused. How could they? It was old. But they couldn't throw it away.

A book had marbled board covers and a leather spine, with a spangled sheen on the edge of the thick, rough pages. The spine creaked when he opened it and clumps of pages fanned out with a sigh. He pressed it to his face and breathed in. It smelled of damp earth.

I know I said it was simple, but you won't learn it by sniffing it, said Cate. If you could, all the cokeheads would have discovered perpetual motion by now.

Ellsta, he said, and leaned over to kiss her.

Ellsta! she said, wrinkling up her face.

El-lsta.

Closer but still way off. Ellsta!

He flipped through the pages. There were no pictures. There were desires and needs in other lives that had never even come within sight of their own, before electricity, when the servants had no artificial servants, and couldn't fool themselves. Mayryng, would you adjust the bedspread? Yoshua, would you bring fresh coals? Mr Ocksyng, would you shoe the brown mare?

Brymdon anches ytr gastorst, he read out. Instead of laughing at his version of Ask that lamplighter to step over here she looked at him gravely and corrected his pronunciation.

Is there a section where the master seduces the serving wench? he said. Come thee hither, bonny lass, and rowp thy postillion?

Cate rested her head sideways on her bare arm, kicking, looking at him. Try page 228.

He turned to page 228, quarter of the way through the book. Present pluperfect, he read out. Mercian tense structure in the present follows the pattern laid down in lesson 25: the future. I thought Mercian didn't have a future.

Read to the end and you'll see, said Cate. Don't be so fucking smart. If you read it to the end there will be a future, won't there?

Rowp thy postillion, said Adam, putting the book down carefully and moving over to Cate. He put his left hand into the fair curls of her hair, warm from her scalp, and it made an ultrasound like foil streamers a million miles long and a millimetre wide, crinkling and billowing in a solar wind, which only he and dogs could hear. Their tongues tasted each other and the fingertips of his other hand were running up the back of her leg.

Y tess ley, he said. It was the only Mercian phrase he knew, the one he'd asked her to teach him the first time they went out, which was also the first time they slept together, and had learned straight off.

Y tess leya, she said, and started to take off his jeans. Before he entered her she took him in her mouth, which he didn't like, but this time he did, he barely stopped himself coming there, her grip between the tongue and the palate was so determined. Afterwards they lay on the settee together for half an hour, dozing off and on, watching the lights blinking stupidly in the branches of the tree, the fanheater thrumming against their thighs and creaking.

It's so old, said Cate. I was lucky to find it. A library was being merged out and they were selling off a load of old books.

It's great.

Will you study?

Of course.

I'll help you.

Yes.

I bought you a shirt as well.

Food for the mind and food for the eh, the other thing.

If you don't want to learn it, it's fine, there's no reason for you to.

I said I would, I want to, I want to be able to speak it.

I know, it's that I saw your face – not like you were disappointed, but that the book was old, like it'd been dug up and it'd been supposed to have stayed buried.

I was hoping there'd be pictures.

That's because you're a moron.

They left the house at noon and took a cab to where Cate's dad lived. As the last but one native speaker of Mercian he was to have been living in a beehive-shaped wattle and daub hut, strengthened with stone and brick in the latter generations, on a ridge among derelict cattle-pens, out poaching in all weathers, keeping the Sabbath and standing stock-still of a late summer afternoon in a cropped meadow of thistles and cowpats and horse-flies, scoured by the shadows of the clouds passing across him.

Instead he lived in a one-room council flat in a cubic four storey block in a street with lots of space between the cars, a gasholder at one end and a triangular park with grass at the other like badly laquered hair. He had the family's Mercian bible which he'd told Cate and Adam he didn't read and a bronchitic black labrador. He hoarded specific items at Christmas: cans of McEwan's Export and tins of Fray Bentos steak and kidney pudding.

I wasn't expecting you so early, he said. He had the kind of face that everything which had happened to him in the past sixty years had been unexpected, but he'd made the best of it. He was astonished to find his fridge full of shiny red cans of fizzy beer, and astounded to see the size of the pot of simmering water on the cooker, and the number of inverted pudding domes hottering inside it. He was incredulous that his daughter should turn out to be married to a man called Adam, and sceptical that they should decide to visit him on December 25, of all days. When Adam recognised the theme to the Guns of Navarone, as played by the band of the Coldstream Guards, he twisted round and looked at the Bush mono player in amazement.

Happy Chrismas, Dad, said Cate, handing over the socks. The incredible act of gift-giving just about sent him doing a double somersault backwards through the window. His mouth dropped open and his eyes bulged like a fish in a net. It's from both of us.

Thanks very much, he gasped. He'd barely sat down in his armchair and started getting over the shock when he was sent reeling again by the discovery of two small parcels on the windowledge, hidden by a line of cards. He issued the gifts, a leather wallet for Adam and a gold chain for Cate. Cate went over and kissed him and Adam tried to make a joke about money not included, eh.

Anyway, he said. Eh . . . Ellsta.

Cate smiled and looked at her dad. He shrugged and wrestled with the arms of his chair, looking down and away, trying to smile and looking like a condemned man waiting for the second buzz after the first application of 2,000 volts had failed to finish the job.

Ellsta very much, said Adam.

Adam, said Cate.

Anyway, Mr Finzy, Cate's given me this brilliant book so's I can learn Mercian and next Christmas I'll be speaking it properly.

Cate's dad nodded slowly, calmer now but more worried-looking. It'll take up a lot of your time, he said. It's not going to help you find a job.

He wants to, Dad. We've got time.

It never helped me.

Adam took a drink of Export. There was silence in the room. Cate was checking her nails, frowning. Her dad was looking into the middle distance, nodding his head as if a spring had broken. He coughed.

Did you put the vegetables on, Mr Finzy? said Adam. Those puddings'll be ready before long.

I forgot. Cate's dad didn't make a move.

Mm? said Cate, who'd been looking out the window.

I'll go and see to it, said Adam.

I'll do it, said Cate, not making a move.

Adam got up. Cate and her dad were looking at him. He let them sweat for a couple of seconds. The sun came out and all the glass in town blazed with cold reflected fire. He went to the kitchen, leaving the door open. This also had meaning in their festive entertainment.

He put a couple of pots of salted water on to boil, located the frozen sprouts and started peeling the tatties. The dog waddled in and collapsed panting on the lino with the effort. Adam tossed a scrap of potato peel in front of his nose. The beast didn't even sniff it, he just looked at Adam pityingly. Don't look so superior, said Adam. Your children will eat scraps and be glad of them. They'll make a dog that eats all the rubbish we throw away. Eh Samm? Want to have your genes altered and eat teabags? He knelt down in front of the dog and scratched it behind its ears. You're not a Mercian dog, are you? he whispered. Just keep listening to me havering. We had this same conversation last Christmas, eh. It's crap, isn't it?

Samm got up and walked out of the kitchen. Cate and her dad were talking. You couldn't make out the words, not that you'd understand them if you could. Adam stood still for a while, listening, with his hands in the water of the basin, gripping the knife, the slivers of peel rocking on the surface tickling his wrists. Great long speeches they were making to each other. What the fuck about? It sounded eloquent and interesting. He only heard his own name mentioned once. Ad-dam. He'd never be able to prove she spoke better in Mercian, even if he learned it, especially if he learned it, what could he do but slow her down, but he knew for certain, even though she denied it, that she was better in Mercian. Her English was perfect of course in a way that you didn't think about it but her Mercian was perfect in a way that you did. It was like an otter, there was nothing to prove they preferred land or water, but you knew they liked pussing about in the river more, you just had to look at them. Dryk, the in-law kept saying, dryk.

Adam stuck the peeled tatties in the pot and went and leaned back against the windowsill, looking down the kitchen. He tapped the box in his jeans pocket with the flat of his fingertips and didn't take it out. That was another Mercian word he knew: cygaret. Also televysion, radyo, VCR and wheel. Wheel! That was a giveaway. They hadn't even changed the spelling. What'd they used before, sledges?

It was necessary to get stuck in to the grammar tables, that was all. An idea existed that he was a guest and Cate's real lover was about to arrive and at that time it'd be time to be not there.

If Birmingham was full of Mercians and him and Cate were the only English speakers and they were talking about whatever bulk-buy crispy high-fat diet nuggets of conversation they engaged in, operational stuff, it would sound the same as Cate and her dad. They weren't reciting poetry to each other. They weren't talking about life and death, the limits of time, the origin and the end of things, the areas that didn't tolerate words as English had designed them, the very colours, the very sense of the change of season, the very love there was. It just sounded like it. Dryk. He knew what they were talking about. Dead relatives. Mum. Remember Mum? She was great, wasn't she. Yeah. Remember how she used to make those things, you know, the things she used to make. That was what they were talking about.

He heard Cate say: Y leya tess.

He moved over to the cooker and tipped the sprouts into the boiling water, hoping to blister his hands, not like he was trying, but sometimes a dose of pain and disfigurement was what you needed, that was why people carried needles and razor blades in their pockets, to prick and cut themselves when they needed their mind taking off things. He ballooned his cheeks and rubbed his palms on his jeans, looking round. It was hot. You didn't tell your dad you loved him like you told a lover you loved him, even in Mercian, not when your husband wasn't supposed to be listening and you knew he was.

They stopped talking and after a few minutes Cate came through to where he was standing over the pots and embraced him from behind, her hips against his bum, her cheek against his back and her palms on his chest.

OK? she said.

It's a sauna, a sauna, a steak and kidney sauna, said Adam.

I'm sorry, she whispered. You know.

Aye, I know what I know. Get the knives and forks, eh.

At the beginning of the meal Adam said if they wanted to speak Mercian, that was fine by him, and Cate said no it was OK, and her dad said nothing, and they ate the food and Cate's dad asked about the job hunting and when they were going up to Fife to see Adam's family, and they got on to the price of travel, and then television subjects, and Adam asked if they could have on the Cabaret soundtrack, and Cate's dad put it on and brought a Christmas cake out from the kitchen and Cate sliced it up for them and Adam looked at Cate's dad, smiled and said: Y tess ley.

Don't Adam, said Cate.

Y tess ley, said Adam again still looking at Cate's dad and smiling. Cate's dad didn't look surprised any more. He looked as if he'd known this was coming since before he was born, since before the words were lost in libraries and radiowaves and dumped at the school gates, since before his folk starting coming down from the hills to the honeycombs, since before they drove the painted ones from the peaks, since before one of them said: there's not enough room here, let's go out west to that big island and fuck the Britons, we're that much harder than them, the women. He rested his arms on the table on either side of his plate, cocked his head to one side, looked Adam in the eyes and said: I'm sorry son, I don't understand you.

Y tess ley, said Adam. It means I love you. You know. It's your language.

It's not *your* language, said Cate's dad. You don't anyway. You only come at Christmas.

I'm family.

Adam, shut up, you're not ready, said Cate. It's the wrong place to start.

What's the right place to start? said Adam. He doesn't even answer back when I say thank you.

He's shy! You don't know what he went through at school.

Maybe but I know what I go through every time I'm round here, standing in the kitchen for half an hour listening to songs of old Mercia and pretending not to notice.

It's only once a year. Who do you think you are, telling my dad you love him, Mary Tyler Moore?

I'll tell your dad I love him if I fucking well like.

You will not.

I fucking will. And Mary Tyler Moore doesn't speak Mercian.

How do you know?

'Cause if she did she'd be packing sandwiches for Tesco's in Wolverhampton instead of having her own TV production company and a millionaire lifestyle. Who are you to tell me what I can say to your dad?

Tell him that you love him, then. In English. Go on.

Adam looked at Cate's dad, focusing on the bridge of his nose. I love you, he said.

I'm not sure I like you, said Cate's dad.

Adam folded his arms and looked down into the cake. Cate put her hand on her dad's.

They walked home late after watching a film. Cate was quiet.

It's true, said Adam. You do never see it in the foreign phrase books. Tell us the way to the bus station, give us five kilos of sun-dried tomatoes, escort my bags to the dental office, and I love you.

It's something you know already before you go, and you never learn anything else, said Cate.

What I don't understand is why the TV people never come round and make films about him. You'd think they were waiting for him to die.

They walked side by side through the raw smoky night of small infinite streets and turnings, pattering with the footsteps of the fearful, the drunk and the doubting.

What does dryk mean? said Adam after they had walked for half an hour without saying anything.

It means cancer, said Cate.

It was prostate cancer, advanced, and they would have to operate. There was a high chance Cate's dad would die. She went to see him most days. Sometimes she stopped overnight. Adam went about once a week. He moved a chair into the kitchen and took a book but he couldn't concentrate with the uninterrupted flow of Mercian coming from the next room. He tried sitting on the toilet with the door closed but he could still hear them. There was no doubt. Cate was eloquent in Mercian. English was for the moving of objects and the taking of decisions, for plain reason, the turning on and off of a tap. Mercian was a waterfall, interrupted by laughter. He began taking a cassette player with him and with the earphones clamped on his head and music playing he was free for a time.

At home he would open the Mercian book after tea, with a pen and a ruled notepad on the desk in the bedroom. He began by staring out at his reflection in the window that looked out on the darkness of January, a planet Adam half in darkness, half in lamplight. He went to get a coffee and started watching the news. He came back, sat down and looked through the close print. It was not as old as it seemed. It was a reprint of a book published in 1868. On the inside front cover was a stamp in faded crimson ink saying Property of the War Office, Reprinted 1916 By Order, and at the back, after the summit of Mercian language skills demanded fifty years previously, a squire's speech at a prize-giving for agricultural labourers, was a pamphlet-thick addendum with Serving King and Country written in English and Mercian, followed by lists of vocabulary and phrases. The officers are your friends. They are on your side. Machine gun. Phosphorous shell. Mustard gas. Come on lads, up and at them! Let's smash the Hun/Johnny Turk/Johnny X! Fix bayonets! This man has trench foot. This man has gangrene. This man is a hero. This man is a deserter. This man is a coward. You will be decorated for this. You will be court-martialled for this. Stretcher party. Dear Mrs X, I regret to tell you that your son was killed in action near X yesterday. He died doing his duty for King and country. He was a brave soldier.

He turned back to the beginning and read the introduction. Sundry gentlemen and men of affairs have turned to me in indignation over the truculence of their Mercian servants and day labourers. Their refusal to understand the simplest instructions in English. Pernicious influence of religious tracts in their own language. Ideas above their station. My answer is invariably the same: in the simplicity of their hearts and souls, they are as much God's children as you or I. If you are to claim mastery over them, must you not demonstrate your superiority by learning their tongue, just as they have demonstrated their ignorance by failing to learn ours? Cannot all pretend to the erudition of a Milton or a Pope. Many may feel reluctant to turn once again to the syntax and parsing of their youth for an aim so much less elevated than the enjoyment of Virgil. Yet Mercian is not a difficult language. Anglo-Saxon roots. Baltic influences. Celtic strands. Pleasing rustic airs. Young children will recite their epics with unaffected simplicity. With no more than an hour's application each day, six months will be sufficient for reasonable profiency. The Reverend G. R. Wiley.

One day the sound Cate's shoes made when she threw them down and they hit the skirting board was harder, and the padding of her stocking feet to the kitchen, and her shoulders in a white blouse against the black of the window, her back to him when he came in.

He's going into hospital tomorrow, she said.

For the operation.

I don't think there's going to be an operation.

Why's he going into hospital?

I don't know. She turned round and took the tissue away from her soaking face. She looked into his eyes and sniffed. She looked down at the ground and said something to him in Mercian.

What does that mean? he said.

It means how's it going, she said. You should know that by now.

It's not that kind of book. They start you off with 200 different sentences starting I am a.

What are you? she said.

I am a haberdasher. Sorry, that's the only one I can remember.

She smiled and sniffed and put out her hand to stroke his chest. It's two months now you've been studying that book, she said.

I know.

I thought you wanted to speak it.

I do, but your dad. Unless I speak it like a native he doesn't want to know.

Just for him? It wasn't him who bought the book for you.

But when you thought you spoke the same language and then you have to start again, and one of you is super eloquent and the other one can hardly put a sentence together.

How d'you know I'm super eloquent if you don't understand what I'm saying?

I can tell.

What does it sound like?

It sounds like the sounds the wind makes things make, or a river, or heavy rain on the street.

And what does it sound like when I'm speaking English?

Like words. Like hospitals, and bus timetables, and cups of tea, and a bit short this week, and anything good on.

You're being sentimental. It won't seem that way if you learn more. You talk about just the same things in Mercian as in English.

Then why am I bothering to learn it?

Why are you?

Because I don't think it is just the same.

She liked that. She had to kiss him.

The two of them went into hospital with Cate's dad next day. He was in a lot of pain. The hospital smelled of pain, or of the notice of pain, the smell of disinfectant and pharmaceuticals and sterilised rubber that took on just the form of what it was trying to hide. The doctors were guessing. They couldn't bring themselves to say so, but they wanted the three of them to know they were guessing. There was body language of not having a clue and being gutted about it but that was the way it was with the human body, it was so complicated it was amazing anyone ever got beyond the cell-splitting stage. Towards the end of the day they said they were going to have to operate. Cate and Adam went in to see him together and sat down beside him on the same side of the bed. He looked at them, purged of all surprise. Cate held his hand and Adam put his hand round Cate's waist and the other on Cate's dad's thigh for a moment, then took it away. After the Mercian for machine gun and brown lung it didn't seem strange that Cate's dad had been surprised before. Waking up in your bed at home in your own flat in the morning, that was surprising. Cancer was the hand that ended the surprise. The whip. He was a brave soldier.

Cate's dad was dying. He was ready for it like someone who'd been waiting too long in too many offices for his name to be called. Not jumping up in relief and running to the woman behind the window any more but fed up with processes of any name or colour and wanting them all to be over and just to sleep. He was whispering to Cate in Mercian. He saw his hand tighten on hers. She turned round and looked at Adam.

What's he saying? said Adam.

He's talking about my mum. He says he sees her.

Sees her.

He says it hurts a lot.

Tell him he's going to be fine.

Why?

I can't think what else to say.

You tell him.

What, in Mercian?

He does speak English, remember.

Mr Finzy, said Adam, leaning forward, you'll be fine.

Cate's dad closed his eyes, turned his head towards Cate and whispered in Mercian again. The doctors came and took him away. He died the next day, after surgery, without coming round.

They were in a small room in the hospital set aside for hearing that people had died. Adam tried to hide his anger in the crying of Cate and the holding of her. She'd folded into his arms so quickly, as imagined and laid down: she hadn't noticed. But she had.

You're angry, she said.

No, of course not.

He wasn't trying to hurt you.

I know.

You used to tell us you wanted us to speak Mercian while you were there. So we did.

I'm not angry. Honest.

Don't be angry.

I'm not. But he could have told me to look after you.

Was that what you wanted him to say?

No.

You mustn't think he didn't like you.

He could have said something. I don't know, goodbye.

After you'd told him he was going to be fine?

He could have told me to look after the dog. Adam was angrier now. Cate's dad hadn't mentioned him to her in Mercian either.

Do you know how to say goodbye? said Cate.

Yes.

What is it?

Adam couldn't remember.

What've you been doing with that book open on your desk all this time?

Y tess ley.

That's not enough.

I thought it was.

You know what I mean.

He got up the next morning and stood naked at the table. Rain spat across the window and wind shook the glass. He closed the Mercian book and put it up on the shelf, on top of an album of Picasso paintings someone had given them for a wedding present. He turned round. Cate was sitting up in bed looking at him.

You learned it when you were growing up, said Adam. It was easier. You didn't have to study it. You just picked it up. It takes so much time. It's not as if you've ever sat down to learn French or German. He waited for Cate to say something but she only looked at him. There has to be a reason. A reward. It's not as if once I'd learned to speak Mercian I'd be able to do anything with it. I won't be able to go somewhere and be understood. Your dad said so himself.

Am I not a reward? said Cate.

But there's only one of you.

If you learned it there'd be two, and we'd have children. How many more do you need? How many women do you love?

Adam sat down on the bed with his back to her. She poked him sharply in the side. How many women do you love?

Just you.

But you don't love me enough to learn to speak my language? You wouldn't do that for me?

It's not a small thing.

Would you only do small things for me? And love me? What would you do for me?

Adam turned round. You said my language, he said. You said my language.

It is my language. I've got two of them.

I'm in love with the one that speaks English.

Cate lay down, pulled the quilt over her and turned away from him. Don't tell me you love me in Mercian any more, she said.

He did say it to her again, two or three times, in the couple of days before the funeral. He said it to comfort her but it made both of them sick to hear it. Y tess ley had been his effort and his promise of a great labour, and meant love in itself to both of them and in the promise of what he'd do, and now it was only a sign of his still being there, like a lighthouse without rocks.

Don't, she said, I told you. Tell me in English if you mean it.

The TV people did come to the funeral, they filmed Cate reading in Mercian from the Lay of Kenelm. Walking out of the chapel with his arm round Cate Adam lifted his eyes from his shoes sinking into the gravel to see the legs of the woman walking by herself in front of them. The legs in black tights were slender and moved in short, light steps. Above that was a short black coat and a black wide-brimmed hat. When they had arranged themselves at the graveside Adam was facing her, the same age as Cate but not a friend he'd ever met, and not a relative that he could think of, with her long North African face, black eyes and dark lips. He spoke to her at the buffet afterwards and was reminded how Cate's dad's sister had married an Ethiopian and gone to live in Addis Ababa and had a daughter before she died. The daughter was called Naomi.

Do you speak Mercian? said Adam.

I can count up to ten, said Naomi. My mum died when I was young.

Her eyes were fixed on him. He felt the blood surge through him and his skin prickled.

I've been trying to learn it, he said. But the only phrase I can remember is y tess ley.

She asked him what it meant.

It means I love you, he said.

She smiled and put her fingers over her mouth. He grinned and looked away. He was looking at Cate and he was grinning after her dad had just been put in a hole in the ground and buried in earth for ever.

He went over to her and she wasn't speaking to him. They shook the hands of the guests together while they left. Naomi smiled at them both and neither of them smiled back. She said she was at university in Leicester and they should come over. They nodded and she left.

I see what you mean now about an incentive, said Cate.

What?

Don't be a bigger prick than you are.

If you're talking about Naomi, we were just talking.

I know, but seeing how you were talking it's all become much clearer. It's too much for you to learn it just for me, your time's too precious, your mind's too precious, but if you knew every time you went somewhere there'd be someone like Naomi to speak Mercian with, it'd be worth your while.

She doesn't speak Mercian.

Jesus, it's not the fucking point, is it?

Cate was cold and down for a week and for longer than that Adam would think about Leicester University and went into a bookshop to read a few pages of a book about Ethiopia. But he got a decent job in a print plant and was surprised that Cate didn't show the missing of her father more. One time the guilt got to him and he took the book down again and left it on the table where she'd see it. But she only asked him how he was getting on, and he knew she knew he wasn't getting on, he wanted her to know he hadn't forgotten, and that was as far as it went.

Cate told him she was pregnant.

I found out just after the funeral, she said, only after seeing you with Naomi I decided not to tell you for a while.

God you talk to a stranger.

No you laugh with a stranger when my dad's just died. Anyway you had the hots for her.

Ah but this is brilliant. A baby. With the job and everything. It's too much.

Is it too much? Others have got more. The dog smells bad.

Do you want to move to the country?

Why? Cate frowned.

Maybe it's better. I remember how you told me how the Mercian word for town and honeycomb was the same cause that was what the lights of the towns made them think of when they looked down at them at night from the hills before they lived there. And I thought maybe you were wrong and maybe they called them honeycombs because they found out that when you'd had too much of them they made you sick.

Neither of us have ever lived in the country. You're strange, Adam, I never had you down as a cottage with roses round the door man.

Aye I know, said Adam. It is strange.

He didn't understand what he'd been after, either. But a couple of months later he came home from work, went straight into the kitchen and heard Cate speaking Mercian in the front room. He listened for a couple of minutes. She hardly paused for breath, but it wasn't a song, it wasn't a poem, it was the old eloquence, inspired. He went quietly out into the hallway and looked round the door. She was sitting on the settee with her hands folded across her belly, looking out into the distance, talking. She'd bend her head forward and tuck her chin into her chest so that she was talking and looking down at her navel.

Adam went back into the kitchen and stood still for a while. Then he sat down on the kitchen floor. Cate came in and stopped sharply in the doorway when she saw him.

God, what are you doing? she said.

Sitting on the floor.

I didn't hear you come in. I was talking to the baby.

Its ears haven't even formed yet.

It'll make them come faster.

What language?

I don't even remember. English, I think.

It was Mercian. I heard you.

Are you spying on me? What difference does it make? Don't you want our kids to speak Mercian?

You said you'd been speaking English.

What the fuck would I want to do that for? I can speak to you in English, can't I?

But you can't make yourself speak Mercian when you know I'm in the room.

Why should I when you never bothered to learn it, when you couldn't be arsed cause the only person in the world daft enough to speak it is a nonentity, your worthless wife?

I'd be a hell of a lot keener to learn it if you didn't go stum every time I'm around, if you weren't so ashamed of it. Christ talk to the baby in any language you like, only not behind my back. I just want to listen, even if I don't understand what you're saying. I don't want to understand. I just want to be there.

You can't be. You know where the book is, go and learn it, in a couple of years you'll be perfect, but it's not going to take any less, is it? How else can we . . .

What?

I don't know.

How else can we what?

I don't know.

Who is we?

You and me.

You meant you and the baby.

I did not.

You did. The officer is your friend. Let's move to the country.

The country.

Then I'd be outnumbered two to one instead of two to a million and still outnumbered.

Cate turned away and shook her head. I don't understand, she said.

At last! said Adam. He grinned. Good.

The Queen of Ukraine

Off Cape Hatteras the sea arched up to her, a gymnast too perfect to be had but wanting to be wanted. Only a detail of scale stopped the Queen of Ukraine sticking out a tonguetip to tickle the muscled water, make the sea plunge concave with a gasp. The ghost of the taste of salt filled the back of her mouth and she ordered Captain First Rank Gubenko to lower a champagne bucket over the side. A steward brought her the seawater on a tray and ladled it into a tumbler of Lviv crystal. It was grey and swirled with plankton and the dandruff of the deep. She took a mouthfull, swilled it round and spat it over the side, sending the glass after it.

Crystalware overboard, she said, and wiped her mouth with the back of her gloved forearm, making a roadkill-crimson smear on the white satin. She walked towards the prow of the SS *Lesya Ukrainka*, pride of the Black Sea Shipping Company. Twenty-five knots in all weathers, your majesty, Gubenko said each night at dinner, morsing dots of red caviar onto a buttery trencher. Give them money and they could never find the place between vulgarity and frugality. In all Ukraine only the Queen knew where that was.

Forced to choose, of course, vulgarity every time.

She stood alone in the bows among the anchor chains, back to the bridge, and the officer of the watch eye-gorging on her. An optic nerve with fingertips and a mouth, tease the curve of her spine and swallow the fruit of it with a snap and a gulp. Cherry on a stalk. The west wind had a coldness. She drew her shawl, an embroidered tribute from the women of Lutsk, gold fleurs-de-lys merging into trezubi on white lace, more closely around her. The sun wasn't long up. Through clouds like torn strips of sodden cardboard the redundancy of a lit barsign on the empty streets of dawn, or a gleam of noonday hustle from the other side of the ocean, while here, off the cape, night had dismantled America, which could, it seemed possible in the diluting blue, with nothing but a hazy code of buoys and lighthouses to remind it of the order of things when it went to bed, be obliged to build it all again.

From here they could see the justification of her insistence on the approach to New York by sea. Leonid Makarovich had begged her to take the Antonov. She'd been tempted. The pool was charming. How the institutes in Mikolayiv had laboured to find glass strong enough to floor the aircraft and hold the water in place! To plunge in and dive down through the water as the plane swooped towards Manhattan. It would be like flying by yourself, like Peter Pan and Wendy! And then to invite friends for a swim run down Grand Canyon. But it would have meant landing at John F. Kennedy.

The yacht, I think, she'd said.

Steamship, said the president under his breath, his loose jaw beginning to rock from side to side with anxiety. Your Majesty . . . Kennedy was a great man. A democrat.

I'm not a democrat. That's your line of work. I don't like him. I don't like the way he treated Jackie and Marilyn.

But he was a great man.

I've known a few great men. You don't understand, Leonid Makarovich, what it takes to be a great man. It can easily be good. Seldom great.

You mean love . . .

Love?

President Kravchuk's forehead began to gleam. A single strand of white silver sprang erect from one of the perfect oily furrows on his scalp and coiled shyly into itself.

The sea crossing would take weeks, he said. You can't be away for that long. Folk wouldn't understand. Your Majesty knows the currency's in trouble.

Am I an economist? Is this my problem?

The notes have your picture on them.

Print more.

That's the trouble. There are too many already. It's called hyperinflation.

So I'm popular. I don't care. I'm not landing at JFK.

There are other airports in the United States.

You want the Queen of Ukraine to land at La Guardia?

Washington . . .

I'm going to New York. There's only one airport there fit for the Queen. But the plane doesn't put rubber to tarmac unless they change the name back to Idlewild. Do you know of any charismatic American politicians called Idlewild with an agenda for hope and a talent for martyrdom? I don't think so. Prepare the royal train. I'm leaving for Odessa tonight.

The hairs were unfolding from their grooves quickly now, like a time-lapse film of the growth of an undersea vegetable.

We spent a fortune on the Antonov, said the president. Surly, pretending to be hurt. We made it nice for you. The walnut finish round the white kid in the royal suite, it wasn't cheap. People won't understand.

It's not their business to understand. Who said I wanted to be understood? I'm the Queen. I don't come with an instruction book.

Leonid Makarovich pursed his mouth, inhaled deeply and touched his knuckles together. Offended Buddha. The Queen rose and stood by the window, arms folded. She looked at the row of giant cement frogs lining the roof of the Horodetsky House opposite. Great men. Without turning round she asked about Mykola.

We haven't found him, the president said. Everyone's trying, the police, the SBU. Without a photograph, an address, it's difficult, of course. If you could at least give us a surname.

He wears black, said the Queen. Tears crested her cheekbones and coasted chinwards. She bit her lip and sobbed.

Your Majesty, said Leonid Makarovich, pushing his chair back and trotting towards her over the nomenklatura-standard carpet. He took her in his arms and patted her on the shoulder with a soft palm like a child smoothing a snowman.

Buy a new carpet, she sniffed. It's vile.

We will, said the president. The IMF's coming next week.

The Queen's fingertips plucked at the president's jacket. She was sure that if she kept looking she would find an air valve and he would deflate, sighing.

Leonid Makarovich drew his head back and peeked, fascinated, at the eyeliner swirling down her face in the flood. Many men wear black, he murmured. Perhaps he's a priest?

Mykola stretched his arm out and hooked a slice of tongue with the fork. He slid it over the china and flipped it up and into his mouth.

Gross, said Bohdana.

His head wasn't touching it, said Mykola.

The grand chessmaster snorted in his sleep. A fleck of yellow matter left his nostril, squashed by contact with the plate of cold mixed meats. His head swayed, rose, turned, and fell again. He settled with his cheek resting snug on the salami, roulade and smoked ham and smiled. He began to snore.

Have some more, said Bohdana. Look, his head's not touching it.

Waiters with faces like the corpses of the drowned moved in the distance, heavy, fragile, self-absorbed, rags hanging from their wrists, tight white shirts straining over paunches and shrunken ribcages, faintly blotched with stains hallowed by nightly boil washes. They had as much regard for the diners as Japanese troops for the Anglo-Saxon POWs who dishonoured themselves by surrendering rather than committing suicide. To pay to eat at the Dnipro was dishonour. There could be no service.

Mykola dipped the wrong end of a teaspoon into a Stolichny salad and lifted to his mouth a pea which had been canned under the Ukrainian Soviet Socialist Republic. Now a free pea in free Ukraine. He mashed it against his teeth and took a mouthful of sweet flat Crimean shampanskoye. A shudder hooped up his torso and the supersized bronzey plates set in the wall like bubblebursts shimmered.

I'm getting a fever, he said.

Everyone has flu, said Bohdana. The heating's out in here.

Yes, it's cold, and this shampanskoye's so *warm*. You've got to help me. I had a bad night again.

The Queen? How did she look?

Oh, fabulous! She was on a royal yacht coming up the Hudson at dawn. She was in silver lamé. It looked great on her. Her hair was blowing in the wind, and the sun made her skin look as if it was reflecting torchlight. She was supposed to be at the Met for a Chernobyl benefit that night. Scenes from *Zaporozhets Za Dunayem*.

Supposed to be.

She was going to blow them off and head for Broadway. Tim Rice rewrote *Evita* for her. *Don't Cry For Me, Ukraina*.

And then hit the clubs.

Yeah, and then the clubs!

Bohdana was nodding as she lit up. She ran her hands through her hair and exhaled. It wasn't like her. The Peron reference had scraped something off, rubbed away a patch of Toronto mall girl. So do you do it with her? she said.

Mykola grinned. Fear and age stayed in his eyes. No, he said. I don't know. I'm not certain she's a man. I'm not sure she's me. In the dreams I move in and out of her, watching her, then being her, then watching her again. She's always alone, because she's never together with anyone she loves. Sexually she's like a stone that changes colour when you turn it in the light, always the same stone, always beautiful, but different colours. Is that strange for you? The more aroused I am in dreams, the faster the object of desire changes, but when it changes, it changes to something different. The Queen of Ukraine isn't like that. She changes but she's still the Queen. She's a woman, she's a man, she's a woman with a dick, she's a man with a hole, she's me, I'm her as a woman, I'm her as a man, she's me dressed as a woman wanting a woman dressed as a man.

D'you want to know what I dreamed about last night? said Bohdana, stubbing the cigarette half-smoked. A slice of Brie on warm French bread. She folded her arms and looked down at her lap, letting her fringe hang over her eyes.

Mykola wasn't listening. Freud, you see . . . he thought it was all to do with sex and instinct. He didn't get to grips with the human urges of space and time. He didn't understand the lust for forms other than sexual forms. He didn't get the longing for places and the past. He didn't understand longing or grief, or light. People will tell you it was a sense of sexual inadequacy that led Hitler to invade Poland, but what about the men who sleep around because they're incapable of territorial conquest? Did you ever hear of a shrink diagnosing geopolitical inadequacy as a source of sexual problems? When I'm in New York I dream of the Queen in Ukraine, and when I'm in Ukraine she's always visiting New York. If you told me it's me mythologising places I love when I'm not in them, I'd be offended, because that'd sound like me not being a sexual man. But then if you said it was all about sexual desire that'd be wrong too, because what's sex got to do with the sunlight on her skin reflected off the windows of Manhattan, or her riding to wolfhounds with her court down the frozen Dnipro, trotting in between the ice fishermen, and them not knowing whether to lift their hats or bow?

The Queen of Ukraine's the part of you that's left behind, the part you romance the locals with, said Bohdana, an inner lid raised from her eyes, which were bright now and saw the world. In the States you want them to see you as the one who dared to submit your soul to the hard struggle of Ukraine, and in Ukraine the cool American. You try so hard in New York to look as if you're brooding about Kiev and in Kiev as if you're out on loan from the Museum of Modern Art. You're like all the perfectionist lovers. You pretend you're longing for love when really you're in love with longing.

Perhaps, said Mykola. But she's still the Queen of Ukraine.

There isn't a queen of Ukraine.

For me there is.

Lieutenant Zagrebelny slipped into the royal stateroom, clicked his heels together and bowed his head from the shoulder as she had taught him. He looked superb in the black leather parade dress of the marines, with the collar and shoulder tabs in white and royal blue suede. The Queen crossed her bare legs, stretching out from her ivory chiffon chemise, and nodded at Natalie to leave.

The Statue of Liberty, ma'am, said Zagrebelny. You asked to be told.

Do you have the photographs? Bring them over here.

The lieutenant brought over a slim black album. The Queen drew a cigarette from the gold-chased basalt box on her dressing table and looked up at the officer. He leaned down with the lighter. The Queen took in smoke, looking into the lieutenant's eyes. He was looking straight ahead. The Queen reached out with her left hand and squeezed the long bulge in Zagrebelny's trousers with her fingertips.

Ever anally penetrated a man, lieutenant? she asked.

He looked down at her. For a second a boy seemed to be there and she weakened. Then anger that she couldn't tell whether it was eagerness in his eyes, or ambition.

No ma'am, he said.

Oh, you poor thing, said the Queen, pursing her lips. Well, never mind. They say New York is a wonderful town.

She opened the album. The happiest day of her life! The day-long Freedom Parade of a thousand floats down Kreshchatik, and the carnival queen a real queen, at the head of her people, Donbass miners in gold overalls with silver helmets carrying bouquets of coal-black tulips, Crimean Tatars in azure and crimson robes with curled and scented beards, Zaporizhzhya Cossacks on chestnut mares, their khokhli waving like horsetails as they sang, their spurs and harness and scabbards loosened to make them jingle. A dozen perfect Poltava girls on a float themed Broken Hearts, all weeping together, an amazing sight. A procession of blind minstrels, led by river fleet cadets from Izmail in white blouses, singing Taras Shevchenko ballads. Hutsul pipers from the Carpathians, gipsy dancers from Uzhhorod, nuclear workers from Chernobyl with a model of the power station under a giant condom and a banner proclaiming: Safe Nuclear Power, Safe Sex. Free borshch, cherry varenyki and Pearl of the Steppe wine on Andriyivsky Uzviz and an all-night rave in Hidropark in the middle of the Dnipro where by dawn all the Poltava girls' broken hearts were mended, and broken again.

By then the royal train had reached Odessa, where the Joke Festival was breaking up and the last laughers were rolling down the Potemkin Steps towards the Black Sea in the dawn, smashing empty shampanskoye bottles as they went and wrapping themselves hysterically around the ankles of ascending cohorts of Orthodox rabbis just disembarked from the Haifa roro. The royal quay had been resanded and varnished and blue and yellow pennants flew its length. The Cossack guard of honour presented sabres as the royal party stepped from its dazzling azure carriage and boarded the *Lesya Ukrainka*.

Look, ma'am, said Zagrebelny, touching her on the shoulder and pointing through the porthole. A green woman hanging from a torch on a little island.

You're too familiar with me! said the Queen in a rage. Take your fingers off my shoulder! The devil, who made you one of my officers?

Zagrebelny stood straight, clicked his heels and bowed. He began to apologise.

Never apologise to me! Never! said the Queen. There can be no apologising. You have to *be* an apology.

Ma'am.

You'll find what you need in there, she said, nodding to a box of silver filigree and birchbark on the pink granite coffee table. One of the Rivne labourers who had manhandled it into place had crippled himself doing it. She'd made sure he had a comfortable pension. Or had she? She'd certainly intended to.

The Queen stood up and moved over to a larger porthole. There was a soft, plump couch under it, upholstered in black silk, with details from Caravaggio rendered in dark grey thread which only showed when the light caught them, and were more felt with the fingertips than seen. She knelt on the cushions with her back to the stateroom, elbows on the wooden rail below the porthole, and watched Liberty doing her duty. Behind her she heard Zagrebelny open the box. There was a pause while he sniffed and cleared his throat. She smiled. She heard his zip and slippery, sticky noises as he lubed up. He walked towards her.

What do they know of liberty here? said the Queen.

Land of the free, said Zagrebelny, lifting the hem of her chemise. She felt the cautious invasion of a nicely-manicured finger.

I hope you don't think you're going to be some kind of court favourite, she said. I don't have them. Especially if they don't know what's a rhetorical question.

Like, What's it all about?

That's what you're going to try to show me. We'll make another statue for the Americans. Like our monument to Leopold von Sacher-Masoch. We distilled freedom into pain and pleasure while the Americans still drink the mixture. We should teach them. Not a Statue of Liberty. A Statue of Liberation.

Lieutenant Zagrebelny did his very best to show the Queen what it was all about.

Mykola left the hotel alone. The doorman who reared up to abuse anyone trying to get into the restaurant, like an old blind farm dog still chasing cars, watched him pass, the bottomless spring of hate bubbling up within him. In the suspended influenza of Kiev's March nights, impregnated with the fragrance of damp, smouldering coal, the depeopled crescent Kreshchatik shrank back from its own weak streetlights, shamed by its dark, blind shopfronts and its freakish towers, cupolas and friezes. Mykola began to walk home.

He entered the tunnels under Kreshchatik and strayed. Stunted teen souls in cheap Turkish leather and woollen hats shivered in the yellow-tiled catacombs, drinking bottles of Obolon. Moist scarlet mouths glistened in white faces and they laughed, shivering and tapping their heels with the cold. The flower-sellers squatted on camp stools, ziggurats of layered clothing. Trash burned and smoked in bell-shaped cans and a crowd horseshoed round a guitarist and a trumpeter playing selections from Soviet films of the 70s and 80s. The trumpeter was playing the theme from *A Stranger At Home, At Home Among Strangers*. A pair of naval infantry conscripts from the Black Sea Fleet marched down the tunnel, faces ravaged by acne, boots two sizes too big, sleeves of their greatcoats hiding their hands, synthetic fur hats pushed back nearly vertical. They were small and crooked in the middle and the brass buttons on their greasy black coats swung loose like the eyes of old toys as they strode past bandylegged, chickenwise.

Givesa smoke, said the fair-haired one to Mykola in Russian. His eruptions were the angriest but for that his eyes were blue like forget-me-nots.

Sorry, said Mykola in Ukrainian. Don't have any cigarettes. He smiled. The conscripts hesitated. It wasn't the no they knew. It was a where do we go from here? and a whaddawegonnado about it?

Foreigner or something? said the dark one to the fair one.

Where you from? said the fair one to Mykola in Ukrainian.

New York.

New York, Fair whispered to Dark out of the corner of his mouth.

Ask him if he likes Dépêche Mode.

Don't be stupid.

They're OK, said Mykola.

Where d'you learn to speak Ukrainian?

Mykola shrugged. America.

The conscripts giggled. America! You're what, doing business here?

Mykola laughed. His eyes ranged up and down the tunnels. All these questions! Don't you want to go somewhere and talk?

D'you drink vodka?

Maybe.

We haven't got any money.

Oh, I've got money. Mykola looked between the two faces. Fair was interested that he was a foreigner. Dark was more intense, interested that he was a foreign man, alone in the tunnels at night, not in a hurry. Mykola looked into Dark's brown eyes. This one was the hustler. I've got money, he repeated. Maybe we could work something out. It's all the same to me.

The two conscripts looked at him. Fair's mouth was a little open. He didn't get it. Dark took Fair's elbow and dragged him away. Mykola stuck his hands in his pockets and walked on slowly. He looked back over his shoulder and saw the two by the wall, close together, chest to chest. The fair one was looking after Mykola with what was supposed to be pride but looked like a penguin spotting something in the distance. Dark was fidgeting with one of Fair's buttons and tapping him on the chest, looking up into his face while he spoke to him.

Mykola heard one of them coming up behind him. Mistr! Mistr! The dark one was walking alongside him, holding his sleeve in his fist, leaning his head and talking out of the side of his mouth.

My friend'll take it in the mouth for a thousand dollars.

Mykola laughed. He sighed. No need, he said. I'm going home.

So, well, come on, how much?

How about ten dollars?

The conscript was quiet for a couple of seconds. OK, he said.

Mykola stopped and looked down at the boy. They were supposed to be seventeen. This one looked younger and older. He looked like he was about to jump straight from teenager to pensioner without bothering with manhood.

How about nothing at all? said Mykola.

How's that? said the dark one foxily, sensing he was missing the point. Here he was on the verge of a breakthrough into the world of intoxicating deals he'd always thought was his due but how to push through the cunning American's negotiating screen?

I don't like to pay, said Mykola.

What are you, greedy?

Money doesn't settle everything.

It's only people who've got it who say that.

Mykola looked into his eyes and said: I'm into it if you're into it, otherwise forget it.

The fair one was coming towards them. Mykola asked the dark one's name.

Petya. He's Taras. Don't think I'm a shirtlifter. Petya worked his shoulders and smacked his fist softly into his cupped palm. A man should try everything once in his life.

Mykola told them his name and shook their hands. There was a silence while they looked at each other. Petya whispered in Taras' ear. Mykola said: I've got some vodka and food back at the flat if you want to share.

Nu, let's go, said Petya. Taras hesitated. There was more whispering.

Mykola . . . said Petya. What's your patronymic?

Cliffovich.

Seriously?

Yes. My father was called Cliff.

Mykola. Kolya. Taras wants to ask you something.

Will you buy some roses for my girl? said Taras, tightly.

Mykola shrugged. How many? he said.

Oh, the Americans and their numbers, said Petya.

It has to be an odd number, said Taras.

The Queen laid the *Voice* on the coffee table and studied the clubbing notes. Everything had changed. What happened to that place where they'd driven a herd of sheep across the dancefloor one night, and Boyz, where in transparent booths along the walls naked boys could be watched as they showered to the beat? In the space of a couple of years she'd missed entire trends and their revivals. It was wonderful to see how fashion slew its avatars. The Queen was impervious to fashion. The camera was her vassal. Her every look was history. She did not dress up or pose. It was natural. She was more than photogenic. She was optogenic. The eyes of others adored her. In every moment they watched her, people around her saw, in the present, the kind of mythologised image that in others took the distance of a twenty-year-old photograph to create. If not death. That was why the Queen always got what she wanted. Even if they hated her when they were out of her sight.

She tore the club pages out of the magazine one by one and crumpled and squeezed them into tight balls. She moved the firescreen away from the fireplace and put them on top of the plastic logs. She lit a match from the hotel's complimentary matchbox and set fire to the paper. She rang for Natalie.

Send down to reception for some raw pork and get Zagrebelny's people to make some shashlyk, she said.

Yes, Ma'm . . . where? said Natalie.

Here, said the Queen, nodding at the fireplace. A stink of smouldering plastic was beginning to come up off the artifical logs.

Of course, Ma'm, said Natalie. The park might be even better.

D'you think? said the Queen, stepping through the open balcony door and leaning out over the parapet. The sun was just down and Central Park was dimming. Muggers, she said. Dealers, policemen. And you know how they love arresting people for the strangest things here.

As you wish, Ma'm, said Natalie. I'm sure the law doesn't apply inside the hotel.

This is the best suite in New York, isn't it? said the Queen, raising her voice.

Yes Ma'm.

Well, get about it.

Ma'm, your press attaché wishes to see you.

Tell him to wait. Get Kiev on the phone. I want to speak to the SBU.

Natalie went out. As she opened the door to the reception room the press attaché, Vasily Hrynyuk, slithered in through the gap. The Queen looked at him and as he opened his mouth put her fingers to her lips. She pointed to a chair in the corner. He sat down. The room was filling with white smoke. Hrynyuk began to cough and the smoke detectors went off with an eardrum-drilling *wheee wheee wheee*. The Queen took one of the phones and went out onto the balcony, closing the door behind her. Turning up the collar of her Prada jacket she sat down in a lounger as the phone rang.

I'll tell you what time it is, she said. It's not Kiev Time, it's not Eastern Standard Time, it's Royal Time. Which just now is seven pm. Time for a snack and a drink before changing. Not Kiev, New York, New York, if I was in Kiev I'd tell the general to come to the palace. Yes, I'll wait.

She lay back in the lounger, laid the phone on her heart and closed her eyes. She heard tapping on the glass of the window. She opened her eyes. Swirls of smoke and spurts of foam could be seen, and faces, swimming up to the glass with wide eyes and strangely working mouths like fish.

Good evening, General.

Your Majesty.

Say it again.

Your *Majesty*.

Oh, it was better the first time. Are you in full dress uniform?

Your Majesty, I regret . . . I'm naked, apart from the bedsheet.

You spies! You know why I'm calling.

The missing one.

Mykola.

We're trying new approaches. We contacted ZAGS and the residence registration bureaux and we've drawn up a list of men in Ukraine named Mykola aged between 25 and 45. We could fit them all inside the Republican Stadium.

Then what?

Well, they could file past you. It would take a few days.

It's very sweet of you. I can't allow it. The humiliation would be intolerable.

They'd have to put up with it.

Don't be a fool. For me! It can't be known that there's such an emptiness in the Queen's life. You'll just have to find him.

The general said: We had another idea. There was a KGB research department in Bukovina where they experimented with trying to synthesize the dreams of dissidents and western leaders. The operatives would be supplied with hypnotically introduced false memories to correspond with their targets and dressed and fed accordingly. In the morning they would report on the dreams of Ronald Reagan and Andrei Sakharov. The data wasn't reliable and most of the researchers have gone into advertising now but perhaps we could try it with you.

What did Reagan dream of ?

The Lone Ranger was queuing for sausage and there was a college football quarterback played by James Stewart who started reciting Pushkin in a Georgian accent every time he made a touchdown. As I say, it wasn't reliable.

Why did you never get married, General?

I did, your Majesty. Don't you remember? We live in separate parts of the flat now. I still love her, but she won't sleep with me. Our children carry messages between us.

Stay on the line. But lie back. Put your head on the pillow, said the Queen. Here's what I remember. Perhaps it was a vision. Mykola's in Independence Square, in black jeans, teeshirt and an open black cardigan. He's tall and thin, not muscular but not flabby. He's in his late thirties, early forties. He's standing there by himself, listening to a soldier just demobbed who's sitting on the edge of the fountain, playing a guitar and singing. It's May, there's that long, slow, bright twilight that never seems to end. The first thing you notice about him is how he can stand alone and not look alone, as if the whole world was keeping him company but was too shy to step forward. All the young girls are looking at him, of course, but he doesn't notice. All his attention goes to the guitarist and the guitarist feels it, it inspires him and he sings better. When his song's finished Mykola goes over to the guitarist who gets up and shakes his hand and they talk for a while. After a few minutes Mykola wishes him well and walks away by himself, with his beautiful walk, looking to one side and the other like if there's anything good to be found in the city, he'll be there. The guitarist looks after him and even though his friends are around him, it seems as if the world is following Mykola, a few steps behind him, and the guitarist has been left behind. He thinks about running after Mykola but he doesn't, he's too proud, and he doesn't have anything to say to him, he just wants to be with him. He knows he's lost something and the next song he plays is a Russian lover's lament.

> *My sweet, take me with you*
> *And there in the far places*
> *I'll be your wife*

She could hear the general snoring. She put the phone down and wiped her face with a tissue.

The balcony door opened and a fireman with a mask and breathing apparatus, drenched in foam, stepped out of opaque curls of smoke. He looked at the Queen for a while, hands on his hips. He reached into the fog and pulled a choking, writhing sinner out of the cauldron. He shoved Hrynyuk into a chair. Next he ushered in a hybrid imp, half maid, half fireman. Natalie wore the black skirt, black tights and heels and a fireman's jacket and mask. She was carrying the cooked shashlyk on a tray. She laid it down carefully on a table next to the Queen, forked the meat off the skewers onto a plate, arranged it with bread and green herbs and hot sauce and a white napkin, pulled off the mask and collapsed onto the floor. The fireman went over and began administering artificial respiration.

Press conference, croaked Hrynyuk. They're waiting.

The Queen stood up. The fireman had one knee clamped high between Natalie's thighs. Her fingernails were picking at the fastenings of his suit while they ate each other.

Give the meat to the poor people of New York, said the Queen.

Petya and Taras followed Mykola down Karla Marla, through an arch into a dark yard lit only by the light from upstairs windows. Cat kings of the wheelybins scattered at their approach from mounds of potato peel and carrot scrapings. At the entrance way Mykola felt for the doorknob and the conscripts closed in behind him, their hands reaching for his back and elbows to reassure themselves he was still there. Inside it was still dark, the bulbs stolen. There was a stench of urine. They shuffled up a set of steps like the newly blind and by memory Mykola found the lift button. The rough, time-chewed plastic wobbled under his fingertip and glowed cigarette-weak when the lift began to descend from its station above, clanking like an iron horse.

In the lift there was a smell of old vegetables and rancid stains on old blankets. Taras put his nose into one of his five red roses and inhaled. From Azerbaijan, he said.

No, they bring them from the west now, said Petya. Africa or something.

Africa? said Taras, sniffing the flowers again, suspicious. Do they have roses in Africa?

Petya laughed. America! he said to Mykola. This probably seems like Africa to you. D'you have lifts like this in America? Bet you don't.

Oh, we have all sorts of lifts in America, said Mykola.

Even before the lift opened they could hear the sounds of a woman screaming. They stood in front of the padded steel door to Mykola's flat, Mykola with the silver key held out, Taras with his face half-hidden by the roses, Petya taking his hat off and holding it protectively in front of his heart. The door was shaking. Every time it shook, it rattled, and every time it shook and rattled, or just before, they could hear a woman screaming No! and a man shouting You bitch, I'll kill you!

Mykola turned to the conscripts. You couldn't go and wait in the yard? he said. It's my roommate. She wasn't supposed to be back till next week. I'll be down in a minute.

Is it your wife? said Petya.

It's a friend who lives in the same house, said Mykola.

Ah, a friend, said Petya. It's a friend, he said to Taras, tugging his sleeve and turning to go.

Can we help? said Taras, waving the roses towards the door so the leaves and petals rustled.

Mykola smiled and shook his head. The door rattled and the woman screamed again, not a word this time, a higher scream. I'll come down in a minute.

The boys went back to the lift and Mykola rang the bell. It's Mykola! he shouted. I'm coming in.

Your mother, said Oleg. What the fuck do you want?

Mykola! called Stella. I came back early.

I'm coming in, said Mykola, pushing the key in the lock.

Tell him to fuck off, whispered Oleg. Tell him we're busy. He shouted: We're busy!

Mykola turned the key. He heard feet moving quickly across the carpet, a slamming door and running water. He went inside the flat and closed the front door. He held up his hand in front of his face to see what the stickiness on the doorhandle was. It was that.

Stella had locked herself in the bathroom. It's Mykola, he said. She let him in. She locked the door behind him and sat down on the edge of the bath. She had a bloodstained wet towel wrapped around her head. She sat there with her back hunched and her hands between her legs. She smiled at him.

Hi, she said. How's it going?

I thought you were in London for another week.

Yeah, said Stella, hunching further forward and lowering her head. But I couldn't get his penis out of my mind. So I came back.

Are you OK?

Yeah, I'm OK.

Was he beating your head against the doorhandle?

Stella nodded, folded her arms across her stomach and sniffed.

Here, let me have a look. Mykola put out his hand and Stella pushed it gently away.

I'm fine, Mykola, honestly. He gets jealous.

He's psychotic. He could have killed you.

Yeah, I suppose he could, said Stella. She smiled.

You've got to stop seeing him.

I couldn't do that! What'd I do then? I'd just be thinking about him all the time. You think I'm crazy. He loves me, you know. I used to think once you were crazy that was it, you were crazy everywhere all the time. But it's not like that. Now I know what my mind's like, it's like a big hotel. Down there in the ballroom it's murder. But up in your own room it's all quiet, and peaceful, and organised. You just lock the door, and take a shower, watch some TV, make some calls. She laughed. Then you're all ready to go back to the ballroom again.

Hard and loud as a gunshot, the heel of a boot smashed against the door. You come out of there, you bitch! screamed Oleg. You and the shitstabber!

Go fuck yourself, you sick bastard! said Stella. Have you got a smoke? she said to Mykola.

No. I think we should call the police.

He'll be fine, said Stella, putting her hand on Mykola's wrist.

The boot went in again, twice. The wood began to splinter. Mykola pulled a cylinder out of his jacket pocket and when Oleg smashed through sprayed him in the face with Mace. Oleg screamed that he was blind and spun back through the corridor, stotting against corners and bookcases like a pinball. Stella ran after him, crying his name.

After a couple of minutes of the two of them shrieking together it went quiet. Mykola got up and went to the kitchen. He switched on the light and the roaches scattered across the table like a gang of nightbirds surprised by a helicopter. He rooted through the cupboards and shelves and poked around in the fridge. She'd brought back a stack of Marks & Spencer's ready-to-eat curries but no coffee. He pulled the bottle of Stolichnaya out of the freezer. It was half empty.

He gathered up the vodka and a loaf of bread and filled a mug with some pickled cucumbers. He went out. On the way he passed Stella's room. She was sitting on her bed, stroking Oleg's forehead with one hand and fumbling inside his trousers with the other. The bloody towel lay on the rug. Mykola could see how her own forehead was messed up.

My little sweetie, baby, I love you, I love you, she was saying. Oleg moaned. Oh don't worry, be quiet, don't speak, I love you and I know you love me, I couldn't leave you, I couldn't live without you, I'm going to be with you for ever, don't worry, my sweet, my dear, I'm yours, you're mine, just lie still, my love, I love you and I'm going to make everything all right.

Mykola stepped out into the rotting darkness and into the lift.

He leaned against the flimsy veneer walls as it spooled its slovenly way groundwards. He closed his eyes and stopped breathing. Like a heroin rush the memory of the scent of a stranger's perfumed body in the Hamptons one hot blue and white day sluiced through him and burst, a divesplash from sphincter to shoulderblades. He was immersed in the cool sunlit shallows of lost time and shoals of sensation darted away from his fingers, dust motes carouselling in the beams slanting through the SoHo window and coffeemaking lovers architecting his days, the warm peppery air of Manhattan evening on his face coming out after a matinée.

The yard was darker than before. Mykola called the conscripts' names. A cat answered. Mykola clinked the bottle and the mug together.

Come and get it, he said. He sniffed the air. In the interstices of decay and smoke bulged the smell of roses.

The panther in the coal cellar. They had known what they were about, the makers of Soviet uniforms, aiding the assignations of adulterous admirals in the dimly-lit backyards of Sevastopol and Vladivostok. The Hard To See Fleet. Now he could make out buttons and faces.

Hey, he said.

The boys, suspicious again, came over. There was a playground with benches around it. They sat down, Mykola in the middle, the boys on either side. They passed around the spirit and zakuski. Taras and Mykola drank a few mouthfuls. Petya drained the bottle, belched and snatched a petal off one of Taras' roses. He put it in his mouth, chewed and swallowed.

Son of a bitch, said Taras.

Dessert, said Petya. To make me sweeter for the girls. *Nu*, ready? he said, slapping Mykola's crotch.

I suppose, said Mykola.

Brother, said Petya, the American wants service.

Taras found Mykola's zip. He got Mykola out, let go and looked at Petya.

Couldn't do it with my hand? he said.

Business is business, said Petya.

It's OK, said Mykola, if he doesn't want to.

No! said Petya. A deal is a deal. That's capitalism, isn't it?

Devil, said Taras. He turned his head, hawked, held the bouquet away from Mykola and went down on him. He started chewing like a dog on a bone. Mykola felt an icy touch on his scalp.

Oho, said Petya. It's snowing. He held the last cucumber out to Mykola. D'you want it?

No thanks, said Mykola. He winced as Taras nipped a bit of skin.

America, America, said Petya, chewing and nodding. I'd like to go there. I don't understand why you came to Kiev. I'm a patriot, of course, but it's shit here. Don't you like New York? Are the girls pretty there?

It's a wonderful place, said Mykola. It's the centre of the world. Everything is there. He pushed Taras' hat off and ran his fingers through the boy's hair, the snowflakes slipping between his knuckles. He came in the conscript's throat. Everything.

So why did you leave?

So I could miss it.

Taras got up, took his hat and walked away, coughing it up.

So I could miss it, and so I could go back, said Mykola. It's good to be there but it's even better to keep on going back.

Ah, Kolya, you don't want to do that. It's unlucky to go back. You shouldn't go back if you've left something behind. That's what happened to Yuri Gagarin. He went back, and he crashed his plane.

People leave to change, said Mykola. But it works the opposite way. It's like travelling at almost the speed of light. The faster and further away you go, the quicker the people you leave behind get old. It's the law of Personal Relativity.

Better put that away, or it'll freeze, said Petya, patting Mykola's prick. He got up and walked off. Thanks for the drink, he said.

You're welcome, said Mykola.

Petya started running towards the archway, shouting after Taras. He stopped under the arc and called to Mykola: Whose was that law?

The Queen's, said Mykola. It was the Queen of Ukraine.

The Queen stopped outside the door to the function room. Hrynyuk introduced her to the cluster of people: the hotel manager, the representatives of the fire department, the mayor's office, Human Rights Watch, the Ukrainian National Assembly, the World Bank, the Ukrainian parliament's finance committee and a couple of dozen lawyers. The Queen smiled at them all and shook their hands.

They seem angry, she murmured in Hrynyuk's ear.

Don't worry, your Majesty, we'll sort it out after the presser.

She walked into the lights and sat down. She began counting the lenses in the camera wall in the middle of the room. She lost track at twenty. Apart from Hrynyuk, she was alone. The ambassador hadn't come. Natalie, Lieutenant Zagrebelny and Captain Gubenko were to have been in attendance. Their chairs were empty.

Ladies and gentlemen, Her Most Royal Majesty, the Queen of Ukraine, will now take questions, said Hrynyuk, getting to his feet. He leaned down and whispered: I'll slip outside and start spinning those lawyers. He vanished. The questions began. The Queen felt her lips cracking.

THE NEW YORK TIMES: Hey, how're you doing? I thought maybe you'd decided to stay out there for ever.

HM THE QUEEN: Thank you. Naturally my people are suffering great hardships but with the help of our friends abroad, particularly in the United States, we are confident that the present crisis can be overcome.

THE WASHINGTON POST: Good to see you, man. I'd forgotten what you looked like. Hey, you know how Meryl said she was going to keep your job open for you? Well, she didn't.

HM THE QUEEN: Thank you. My visit here is essentially private. I shall be meeting with some very dear acquaintances. Nonetheless, I shall be attending a number of public functions, most of them connected with my post as honorary chairman of important Ukrainian charities.

THE BOSTON GLOBE: Son, we're willing to overlook what's happened, but how about you hold the gay deal for one weekend, and take your father bowling or something? He won't mention you being a faggot if you don't.

HM THE QUEEN: Thank you. There are a number of pretenders and communists who dispute my claim to the title, and even question whether the monarchy has a role in Ukraine in the 1990s. I need only point to such stable, prosperous societies as Holland, Denmark and the United Kingdom to illustrate my conviction that it has.

CNN: I was afraid this was going to happen. How can I put this? You've been away for so long and now you want just to jump right back in. We're older now, we're not as multi-partner as we were. I'm not saying I'm monogamous. It's a kind of partial celibacy. I sleep around but I abstain from sex with you.

HM THE QUEEN: Thank you. The story of my discovery in a wicker basket among the reeds of the Pripyat Marshes, my upbringing by a collective farm director and his secretly

Banderovite wife, my teenage years in Brooklyn and the establishment of my descent from Ryurik of Kievan Rus are too well known to be retold here. In response to your second question, the documents mentioned in the Komsomolskaya Pravda article have been shown conclusively to be second-rate forgeries. There is no sex-change clinic in Yalta, and it is clearly absurd to suggest that anyone would attempt to change sex more than once. On gender, I reply as I always do: it is the privilege of a sovereign to strive to be loved without being desired, to be wedded to her people rather than a spouse to a single person. That said, anyone may desire me, if they dare.

THE LOS ANGELES TIMES: You don't find me interesting enough any more, is that it? Is that why you never call when you're in town.

HM THE QUEEN: Thank you. I do not accept comparisons with Imelda Marcos. It is not the quantity of shoes which matters, but the quality. I can assure you that in both respects I have left Mrs Marcos light-years behind. As for the economy, I hardly think that a proper subject for a queen to concern herself with. I can tell you that shortly before my departure I met with members of the government who assured me that they were increasing the production of money by all means at their disposal. I regularly go among the poor, dispensing small baskets of currency, but I am sure you understand my busy social schedule allows me to distribute money only to a limited percentage of the population. Alas, I cannot solve all my country's problems singlehanded.

THE WALL STREET JOURNAL: Just the person I need to settle this argument we've been having. Now I know Kiev is in Crimea, but where the heck is Siberia, is it Ukraine or Russia?

HM THE QUEEN: Thank you. No. I am not an ambassador

for my country. I am a hostage against my own reception. If America doesn't love me, it'll never see me again.

NBC: Are you OK?

HM THE QUEEN: Thank you. There is one man. His name is Mykola. I can't tell you any more about him but if you want to write about love, write about him. Make it up. He does. Only make it up well. I know he's there now, in the dark yard on Karla Marla, in the snow, thinking about me. Of course I wish he could have been with me when we sailed up to the lights of your island in the evening, with the crowd and the orchestra on the wharf and the helicopters squinting at us as we docked, but he chose to dine with a woman friend in the unheated hall of the Dnipro. He should have been with me in Kiev on my birthday, when we raced reindeer sleighs on the reservoir and roasted oxen on bonfires of old Soviet passports. He was here, watching *L'Age D'Or* in some arthouse fleapit. Does he care for me? I don't know. I care for him. Perhaps he's afraid of me. Perhaps he's afraid of the scale of my style. I am difficult. I am beyond the limit. I am the Queen of Ukraine.

Smoked

I drank and slept and dreamed I was a poisoned angel, with feet like a bird's, standing on the edge of a crater looking down at an ocean of clouds boiling with bruise-coloured folds. I was poisoned by the thought that in one of the alternative moments the angels lived through, God had made a world other than the one we knew, our existence where the only tendency was towards an infinite complication in artefacts and deeds. I asked him, he was everywhere, but he didn't pay attention, he wasn't even aware of the nature of the question. I watched the lightning shooting upwards into the firmament from the clouds, and other angels darting like gnats around the flashes. I'd shoulder-charged the ends of time and broken through to the circularity of it, meeting myself each way, and still there was no trace of the world, no clue God had ever made it, only a memory planted inextractably, like the traces of poison, of a blue and white sphere of seas and mountains and beings. I pushed myself off the rock with the sound of claws scratching against it and dived towards the clouds. I wanted to be the first angel to commit suicide.

I woke up. I lay in bed petting my grief that something had been lost, something which could only be the world I suspected God of having made, in an alternative course the angels had been forced to pass by without looking back. I felt as bad as if a woman I loved without her noticing had told me about another man. A better man.

Outside the window was the world I was mourning the loss of. The mountains were to the west side and the sea was to the east, the green fields to the north and the river to the south.

There were two things I admired Helmet for: wearing a fox fur hat in bed, and teaching his dog to fetch his newspaper from the shop. I thought the hat was a pose before I found out how cold it could be where he lived. He lived in an old fisherman's cottage near the stony beach. I could see it from my window on the hill. With some people the hat would still be a pose, even if they were cold, but he wore it because it was what he had. It wasn't like he'd killed the fox himself, either. As for the dog, there must have been a lot of training involved. And if I'd seen him doing the training, I would've thought he was a right wanker. But I hadn't. That's the secret. Never let anyone see you practising. One day I was round and the dog burst through a flap in the door, trotted in, bounded up on the bed and laid a neatly folded copy of the *Courier* on Helmet's lap. And it was like with the hat. Helmet didn't make an issue of it. He put on a pair of reading glasses and offered to split the paper with me. He turned to the death notices first, hoping to find the old fisherman's name there.

He wanted the old fisherman to die and leave him the house. Helmet had been paying him ten pounds a week in rent for five years and they split the two-room effort down the middle but Helmet wanted more space for his records. Sometimes he left a few albums on the fisherman's table by way of a hint but the fisherman would always find something in them that interfered with his sense of taboos and would throw them out the window, where they could carry a fair way if the wind was right. I once came across an astounding LP wrapped up in the dried kelp and bladderwrack on the beach. The cover was shot but the vinyl was fine. I kept it. All items washed up on the beach are the property of the Queen. If she ever comes round to pick it up, she can have it.

The fisherman was in his late seventies but didn't seem to be about to die. Helmet claimed he had no relatives but I told him there was no law that property passed to a tenant on the owner's death. I said he'd have to be nice to him. Helmet didn't say anything to that, he folded his arms across his chest and looked through the window at the sea.

He never even helped the old boy build his smoking shed. The fisherman had decided he would supplement his pension by making smokies on his back green like they did in Arbroath. He did build the shed, about the size of an outside toilet, but he never organised a proper fish supply and used to go to the fishmonger for packets of filleted haddock and fix them to racks with clothes pegs. Then he'd start faffing round with firelighters and bundles of firewood from the filling station. We came into the kitchenette once and found him trying to eat one of his smokies. It looked like a lung cancer autopsy. And Broughty Ferry wasn't about fish. It was about gardening, retail and sheltered housing. The old fisherman was as popular with the neighbours as a naked aborigine walking onto the stage of Sidney Opera House during a performance of *Die Niebelungen* and asking the audience to leave so he could reestablish the site of the Kookaburra Dreaming.

My work as a seal counter left me with time on my hands. I was supposed to bike over to Tentsmuir every day at dawn and count heads but I found it easier, after a few hours' research in the library, to work out a likely population curve and fabricate the figures on a daily basis. When I went down the Ferry I'd use the people I passed to incorporate a random element. A young child meant fecundity among the seals. Two white-haired pensioners together meant a low death rate. A good-looking boy or girl meant a population explosion or a deadly epidemic. If I fell stricken in love on the street I intended to create billions of seals. I was waiting to be stricken. I was expecting it. If she wasn't interested, I could always kill them later.

The morning after the dream Helmet called to see if I was coming over. He asked me to buy some pies on the way, and a couple of strawberry tarts. At the counter in Goodfellow & Steven the girl handed me the bags, I paid and left the shop. A gull sprang off the edge of the pavement, perfectly white, and stroked my jacket with the edge of its wing when it spun up towards the cloud. I stopped and looked in the bags. The baked goods nestled in unchanging twos. I went back inside.

I didn't ask for these, I said.

The girl put her hands on the counter and stood on tiptoe, peering into the mouths of the bags.

I made them up for you, she said. Did you want something different?

It's what I wanted but I didn't ask for them.

The girl settled back on her heels with a squeak of shoeleather and a rustle of her smock and we looked at each other. These seconds would be the best of the day. The seals were to have a hard going of it later.

You come in here every morning and ask for exactly the same thing, she said. Two pies and two tarts.

I looked at her.

I was trying to save time, she said.

Everyone does that here. You can't, though. It loses its value.

That was how I found out that Helmet never left the house.

He lived off a pie and a tart and tapwater six days a week. I was keeping him alive.

He came to the door bare-chested, wearing the grey leggings and the fur hat. We went through and lay side by side on the bed in his room. He'd been in it. He had a beautiful narrow chest, and a flat stomach, not by exercise, but by luck. He had tiny hard nipples sticking up like the backsides of buttons. I often felt like laying the flat of my hand on them, to see what it felt like, but I never did, not because I was afraid he'd think I was a poof, or'd scream or SAS my windpipe, but cause I was afraid of my bigoted future self giving me a good kicking for it ten years down the road.

I arranged the baked items between us on the bedcover and we lay on our sides on one elbow.

I dreamed about God last night, I said.

Did he tell you to kill a fisherman? said Helmet.

No.

Helmet hooded his eyes and tore off a piece of pie with his teeth. There was a thunder of jet engines over town as the fighters from over the river headed out to sea.

Helmet's dog came in with the *Courier* and we divvied it up. The room had two windows, one looking on to the shore and the other into the back green. The old fisherman was to be seen pottering about so it was pointless for Helmet to be checking the deaths.

It's pointless for you to be checking the deaths, I said. He's out there. He's alive.

Helmet levelled his heavy blackframed glasses at me over the top of the paper. If it says in here he's died, he's died. There's nothing he can do about it.

Does it say he's died?

Yes.

There were two things I admired Helmet for: the hat and the dog. It wasn't much. Everything else about him was repulsive. I looked in the paper. Sure enough, there was the old boy's name, George Brynie. Peacefully, on 10 October, and a poem. We think of you most every day/ But now that you are gone/ There's really not much else to say/ We must be moving on.

I got up and went to the back window. The door of the shed opened and the fisherman came out, coughing in waves of smoke. He caught my eye and raised his hand. I waved back. I looked at my watch. It was the tenth of the month.

If you can pay for a death notice, I said, how about paying me back for the food?

Helmet lifted his finger and held it still in the air for a second, his way of smiling, went over to a box on top of one of the shelves of records, took out a fifty pound note and gave it to me. I'd never seen one before, but that wasn't going to stop me pocketing it.

I wonder how this death notice is going to be enacted, I said.

There's a good sharp kitchen knife, said Helmet, taking off his glasses.

I looked into Helmet's eyes. We were standing in the narrow space on opposite sides of the bed. He'd always been calm, certain and determined, but nothing had ever seemed to come of it. It'd never been possible to believe that the only goal towards which his self-conviction was taking him was finding more space for his records, even in the days when he'd still lived with his parents and he'd only had a few hundred. I tried to remember all the trivial things we'd talked about. They were trivial. And if I'd known they were trivial even then it meant I'd always known there was something not trivial which was not being spoken of. If the trivial things had been about money and entertainment, the thing not spoken of was a man's life. Helmet was sober and calculating now in his record-lined room which was more to him than the world he didn't enter any more and so it was the man's life, perhaps, that was trivial now. I feared for the fisherman. But I was wondering about the money too.

I opened my mouth to speak about the law and understood for Helmet it would be necessary to go deeper.

He hasn't done you any harm, I said. You can't do it.

I won't get found out.

That's not what I mean. I mean it's wrong.

Why? Is this something to do with your dream?

It's to do with thousands of years of human civilization.

I haven't been around for thousands of years. I'm only 29. He's lived long enough. He takes up too much space. He stinks of smoke and fish.

You're exaggerating. He doesn't get in your way. Killing him is too extreme.

You're only saying that because you think I'll get found out.

No! I'm not! I was trying to convince myself, and trying not to think about Helmet with a kitchen knife in his hand, coming up behind old Brynie in the kitchen while he was frying his supper that evening. It's wrong, I said, it's immoral, murder is wrong.

Why?

I looked out of the window at the sea. The edges of the waves slid up sharp and solid as the jags of a broken bottle. I tried to think of reasons for things we don't usually seek reasons for because if we did we'd realise how badly we needed them at the same time as we realised how hard they were to find, as if you'd become addicted to a drug in your sleep and woken up to find it hadn't been invented, as if you suspected a better world had been made and unmade behind your back before you'd had a chance to savour it.

He's a human being like you, I said. What if everyone killed anyone who got in their way?

They won't, said Helmet. Everyone's afraid of getting caught. And the rest are afraid of having to clear up the mess.

Jesus, I said.

Is that your dream again? Is it religion, is that it?

No! You know I don't believe in that. Listen, Helmet, you're a human being, it's what you are, you can't help it, and it's in your nature to be angry, but it's also in your nature to be merciful and feel pity.

He doesn't deserve any mercy.

But he hasn't done anything wrong!

He has, he's stopped me taking his room for my records.

The whole house belongs to him!

Exactly, said Helmet. That's why I can't go on like this.

I sat down on the edge of the bed. I felt as if the blood bank'd just tapped me for all I had.

When are you thinking of doing this? I said.

After tea, said Helmet.

All the blood came flooding back, with interest on the loan, and if the knife'd been there on the bed I would have filleted the boy on the spot. You're fucking ill, you are, I said.

Easy, said Helmet.

You don't see the seals killing each other.

I'm not a seal. They don't collect records. I could see his brain working in the flexing of the flesh of his forehead.

And if they did, they'd have more room for them out there.

The phone rang. It was out in the hall. The fisherman answered it. He knocked and put his head round the door. Phone, he said flatly and disappeared. He was a small man, bony. Getting the point of the knife through his dungarees and sweater and through between the bones would be hard. The worst moment would be halfway when Brynie was still alive but the blade was half in and it was too late to change your mind and say: God, sorry George, didn't mean it. Especially if there'd been no row beforehand.

Forget it, Helmet, I said. They'll catch you anyway.

Oh! he said, pointing at me as he went out. Like I said. And they won't.

I picked up the *Courier* again and leafed through. I shivered. Someone had draped my chest in a soaked bedsheet. The text blurred on the white. Scientists shocked by latest seal numbers, said a headline on a single column story. The rest of it was punched through by canine teeth and smeared with dog saliva. The worst thing was his trust in me. No, the worst thing was that his trust might be justified. That I'd wait until he did it, because surely he wouldn't, and afterwards it'd be done, and Brynie would be dead, and there'd be no bringing him back, so what would the point be in destroying Helmet, let his conscience be his executioner? Not that he had one. And where did you go to denounce your friend for planning to murder a stranger? The victim? The police? His mother?

Helmet came back. I could tell there was someone still on the line from the way he stood in the doorway. It's the man, he said. D'you want to put something on the 1979?

Tell him to call back. Let's talk more about your plans for tonight.

I'm putting a tenner on Callaghan.

I got up and went out into the hall where the receiver hung bobbing on the end of its wire, stotting gently against the woodchip. Helmet watched without saying anything while I picked it up.

Could you call back, I said.

Minimum stake's a fiver, said a voice like stones grinding

together. Callaghan 5–1, Thatcher 3–2, Steel 100–1, Wilson 100–1. Ten minutes to the off so make up your mind, eh? Your pal took me for fifty quid last week.

Fifty, eh?

Backed Reagan in the 1980 at Washington on 2–1. The old guy was ahead by three furlongs. So're you in or what? The voice went into a coughing fit. It sounded like someone was stirring his guts with a poker.

I asked Helmet what the year was. He said 1997. I asked him what we were betting on.

1979 general election results, he said.

It was Thatcher, I said. Thatcher won it. You remember. You were already born then. Was he born? You couldn't imagine him with an umbilical cord. With some people you could. With some people you didn't have to imagine, they still had it, they were sitting in the pub and you looked down and you noticed this long, manky, trodden-in bit of fleshy string leading to the door, and you'd see it twitch a couple of times, and your drinking companion'd drain his pint and say must be getting back, they'll be starting to worry. And off he'd go, coiling it in his hands as he went.

How d'you know she won it? said Helmet.

I remember, I said. It happened eighteen years ago. It happened. It occurred. Callaghan lost. He did. He wasn't prime minister any more. You can't go back. It's already been. You know what your trouble is? You don't go out enough. You sit in here with your records and you think it's acceptable to murder people and time loses its meaning for you, you can't tell the difference any more between good and bad and right and wrong and past and future. Don't think you'll convince me there's money to be made betting on Callaghan to win the 1979 general election because these things happen only once, they've been already. D'you think it's going to get to me because I sit here with you inside your four walls, inside your record collection, for an hour or two? It's not, because I go outside and I see that what's broken stays broken, and what's dead stays dead, and what gets old doesn't turn young, and that people live with that, they get so used to it they don't even think about it, and they get by without killing each other and without trying to cheat the past. It can't be done. And you will get caught if you kill the fisherman. Come out for a drink tonight.

Helmet covered his upper lip with his lower one and looked down at the floor. He went over to the phone and told the guy to call back when he was ready to start. He stepped back on to the bed, scratching his stomach, and lay down. I sat down on the edge, facing away from him. Neither of us said anything for a while. From where I sat I could see a long red freighter gliding at speed upriver, powering flatly through the waves behind the delving pilot boat.

So who d'you reckon's going to win? said Helmet.

Thatcher, I said. She wins the 1979 general election every time.

Why don't you put money on it if you're so sure?

Who's the bookie?

Don't know. Just started ringing up. He sends a young lad round to collect the stake or give you your winnings. I'm ahead so far. He got skinned on the 1966 World Cup.

You had your money on England, eh?

There was a tip. What about the 1979?

The phone rang.

Go on then, I said.

How much?

Fifty.

Fifty.

We went together to the phone. Helmet placed the bet and held the receiver between our heads so we could both make out the commentary.

There was a sound like a pistol shot down the line and they were off with the old guy doing the live commentary bit. And it's Thatcher in the lead followed by Callaghan then Steel from Wilson and Callaghan going strongly and Steel and Wilson fighting for third and fourth place and Callaghan's pulled level with Thatcher and they're neck and neck and Wilson now, Wilson coming strongly into third but Steel's coming up on the outside, now it's Callaghan from Thatcher and Steel with Wilson trailing, and as they come into the final furlong Thatcher's out in front and she's opening up the gap, it's Thatcher from Callaghan with Steel and Steel's fallen! Steel's fallen, and Callaghan's putting on a sudden burst and he's pulled ahead of Thatcher, Callaghan's in front, he's ahead as they cross the line and it's Callaghan first, Thatcher in second, Wilson coming in a long way behind in third and the vets now moving swiftly over to David Steel, I'm afraid he'll have to be shot, but what a superb finish from Jim Callaghan, beating the favourite Margaret Thatcher in a magnificent race which will yet again have the punters tearing up their form books in despair. Give Helmet the cash.

Eh? I said.

Just give Helmet the stake, the voice said. I'll pick it up later.

That was the 1979 general election.

Plus five quid tax, that'll be 55 pounds.

That's not on, I said. Thatcher won.

Fine. You're barred. D'you understand me? Barred. You heard the result, if you'd like to hand over the money to Helmet there we won't have any further problems.

I want to know who gave you permission to fuck around with history like that.

If it's history you want go to the library. This is the past we deal with here, and we can do what we like with it. It hasn't been nationalised.

I'll give Helmet the money. But admit she won. I remember.

That's your business, sir. No-one's trying to tell you what to put in your memory.

Eighteen years of Tory rule!

It could've been a dream. It's your private business. All we ask is that you don't try to spoil other people's free use of the common past by dumping your memories all over it. The bookie hung up.

I fancied Thatcher myself, said Helmet, taking the cash and sticking the notes into his waistband. He went back into his room, put a copy of *Super Trouper* on the turntable and lay down on the bed with his hands behind his head, looking at the ceiling. I expected to see fox fur under his armpits but the hairs were black, flat and separate.

Come out for a bit, I said.

No, said Helmet.

If you came out you'd see what I mean about the way things are. It'd all fall into place. You'd see that time only goes one way, the past only happens once, and that killing people is too complicated.

You're saying I shouldn't kill him because it's too complicated? said Helmet, frowning at the ceiling.

Yes, I said. That's one reason. The sweat was over me again, hot this time. If you came out with me you'd remember there's more than just you and me and the fisherman. There are so many people, and they're all connected, and if you kill one of them, others are bound to get dragged in.

I can put your mind to rest on that. It's not complicated at all. It's very simple. There's me and the fisherman, and I kill him, and then there's just me. That's it. It's not a problem.

Are you coming out?

No.

Don't do anything, I said. It's not like taking a record off. You can't put it on again. It's not like the ships that come up the river and always go back out. It's not like Thatcher. True enough, we never saw her in the flesh. Maybe she never did win. Maybe she doesn't exist. But the fishermen does.

Not for long, said Helmet.

I went to the turntable, flicked the arm aside, took off the Abba album and snapped it in two.

That's what happens, I said.

No it isn't, said Helmet. I've got a couple more of them. That's a fiver you owe me.

What if I broke them all? I said.

Helmet said nothing but I saw his lips press together and a dark tongue tip zip them up moist.

I'm going out, I said. I'll come round again before tea.

Helmet was silent.

Brynie was working on fish in the kitchen. I saw the big knife hanging flat vertical on a magnet.

Hi, I said. How's it going?

All right, said the fisherman.

Helmet said it'd be OK if I borrowed a knife for a couple of hours.

Help yourself.

I took the knife off the magnet. It was shiny stainless steel with a black plastic handle and a broad ten-inch blade. I held it suspended, holding the handle between thumb and one finger.

Take care, then, I said.

Brynie looked at me over his shoulder with his eyebrows arrowed into his nose and went back to his fish. I went out into the street.

The sun had come out. There weren't so many folk down where I was, near the old lifeboat shed. I saw a rapid movement across the wall of a tenement opposite, like a cursor fleeing across a screen. It was the light reflecting off the blade of the knife swinging in my hand. I was wearing a red woollen jumper and black jeans. I lifted the hem of the jumper and started pushing the blade down the front of my jeans, blade turned out. The thigh cringed from the cold of the metal as it went down. The point pricked me and I drew in breath. A white-haired couple went past looking at me and wondering out loud what the lad was doing. I pulled the jumper over the knife handle and set off for Visocchi's. It was hard to walk without stabbing myself in the leg. It felt as if I already had. I limped along slowly, looking down every second to see if blood was blooming on my jeans. There was no sign but what an idea for a product: tampons for soccer casuals. I used to be afraid to wear white jeans to the game but now with super-absorbent wound-strength Tampax I can go out tooled up with absolute confidence.

I went into the cafe. I saw the girl from the baker's on her own in the corner with a pot of tea and a mini-pizza and asked if I could join her. She looked up from under eyelashes lumpy with mascara, like charred fishbones floating on a rockpool. She managed not to smile. She waved with her hand to the seat opposite. I sat down. The girl screamed and her knees snapped up to crash into the underneath of the table as she recoiled.

I held up my hands. It's OK, I said. There are things which can't be explained but this isn't one of them. I snatched a napkin off the table, opened it and spread it over my lap, covering the two inches of knife blade which had pierced the jeans and poked out into the open air from the top of my knee. I'll tell you about it once everyone's stopped looking.

I need to be getting back, said the girl, pale.

I turned my head. One by one folk went back to their food as they met my eye.

It's not mine, I said, picking up a menu and leaning forward. I just happen to have it on me this one time. And I thought if I walked through the streets of Broughty Ferry with a ten inch kitchen knife in my hands I might cause anxiety.

You could have put it in a bag, said the girl.

I didn't have time. Listen, I'm going to take it out now, and put it on the table. OK?

I need to be getting back.

Just be calm. I don't like it either. That's why I want to take it out of my trousers right now, and put it on the table.

Can't you wait till I've gone?

If I wait any longer I'm going to turn my leg into fajitas. Just be calm.

How should I be calm?

You see me coming into the bakery every morning, don't you?

That's what they do! They keep telling you! It could be someone you know!

Wait, I said. I screened my lap with the menu, slid the knife out and laid it on the table.

D'you have to go back right now? I said.

No. What is it you do?

I'm a seal counter. I count seals.

The girl picked a splinter of once-frozen cheese off the mini-pizza and nipped it with her teeth. Her nails were pink. So how many are there? she said.

Enough.

How many seals is enough?

I don't know. How many people is enough?

Four, said the girl seriously, looking at me and twiddling another bit of cheese between her pink nails. A strand of hair swung in and hooked her lips. She flicked it back behind her ear and put the splinter on her tongue.

A waitress came. I ordered a steak and a pot of tea.

There's one! said the girl, pointing over my shoulder. I looked round. What? I said.

You missed it, said the girl. There was a seal coming out the charity shop with a drip-dry brown nylon top. She grinned and looked pleased with herself.

The waitress came back and tried to lay down a steak knife at my place. I lifted Helmet's blade. It's OK, I've got one, I said. The waitress opened her mouth, closed it and walked away.

The girl was angry with me for not being good about her joke. She rested her chin on her hand and looked out the window. I asked her what her name was. She didn't pay any attention.

Listen, I said. I have this friend. He wears a fox fur hat in bed and taught his dog to fetch the newspaper for him. He's been indoors for too long. He says he's going to kill a man tonight. His landlord. It was going to be with this knife. But there are other knives in the house. His landlord's a fisherman, and they always have a lot of knives about the place. Now I'm wondering how we became friends. I can't remember how it was an hour ago, before he told me about what he was going to do, whether I thought better of him, or if I always knew he was going to show me one day he didn't care about other human beings. I can't remember.

It's Liz, said the girl.

Wait.

You haven't told me yours.

Wait. Suppose your friend is about to kill someone. What do you do? This is what I'm most afraid of, that I go to see him later and there's no fisherman. No blood, no weapon, no clothes, no possessions. And I say to Helmet: what happened to the fisherman? And he says what fisherman? You're remembering something that you dreamed as if it really happened. And I say: but Helmet, I remember. And he says: a memory of a man doesn't make the man exist. D'you see what I'm saying?

He sounds like a right wee bastard, this Helmet.

He's not wee.

I know the dog. I've seen it coming out of the newsagent with two copies of the *Courier*.

Two, I said.

I thought it was weird there were two. I followed it once and I saw it going into the house with both papers.

Christ, I always thought the fisherman hated the dog, I said. The trouble with Helmet is he's a psychopath, but he's too thick to be good at it.

I got up. Liz raised her head and her hair fell back, and she looked at me and blinked. Sometimes it's only when the looker blinks you realise how hard they're looking at you and how deep back the heart of the look lies. And that's in Visocchi's, over a half-eaten mini-pizza, a stainless steel teapot and a ten-inch kitchen knife. The seals were thickening. I took out five pounds and left it on the table.

I have to go, I said. That's for the steak. You have it.

Are you going to count seals? said Liz.

Later, I said. I go across to Tentsmuir. But there's others out on the sandbanks, closer to Monifieth. I was going to walk out there this evening. You could come.

OK, she said.

I made for Helmet's place. I left the knife on the table where

I'd put it. I was trying to think how much I cared about Helmet. Not much. Hardly more than the money he'd cost me that day. Maybe I'd cared more before lunch. Liz was millions of seals, billions, just the way her hair bobbed against her bare neck, and those tiny golden shaved hairs, on the curve at the back.

At the cottage there was no answer when I knocked. The door wasn't locked. I went in. The house stank of smoked bacon. The dog ran up and started doing figures of eight round my ankles. I went through the back green and saw the fisherman sitting on a chair outside his smoking shed, reading the *Courier*. He had reading glasses like Helmet's. Smoke wisped out from the edges of the shed door, held shut with a wooden twist latch. I stood in front of the fisherman for a while. He took no notice. A gull screamed on the glide over the shore, as if in ecstasy, or on Ecstasy, after all, they must get dropped in the gutter sometimes. The smell was rich.

Where's Helmet? I said.

The fisherman said nothing. He didn't look up. Only his eyes moved, scanning text.

Where's Helmet? Where's Ian?

Eh? said the fisherman.

I was expected to remember the tosser's surname as well. Ian Colwell. Your tenant. I'm looking for him.

No tenant here, said the fisherman. I live on my own. Me and the dog.

You had a tenant. I was here this morning. I borrowed a knife from you.

I don't remember. Have you got it with you?

No. Where's Helmet?

Are you wanting to do business, son, 'cause I'm busy.

I heard you were branching out from smoked fish into smoked

pig. I was thinking of making an order. D'you mind if I look in the shed?

I'm not taking orders, said the fisherman, lifting his eyes from the paper for the first time. It's all still at the experimental stage. I'm getting a grant from Brussels. I need to expand. There's not enough room here. He took off his glasses and tapped the inside pages of the paper. It's a communist paper, the *Courier*, he said. They're against private enterprise. They've been running a campaign against me. They're hand in glove with the council, you see, against the business. If they can't get you on planning permission, they get you on the fucking Clean Air Act.

I'm not saying I want to look in the shed, I said.

I'm not saying I'm going to let you, son.

Maybe someone walked in there by mistake and got locked in.

The fisherman folded the paper and put it down on the flagstones beside his chair. He took a tin out of his shirt pocket and started rolling a cigarette. He really did like smoke.

You can see the latch is on the outside, he said. If anyone's in there, it means I locked them in, right? D'you think like there might be a market for smoked folk? He laughed and lit the cigarette. With yellow skin like haddock! He laughed. See that commie rag? They ran a death notice of me this morning. It's part of the campaign against me. I wasn't too chuffed when I saw the death but then I thought hang about, if they all think I'm dead and I'm alive, there's bound to be some poor bugger who's died and nobody knows.

Why?

You think they can put a death notice in the paper and there's no death? I signed up once on a deep sea trawler, split-new, superb, radar, sonar, stabilisers, it was like a space shuttle. A million and a half it cost. There were a dozen partners and it was named after the skipper's daughter. The Tamsin L. We were set for the first trip and the girl goes and gets herself kidnapped in Kashmir. Kashmir, aye. She was hiking there and they took her, the rebels. And nothing was heard for six or eight months. And we went to sea all the same. And the skipper too. We had two good trips. Listening to the radio, keeping in touch, but thousands of miles from shore nonetheless. I was on a fixed rate, the partners were on a percentage. I was doing all right and they were making an absolute mint. So we were back on shore and the news came in that the girl had been killed. They'd found her body with some others in the mountains with a message saying why they'd done it.

Why?

I can't remember, said the fisherman, shaking his head and waving his hand. They wanted to be free.

Free from what?

Free from having to kill people. They wanted the place to themselves. Anyway so the skipper had to fly out there, poor bastard, and identify the body. He was all set to go and he went to his partners and said look you're due to sail the morn, go anyway, go by yourselves, this is hard enough on me, why should you lose out. And they didn't say anything, they looked away, looked at the ground, they couldn't look him in the eye. They refused to sail. Eventually he realised it was the name: they'd never set foot in the boat as long as it was called the Tamsin L. So he said OK, we'll recommission her, she'll be another boat. But not till I get back. Till then you can just sit on shore and drink your savings. And he flew off to Kashmir.

Only when he got there, who should he see waiting at the airport to meet him but the fucking lassie, his daughter! The local polis had screwed up and it wasn't her who'd been killed, they hadn't killed anyone, I can't mind now if she was ever even kidnapped or if she maybe just hiked around the Himalayas with them for a few months. So it was a big happy ending and they rode off on the 747 back to bonnie Scotland, five pages in the *Daily Record*, TV interviews and everything. And when the partying and the drinking's all done the skipper rounds up the crew and says right lads, we've got some ground to make up here. And it's the same routine again with the eyes, you know, they can't look him in the face. They still won't go. And he tries to tell them she wasn't killed, no-one died, it was a mistake, no need to change the name, everything was back to the way it was before, like they'd dreamed it all. It was no good. None of them could explain it, or maybe they could've, but nobody tried, they knew they couldn't go on the boat any more. He couldn't persuade them. There'd never even been a funeral, but as far as they were concerned they'd lived through the death of Tamsin L, and that was it.

Is it true? I said. The fisherman shrugged and went back to his paper. I walked to the shed and unlatched the door. The hot salty smoke smothered me and I took a few paces back, intoxicated and coughing, eyes stinging. When it cleared I saw the dark space empty except for half a dozen rashers of supermarket streaky bacon pegged to the racks.

I turned and walked back into the house. Brynie didn't try to stop me. I opened the door to Helmet's room. Helmet wasn't there. The bed was made and the records were gone and without them there was no sign Helmet had ever been there. I looked out the window at the fisherman. He was sitting where I'd left him, reading, though he'd closed the door of the smoking shed. I left the house and went home.

I rang Helmet's number a couple of times in the afternoon and hung up without saying anything when the fisherman answered. I couldn't sit down or eat. I made a pot of tea and watched it get cold. I stood at windows with my palms on the glass, breathing on it, drawing crosses, hearts and smiley faces with the tip of my finger. I watched Gray Street through the binoculars, not knowing if I was looking for Helmet or Liz. I couldn't remember when I'd last seen Helmet in the open air. The pedestrians looked anxious and placid until two of them would start laughing for no clear reason. The sun was on its way down. I should have done something about Helmet. It was making me feel bad that I hadn't. It was only so bad as to be strong spice for the feeling good about meeting Liz later. And the planet'd spin like a tennis ball and get kicked off the wall of sleep four or five times and lose its energy and which of them'd be first to fade? I didn't know. But the thought of not breakfasting with the fur hat worried me less than the thought of not having a reason to go to the baker's in the morning.

I went down the road at six with the binoculars round my neck and a seal sheet in my pocket and saw Liz in a print dress sitting on the bench near the lifeboat shed, looking out across the river. The sky was still light from the afterglow of the sun but pricked with a blinding white Venus it looked a darker blue than it really was. Liz looked up and smiled and turned back to the river. I sat down next to her. Her hands were on her lap and she was playing with her fingers.

It's too dark to count seals, she said.

I know, I said. D'you not want to go for a walk?

No, it's OK, she said. I thought maybe you had special equipment for seeing in the dark.

I don't. Just these, I said, holding out the binoculars. She took them and focused on Tayport. She watched the cars scudding along the coast road for a bit. Then she stood up and tried to look at the dark light-speckled humps of Dundee upriver.

The lights keep skidding, she said. It's hard to keep still.

Here, put them on my shoulder, I said. She came round behind where I was sitting on the bench and put the binoculars on my shoulder, leaning her body against my back.

There's a plane landing at the airstrip, she said. I could feel her breasts press into my back and her heart beating as she tracked the plane in. She moved away and handed the binoculars back.

We began walking along the top of the sea wall. It was easier than I expected to ignore what was coming in on the tide as long as she hadn't noticed it. She said there'd been something on TV about the seals: too many old ones, not enough pups being born, they couldn't understand it. I told her how I made up the results.

Is that not really bad? she said.

If they knew the truth, it'd be worse. The real seals are having millions of kids, and most of them don't survive to be old, and the old tough ones get to be that way because they survived and know how to beat the young ones back until their teeth fall out and they're too weak to fight and feed themselves any more and they go away and die. I've been counting people instead of seals and it's the other way round. Too many old ones and not enough pups. And the pups start to think they're the tough ones. Time runs backwards and the young ones try to teach the old ones, try to share their wisdom, and if they don't listen, or they get too cocky, or they get in their way, they go out and fight. The scientists are looking at my figures and they can't believe the young seals are so special and the old ones are so common. They should start counting their own.

What are those? said Liz, stopping and putting her hand on my shoulder. She'd noticed. She pointed at the flat waves lapping the stones, pushing a zig-zag graph of sodden album covers up the beach.

I put my hand on top of her hand. It was cool and soft. I love you, I said. She turned round to look at me.

What? she said.

I leaned forward and kissed her and found her mouth slightly open. Hers was the tongue to enter, buzz on mine and slip out. We separated. I heard the sound of marine engines on the river, cars and the hiss of the city as if my ears had just been unblocked. She looked at me like a nurse who'd had to jab a bucketfull of adrenalin into a cardiac arrest case and was interested to see what was going to happen next.

You're going too fast for me, she said.

Yeah?

That only happened because of me getting interested in those LPs being washed up on the beach, didn't it?

No, I said. It was because of that, but it was also bringing forward something I was going to do anyway.

Fuck you, said Liz. I'll go away and come back later, would that be more convenient?

No, but don't let's talk about those albums. I did want to change the subject but would I have thought of saying I love you if I didn't? It would have taken longer otherwise. Did I not sound as if I meant it?

Liz began moving on and I walked beside her. She didn't look at me to begin with. She said: Maybe you sounded like a man who finds it easier to change the names of things than do something about them. Like you're afraid someone you know's been murdered, and because there happens to be a girl next to you, the easiest thing is to cross out I fear it and write in I love you. But it's fear all the same, not love.

It's not like that, I said, and went quiet, because I couldn't think of anything else to say, because she was almost right. But we were walking on, leaving the records behind. We passed the harbour and approached the floodlit castle. It was a clear night. It would have been good to have lain with Liz on the beach, watching the stars and all the cosmic furniture. The floodlights and the streetlights were too bright. Through the fog of lights only the very brightest planets stood out. Years back the energy makers had gone on strike and there'd been power cuts across the district. We'd been grateful those nights, when we'd hung our heads back with our mouths open and tried to cover the whole speckled glory with our narrow eyes, and the powdered field behind the constellations had seemed to drift and not drift, move and not move. Then the lights of the ground came on again. The energy makers had dared to strike then. They didn't know Thatcher was coming. I was as angry with them for a moment as with Helmet for not accepting that she'd ever been. It was easy enough to confuse the past with the future. I did it all the time. Liz was right. My mind was as weak as Helmet's, it was filled with storms that had no names or directions, colours that could never be remembered, events with faces and dialogue that shifted with mood and age.

Is that a seal down there? said Liz. We were on the beach, walking on the dry sand firthward of the dunes, the tide half-out. She pointed to a blubbery tube rolling from side to side in the surf. We stopped.

I don't know, I said.

I'm going to look, she said.

Don't.

You said you came out to count seals.

I told you about that.

You could get one real one at least.

What if it isn't a seal?

Liz frowned and looked down at the sand. We go to the police, she said.

I squatted down like a bird and watched Liz step away alone through the ragged graph of jetsam onto the smooth, wet, yielding sand of the recoiling waters. The first horn of a crescent moon had risen over Tentsmuir, sheening the lower beach, and Liz's feet sank neat black inches into the sand, haloed with squeezed dry grains like charlatan snaps of ectoplasm. She reached the body, bent down, skipped away to avoid an incoming wave, pushed her hair back, turned to me, pointed at the carcass and called: 'One!'

I got up and walked towards the creature. It was an immature seal, not long dead, its eyes missing, otherwise whole. I'd never learned how to sex them.

Thanks, I said. I'm a coward.

Yeah, you are, said Liz. I've never seen one this close before.

Neither have I.

What a shame.

They do die.

I know, said Liz, but it's still a shame. I suppose when my granny was laid out in the lounge you would have been the one to put your head round the door and tell us: Well, they do die.

I wish I could've. Only as you said, I'm a coward.

We walked on and I started telling Liz the dream. I was a detective angel, I said. An investigator. I could go anywhere, even through time, but I couldn't go into alternatives: only God could do that. The thing was I suspected he'd made the world – you know, earth – and then changed his mind, it'd just been one of the avenues he was exploring. But I couldn't prove it.

My dad's always doing that, said Liz. He makes things, then changes his mind and hides them. You should have looked in God's attic.

But I was sure I remembered the world. Even though I'd never seen it, the idea of it had got into me somehow, and it was killing me to think of how it'd been and then wasn't and I never would see it. Then I woke up, and instead of being relieved I was in the world I'd thought I'd lost, I felt terrible about losing the false memory of a real world.

How about not losing me? said Liz. Is there some point to this? What was God like?

Like someone who pretends to be very hospitable, but makes it obvious they can't wait for the guests to leave.

I like the real, real world, said Liz.

You only get to touch it in one place at a time, though, and the rest crumbles away behind you.

You expect too much.

It was the best thing I'd heard about myself for a long time, and the place I was touching, the beach, seemed very wide and deep.

Look, said Liz. There's another dead seal.

Another dark body lolled on the waterline a hundred yards further on.

Let's take a look, then, I said.

Are you not scared? she said.

We have to look, I said, taking her hand and leading her on.

Management Secrets of the Nazi Generals

On the morning of the eve of repeal of the cannabis laws, Leila Menimonie woke early and lay in bed, too afraid to go back to sleep and too tired to get up. A tall man dressed in a dark blue military pullover and sharply ironed slacks entered the room and began to undress. He had the body of a man who did weights, and a moustache the shape and size of a large postage stamp. He was a security guard called Lester Bee. He'd been living with Leila for a little short of a month.

Hi, said Leila, propping herself up on her elbow and watching him.

Hi gorgeous. Lester tossed a carton of Silk Cut on to the quilt. Leila picked it up sleepily and turned it over.

Very nice of you, she said. Since when did they start handing these out to the night shift.

One-off, said Lester.

You nicked them, didn't you. She clawed at the packaging.

I did not nick them. They were trying to get rid of them. They needed the space for a special consignment. I've got 5,000 more in the car.

Leila ripped the carton in half, took out a box and withdrew a cigarette. She put it in her mouth, lit it, opened the library copy of *Heart of Darkness* on the bedside cabinet, ripped out the first page, fashioned it into a cone and began using it as an ashtray.

You shouldn't do that, said Lester. It's public property. It comes off taxes.

I'm not taking it back to the library. It shouldn't be there. It's racist rubbish.

How can it be racist? said Lester. It's a Penguin Classic.

You woke me up.

I wish I hadn't when you call me a thief and a liar after I bring you a present.

Ach, I was awake anyway. Get your clothes off.

Lester hung up his trousers, taking a minute to get the creases exactly in line, folded his shirt, socks and pants, placed them carefully on top of the pile of Leila's dirty knickers in a sports bag in the corner, took off his gold crucifix, kneeled down nude with his back to Leila to pray in a whisper, touched his moustache and lay down in bed facing her. There was a powerful crinkling as his naked flank crushed the cigarette carton wrapping.

Hope you thanked him for your bum, she said. She stubbed out her cigarette and ran her fingers over the freckled skin on his deltoid, over his downy trapezius, down the spine and over the smooth, warm, narrow compactness of his gluteus maximus. Lester gave his moustache a touch with the side of his index finger and let his hand stray to his groin. Leila slapped his wrist.

That's mine, she said. Leave it alone. She lit up another cigarette. What's this special consignment you're dying to tell me about?

It's confidential.

Leila pouted and raised her eyebrows. Confidential? Between Lester and Leila?

Lester frowned and picked at the bobbles on the bedcover. I know you wouldn't tell anyone, Leila, he said. So I'll tell you. The warehouse is stacked with ready-made spliffs to the rafters. They've been trucking them in all week. I don't know where they come from. Word is they've got a floating factory moored off Casablanca. It's incredible. They're all ready to go. They've got them in cartons, in packs of twenty, like cigarettes, only the paper's not white, it's different colours, green, purple, orange. The packs look the same, foil and everything, but inside the purple square there's a silver cannabis leaf and instead of Silk Cut it says Hemp Cut.

Hemp Cut? That's terrible. What's it like?

We're not allowed to touch them.

Lester! She punched him in the shoulder. Who's breaking the law! No-one's supposed to start warehousing the stuff till tomorrow.

Leila. Leila. Lester was earnest. This is a multinational corporation. They're intelligent, responsible people. There must be a good reason for what they're doing.

If only they knew what a treasure they had in you, said Leila, smiling and shaking her head, they'd have to pay you double.

Seven pounds an hour! What would I do with that?

Buy yourself some nice things, said Leila, putting her arms round his neck and tickling the tip of his prick with her slit.

They had sex, which, as long as Leila didn't let herself think about Lester's beliefs, opinions, uniform, job or employers, was unfailingly good. She even managed to forget her fear, until it was over, and she was lighting up, and the fear came back.

There's something I should've told you before, she said, gazing at Lester. I'm expecting a visitor today. Kind of like an old flame. An admirer. I don't want to see him. He's despicable. But he might come here. In fact he will.

Well, we won't let him in, said Lester.

He's got his own key.

We'll change the locks.

I've sort of got to let him in.

How?

The house sort of belongs to him.

Lester's forehead was so contorted it seemed to have a hole in it. He got up, looked around, and sat down again on the edge of the bed, feet on the floor, biting his nails. He would nibble a sliver free and try to tear it off with his other fingers.

Why are you living in his house if you don't want to see him? he said.

Well, I sort of married him. He's sort of my husband.

Lester massaged the side of his head with his knuckles and took deep breaths.

You're living with me in your husband's house for six months, and he doesn't come round once, he said. He can't care much about you.

Leila cleared her throat and licked her lips. He's been sort of unable to visit, she said. He's been sort of locked up. In prison. He gets out today. I'm supposed to meet him. She sat up in bed and ran her fingers through Lester's hair. Want to see what he looks like?

Lester looked down at the floor and shook his head.

C'mon. Take your Jackie Chan tape out of the video. See that cassette there? The one that says On Golden Pond? The one you never touch? Yeah. Put that one in and switch it on.

Lester did as he was told. Noise bars sailed across the screen and there was a sound from the TV speaker of screaming, a scuffle and breaking glass. The picture steadied. The camera was looking down the aisle of a short-haul passenger jet. A dark, powerful figure with a stoop, tangled masses of black hair and a Hawaiian shirt, if Hawaiian shirts could show winter scenes from rural Poland, stood braced at the far bulkhead, trying to stop a drinks trolley behind him from ramming its way past him. Beyond the drinks trolley it was just possible to make out a Hydra of uniformed anxiety waving its hands.

That's him, said Leila. This was taken just before he was arrested.

On screen Melvin began to speak.

Ladies and gentlemen, he said. I'd like to welcome you aboard this Ganja Airlines flight from that desert place smelling of sewage where they can't cook chips, sunburn capital of the world, to your mean, rainsoaked, debt-ridden real lives in the United Kingdom. My name's Lord Lucan, and I'll be your air rage incident on today's flight. Our journey time today is two hours and ninety-nine minutes, but it will seem longer. Before I join my lovely partner and the female cabin staff in a drug-fuelled orgy in the toilets to the rear of the aircraft, I'd like to draw your attention to some of the safety features on board this aircraft, which is a minty Cadbury's Aero. Please keep your safety belts unfastened at all times, since in the event of a crash they'll hinder the task of the police when they come to extract your charred corpse from the wreckage. There are exits to the rear, middle and front of the plane, and they're locked, so don't fucking try opening them, less you want to be sucked out like the lumpy bit at the bottom of a milkshake. Please remember that you are economy-class passengers, and therefore expendable. Babies and small children should be stowed in the overhead lockers or under the seat in front of you with their hands securely tied behind their backs and hankies stuffed in their mouths to prevent crying or chatter which would annoy the cabin staff. In the event of a failure of the cabin air supply, tiny green dwarves will descend from hatches above your head and cover your nostrils and mouths with their sly wee fingers, suffocating you within minutes. Enjoy your flight. I am now proceeding towards the cockpit, where I shall pit my cock against those of the pilots.

You can stop it now, said Leila.

Lester switched the video off and started putting on his clothes. Leila asked him what he was doing.

Leaving, said Lester.

Baby, said Leila, getting out of bed and putting her arms round him. I don't want you to go. I'll just explain to him that things have changed.

Did you visit him in prison?

Couple of times.

Did you mention me?

Nope.

Will he like me?

Nope.

Leila watched Lester's fingers as he stroked his moustache. She bit her lip.

If you're off work sick for six months, will they look after you? she said.

Zebedee unlocked the last locks between Melvin Menimonie and the big world. Zebedee for the moustache but then when he did the rounds at lights out in B wing a Mexican wave of sound boomed around the stale cloister: Time for beeeeeed!

Score me some for the do tonight, eh, Melv, said Zebedee. Mind I did you a few favours.

Melvin stopped with his shoulder resting against the last door. Zebedee had a scrotum curly head of hair on top but the moustache was sleek and straight. It looked like a case of the hot tongs.

You can't send me back inside now, can you? said Melvin. You've got to let me out, right?

I have to, aye.

In that case, fuck off.

The prison officer clucked and drew in breath between his teeth, cocking his head. You're confrontational, he said. That means you'll be back inside. Just trying to do you a favour. Tomorrow they'll be selling it pot-fresh in Tesco like rosemary and folk'll be going up to you getting change for dods of resin out of vending machines.

You'd better open the door, else I'll have the civil liberties on you.

That's got me panicking, said Zebedee. He opened it, though.

In the free world, prickly rain billowed over the land from the boundless sky. Melvin ran his hands over his face like a Muslim before prayer, felt the air and the water, knelt on the shining black car park, bent forward and kissed the tarmac. When he stood up he took in the *café au lait* Rolls Royce parked opposite. The door swung open and a chauffeur in cream-detailed dove-grey livery, with a peaked cap, jodhurs and black patent leather jackboots, unfolded from the driver's seat.

Mr Menimonie?

That's me, said Melvin, hoisting his sports bag over his shoulder and moving towards the car.

Your wife said to tell you she got fed up waiting. She said you could take the bus. She left the fare for you.

A chamois fist bloomed and shat silver.

When Melvin reached the stop there was only an old man with a long coat, a walking stick with the varnish worn away in the crook, and gummy eyes. He was leaning on the stick.

Seen my wife? said Melvin.

The old man shook his head.

Tall, good-looking woman with long black hair. She's called Leila. Leila. Her hair was long the last time I saw it. That was a month ago. She couldn't come the last few times, her shifts were wrong, so she missed a few visits. Maybe she's cut the hair short now. Maybe she's even dyed it. She did dye it once, before I went inside. I went out in the morning and she was a beautiful woman with long black hair down her back, she wore dresses that showed her shoulders and her back. The hair came down between her shoulderblades. I used to get jealous of the hair stroking the skin of her back all day long, every time she moved. One day I came back and it was like she was a different woman, she had short blonde hair. So I say you could have warned me. She says why, it's my hair, anyway I wanted to surprise you. I say it's my hair too, you're my wife, you could have warned me. She says just because I'm married to you doesn't mean I can't change my hair. I say you can you can but you should have told me, it was the woman with the long black hair I was in love with, remember. You're not just for yourself to look at. You're for me as well. I get a say. And she says you're talking about me like the lounge, like we have to agree on my hair like the colour of the curtains. And I say right, right, the next thing is you go back through our photos, like Stalin with his big fucking moustache, and you make all the old pictures of you with the long black hair disappear, is that how it's going to be? And she looks down at the carpet, 'cause by this time of course I'd broken something, a vase or something, and she says: You're weird and dangerous. D'you think I'm weird and dangerous?

The old man swallowed, hunched his shoulders, sniffed and stayed silent. The bus came. Melvin took the old man's arm, led him on board, dug into the coat's big pockets with their moist, gritty interiors to find the bus pass, chucked his cash in the slot and moved down the bus.

Let's sit upstairs, he said.

No, said the old man, wrapping his fist like a sucker round a silver pole as the bus whined into motion. Melvin tugged at his wrist, then prised the cold fingers off the pole one by one. He took his bag in his teeth, hooked his hands under the old man's tobaccoey armpits and started climbing the stairs backwards, dragging the old man after him and explaining what a grand view was to be had from the top deck. The old man struggled. Melvin warned him to keep a tight hold of his stick because he didn't want to lose it. When they reached the bend at the top of the stairs the bus took a tight curve and Melvin teetered. The old man looked up sharply and they saw each other's faces in the round mirror, Melvin wide-eyed, saliva dripping from his mouth on either side of the bag handle, like a crazed stallion champing at the bit, the old man being forced to believe that only he could save them. Before the bulk of the falling Melvin could send them both to the floor far below, the old man gripped the rubber end of his walking stick with both hands, raised it above his head and grappled the crook onto the chrome rail. For a few seconds Melvin rode like a demon on the old man's back, then recovered and hauled the old man up and into the front seats.

There you go, said Melvin. Great view from up here, eh. What was I saying?

Did I think you were weird and dangerous.

Aye, right. You know me well enough now to form a judgement. Melvin drummed his feet on the floor, rubbed his hands together, folded and unfolded his arms and beat out a free form mambo rhythm on the screen of the driver's periscope. He kept throwing his head sharply round to look out of the window while he was talking. I'm just out the jail. Not going back. Didn't like it. On my way home to my wife. I love her. I really love her. Been inside six months. Didn't milk myself once. Holding myself back for her, you see. We did have problems but not any more. From now on, I'm going to make her happy all of the time. I'm going to be an entrepreneur. I did a course in the jail. I've got an idea. It's WHY NOT PLANT A FUCKING SHRUBBERY ON YOUR FACE, YOU FUCKING ARSEHOLE. Melvin was on his feet, pressed against the glass, screaming at a guy in an anorak walking his dog along the pavement below. They left him behind and Melvin sat down, tugging at his lower lip and frowning.

See the fucking 'tache on that one? he said. Jesus. I didn't like moustaches before I went into the jail but once I was in there and saw what the *hombres* with face furniture were like, screws and prisoners both, my eyes were opened. I saw the whole thing. Moustaches equate with evil. By the way, don't try and catch me out when I'm on moustaches. Don't try. Are you going to try and catch me out? Eh?

No, said the old man.

Good. Melvin brooded. Stalin – moustache, he said. Hitler – moustache. Saddam Hussein – moustache. It's so fucking obvious. Lord Kitchener – moustache. Neville Chamberlain – moustache. Lord Lucan – moustache. Genghis Khan – moustache.

Ringo Starr's got a moustache, said the old man. He's a nice fellow.

What did I say? said Melvin. What did I just say? Did I or did I not say don't try to catch me out when I'm on moustaches? Eh? And now what are you trying to do? You're trying to catch me out, aren't you? OK. Listen. When did the Beatles start to go down the toilet? How did they mark their descent into pretentious wankery and destructive egoism? Eh? By growing moustaches. And who was the least useful of the Beatles? Was it the one who had the 'tache first and kept it on for ever? It was.

It was Ringo fucking Starr. Do you agree with me? Do you get my point?

I suppose so, said the old man.

Aye. Now I've warned you. Don't try to catch me out when I'm on moustaches. You can catch me out when I'm on anything else. You can catch me out on politics, football, the horses, philosophy, music, whatever you like, but don't try to catch me out when I'm on moustaches. See I know what's going on. Cast your mind back to puberty. My guess is we're talking about the Thirties, right? Excellent. So the big day's arrived, your balls drop and your voice drops and then something else happens. Down there, on that wee soft bit your prick hangs out of, bristles appear. What an exciting moment that is. At first the skin's a bit rough, then downright coarse, and hairs start sprouting. The young lad is fascinated. He keeps reaching down inside his pants to touch the place where the hair is. He can't leave off stroking it. It's at this moment that mankind, the sex to which you and I belong, divides into two separate halves. One half grows up. They lose interest. They stop stroking the hair. They forget the days of first growth. They don't have the urge to put their hands inside their pants any more, except to employ the tool there for its various natural uses. But the other half, they don't lose interest. They can't shake off the memory of those days when their fingertips first stroked those tender, springy curls. They try to forget. They try to put it out of their minds. But in their every waking hour it's there, needling them. They want to be running their fingers through their pubes. Their hands are always straying to their crotch. Socially, it's problematic. What chance d'you have at work, making friends, getting into college, getting the interest of the lassies, when you're going round with one hand stuck down the front of your trousers? On the other hand, if your deprive yourself of that scrotal buzz, you're fit for nothing, your nerves are shot, no confidence, nothing. What's the answer? Melvin slapped his hand and snapped his fingers. A pubic substitute in a socially acceptable place. Pubic in public. That's it. That's the definition of a moustache. A beard! A beard's no good! It's too much! But a moustache, now, that's just about the right size, and with the nose and the mouth, what you've got there is a complete mirror image of the arrangement down below. What a comfort! What a relief! You can make sure everyone knows how proud you are of your little scrotal bush, you can reassure the girls of your manhood, and most importantly, when the going gets anxious, you can raise your fingers to your upper lip and . . . aaaaahhhh.

As the bus languished in centre traffic, Melvin laid it out for the old man. Apart from the shouting, the breakages, the tendency to mix drugs, incompatibility of friends and irreconcilable views about Joseph Conrad, he and Leila had been perfect together. The missing ingredient in their life had been money. He had started out as a concert promoter, moved into dealing coke and grass in a small way. She had failed to weld the rich fragments of her education – the convent school, the unfinished psychology degree, the half-done farrier apprenticeship, the self-taught Polish – into a professional career, and took jobs in call centres.

The jail sentence was a blessing, a kind of sabbatical for Melvin, a chance to refine his drugs use and reflect. When they offered vocational classes, he took them up. He took a course in word processing and a course in writing. After six weeks of the writing course, the tutor asked his students to talk about long-term projects. Chutney, the recidivist car stereo recycler, waved a page torn out of a glossy Brazilian homemaker's journal, showing a cod flan with Ronnie Biggs' signature scrawled across it, and said he wanted to write a book of recipes by celebrity criminals. McKeldy, a lifer who'd been unlucky enough to stick his kindergarten-sized blade in the one place in Concrete Shelbo's body where it'd kill him, had never read anything written after he was sentenced in 1990 and had started work on an upbeat, episodic, autobiographical novel about young Edinburgh junkies struggling to deal with violence, addiction, AIDS, sex and their parents. Saldino, who was there for kicking somebody's head in, wanted to write a cheap advice booklet for teenagers called How To Avoid Getting Your Head Kicked In. Wetherburn, subsistence dole farmer, was agreed by C wing to be a fucking excellent poet, and was already acknowledged to have played a blinder with his epic work in the style of Hart Crane, A74(M).

All sounds brilliant, said the tutor. How about you, Melvin?

I'm going to write a best-selling business book, based on my experience of the prison and justice system and the management of holiday charter airlines, said Melvin. It's going to be called Management Secrets Of The Nazi Generals.

After several days, they managed to talk him down from his inspiration, and Melvin enrolled for classes in starting your own small business.

That's where I sorted out the idea that's going to put me and Leila on easy street for the rest of our lives, he told the old man. I'd tell you, but this is my stop.

Melvin ran downstairs with a light heart. He didn't see the old man giving him the fingers. He spent his tiny stock of cash in the shop, getting a bunch of red and white chrysanthemums, a box of seashell-shaped chocolates, a couple of baguettes, a carton of humous and a box of deluxe frozen veggie burgers with cheese. He took his purchases to the counter and asked Faisal about the immediate whereabouts of certain key individuals in the community.

They don't do it any more, said Faisal. The bottom's dropped out of the freelance market. What's the point? Tomorrow it's going to be legal.

Very true, said Melvin, winking. I reckon you and me are going to have a chat tomorrow about that.

About what?

Top secret, my friend. All will be revealed. What's that space for? He pointed to a row of empty shelves behind Faisal's head, next to the cigarettes.

Faisal looked round. Marlboro doing a big promotion tomorrow, he said. New line of ready-made joints called Marin. Come to where the high is. Come to Marin County. You know. Reeferettes.

Melvin's jaw went slack and he blinked. Then he creased up and shoved Faisal in the shoulder. You had me, he said, backing away from the counter, farting with laughter. You really had me there. Reeferettes! He fell out of the shop.

Faisal's dad put his head through the bead curtain. What was that? he said.

Melvin Menimonie went mad in prison, but they let him out.

Oh. Listen, when you go to the cash and carry tomorrow, get a couple of boxes of those McVities Chocolate Hashish Digestives, eh?

Milk or dark?

Melvin walked to his house and stood there for a moment, pressing his palm against the maroon gloss paintwork of the front door, stroking the stone chips of the pebble dash, tracing the white grooves in the black rectangle fastened to the door which read: M & L MENIMONIE. He smiled and a tear from each eye splashed onto his chest. He rang the doorbell.

Hi, said Leila.

Melvin stood still and silent. He opened and closed his mouth a couple of times and seemed to be trying to say something. A guttaral moan came from his throat. He dropped the bag, flowers and French bread went flying, and he had his arms round Leila, squeezing the breath out of her, lifting her off the ground. I'm back, he said, eyes pressed shut, head tight against her neck. I'm back.

Too hard, croaked Leila, as Melvin walked her down the hall to the bedroom.

I'm sorry, love, said Melvin. He let her go and she sat down sharp, coughing on the edge of the bed. Melvin knelt beside her, took off her slippers and began kissing her feet and ankles. I'm sorry. He looked up. I was going to sing you something. Guns N'Roses. But when I saw you I couldn't make a word come out. I missed you so much. He hugged her legs, kissed her jeans and promised never to leave her again.

Melvin, said Leila.

Yes, my love? said Melvin, taking her hands.

Leila nodded to something over his shoulder. Melvin looked round and saw Lester standing there in his uniform. Lester put one hand in his pocket and ran his free index finger over his moustache.

Melvin got up. He walked round Lester, scanning him in narrow bands from sole to scalp. He leaned forward and sniffed Lester's jumper. He didn't like the smell. He ran his finger down Lester's jaw and put the finger in his mouth. Tasted bad. He put his hand on Lester's shoulder and gave him a gentle shake, such as you might give a fragile tree on the verge of yielding fruit. He sat down on the bed next to Leila and put his arm round her.

Let me tell you what I want to hear, he said. I want to hear that while I've been inside there've been remarkable advances in the field of sex toys. I want to hear that, understandably, you were lonely without me, and in an effort to recapture some of the lost ecstasy of our time to together, you went out and acquired a large, ugly, synthetic prick, in the shape of . . . a security guard. I want to hear that only because you were very, very lonely, and because this was the very, very last one they had in stock, did you have to buy one with, with, with . . . he put his head in his hand. With one of them on his face.

One of what? said Lester.

Oh! said Melvin. The dildo speaks.

I'm not a dildo.

Then what the fuck are you doing in my wife's bedroom?

She never told me she was married!

I see. So first you go into a strange woman's bedroom and then you ask if she's married?

She's not strange.

I KNOW SHE'S NOT FUCKING STRANGE! screamed Melvin, going up to Lester so the guy could feel the spit spraying on his face. ARE YOU ACCUSING ME OF NOT KNOWING WHETHER MY OWN FUCKING WIFE IS STRANGE? I THINK AFTER FIVE YEARS OF MAR-RIAGE I MIGHT KNOW MY WIFE BETTER THAN A SECURITY GUARD IN HER BEDROOM.

Two years, said Leila.

Eh? said Melvin, thrown off his rhythm.

It's two years we've been married. Not five.

What is it I've got on my face? said Lester.

That Hitlerish patch of scrotal scum infesting your upper lip, said Melvin. Yeah, that's right, touch it.

It's not Hitlerish, said Lester. It's what the top racing cyclists wear.

Don't do that, said Melvin. I'm warning you. Do not try to catch me out on moustaches.

It's true.

I warned you, said Melvin, and lunged for Lester's moustache.

Don't touch it! shouted Lester, dancing back, but Melvin had got a firm grip on the tight short hairs with his thumb and knuckle and was using the other hand to fend off Lester's attacking paws.

Get the scissors, love! called Melvin, tugging at the moustache.

No man touches that, said Lester between his teeth, trying to get Melvin off balance.

No-one tries to catch me out on moustaches, muttered Melvin, who was starting to take punishment and was getting ready to bite his opponent.

Who can say for certain what went into the French sticks in town that day? Nobody who used one for its traditional purpose complained that they were heavier than usual, that the brittle crust yielded to the teeth with anything but the familiar light rain of flakes and crumbs, that the white of the bread was not, as always, an airy, almost tasteless sponge that shrank under incision until the last moment when it and the inner crust formed a tough, chewy pith. Despite that, when Leila smacked Lester and Melvin almost simultaneously on the side of the head with the baguettes, they stopped trying to hurt each other and stood pondering the nature of the thing, the truncheon-shaped object with the serrated edge, which had hurt them. Melvin bled from a cut in his cheek.

Sit down the both of you, said Leila. Listen.

Leila told Melvin that she had been in love with him once, when she'd seen him in rooms full of strangers, making the good ones laugh and the bad ones angry, not to impress her and not to impress them but for the sake of the thing itself, because he could do it, because in those days the things he could do, the things he wanted to do and the things he should do were very close to each other. She'd been in love with him most of all because it was just when he'd captured the kindest, the sharpest and the truest people there that he turned round and gave all his attention to her.

I'll do it again, love, I promise, said Melvin.

Leila went on, saying it was then that catastrophes began to happen. Melvin got so used to winning people over that he started putting less effort into it. He started expecting people to love him before he'd opened his mouth, and got angry when they didn't. When he got angry he raised his voice and mocked people he didn't know. He still drew people to him but they were different people, they demanded more entertainment and maintenance and time, and there was less room for Leila. Melvin was trying to make it as a promoter, it worked at first, but as the crowd he hung out with evolved there was more mutual flattery, more play, more self-indulgence. Melvin's circle got smaller, more brilliant and more bitter, chest-deep in cocaine, and the world beyond the circle got more contemptible. Melvin and Leila's rows escalated to the brink of murder. Melvin's finances imploded in a puff of white powder, credit card bills and half-empty venues, and his friends strolled on without him. He stayed at home, sleeping till the afternoons, never cleaning anything, including his hair, drinking strong tea and weak lager, living off Leila's earnings and occasional small-scale dealing. Leila threw him out several times. He slept in the garden and came back. The holiday, bought on credit, was a last throw. Maybe the sun and the pool and holiday sex would restore something. It failed. Leila came home broke, watched her husband taken away in handcuffs, and felt happy for the first time in a year. She never wanted to see him again.

And I'm being replaced by a security guard with a Hitler moustache? said Melvin.

He's nice, said Leila. What else matters?

Love, love, you don't know what you're doing. I've changed. I'm not going to be an arsehole any more and I've got a business plan. We're going to be rich. No, we're going to be better than rich, we're going to be comfortably off.

Melv—

Here's what we're going to do. Starting tomorrow, we dig up the garden, and we roof it over with plastic. We weed it, we hoe it, we draw furrows, and we plant cannabis. Enterpreneurs, love! You don't think anyone else round here will've thought of it, do you? They haven't got the vision. When they change the law tomorrow, we'll be ready. If we plant next week, we'll harvest by September. We become the number one local producer of legal, organic, top quality, original flavour, ready to smoke marijuana. We supply all the shops and pubs round here. That's phase one. We cover our costs. Then, we start leasing the neighbours' gardens.

Melvin.

I know what you're going to say. How do we make it to September? Love, when the bank managers see my business plan, and my diploma, we'll be fighting them off, begging them to leave because they want to lend us more money than we can possibly use. This cannot fail. The people demand, and we supply. I've designed a logo for us here, look. Menimonie and Sons, Organic Cannabis Growers, suppliers to Fortnum & Mason, by appointment to His Royal Highness King William. I'm thinking ahead with the endorsements, of course.

Melvin.

It could be Menimonie and Daughters.

Melvin, have you heard of a company called Philip Morris?

Aye, run a garage up the road.

Philip Morris, the multinational tobacco corporation which makes billions of cigarettes every year? And BAT? And all the others?

Well.

What do you think they've been doing in the past two years they've known what was going to happen tomorrow? At midnight tonight, the trucks begin to roll, and tomorrow morning, if you're over 17, every newsagent and kiosk and pub from Dover to the Outer Hebrides is going to be able to sell you five different kinds of name brand reeferettes, over the counter, duty paid, in a pretty fliptop pack, foil-sealed for freshness, factory-cut, regular or light, quality guaranteed, government-approved, health warning added, many as you like, £4.99, thank you very much, have a nice day.

No, said Melvin. You're winding me up, like Faisal.

Lester does nights at the bonded warehouse, said Leila. He's seen it! They've been stockpiling containerloads of pre-rolled joints in among the fags.

No, said Melvin. I don't believe it.

It's true, Mr Menimonie, said Lester. If customs and excise found out they'd be in trouble.

You, snarled Melvin. I'm going to shave that groin off your face, so help me. He lunged.

A few hours later, closed circuit TV cameras at the bonded warehouse tracked a man approaching bay 5 and punching in the correct entry code to open the door. The man was dressed as a security guard, but long, tangled black hair flowed from under the peaked hat tilted back on his head. The supervisor in the TV room leaned forward and marshalled his camera views as the intruder crept through the aisles of cigarettes and reached the inner sanctum where the Rothmans reeferette stash was located. He zoomed in. The bogus guard wrenched up the flap of a stapled box, took out a carton, ripped it open and unwrapped one of the packs inside. The changing expression on his face when he saw the reeferettes, took one out, examined its slightly bulbous, filterless form, encased in sky blue paper printed with rosy clouds and passed it under his nose to smell it, was something that would haunt the supervisor for years to come: horror yielded to rage, which dissolved into nausea and grief at the scale of man's injustice to man. The intruder sank to a squat, held the joint up to eye level, took out a lighter and lit up. As he inhaled, his face grew more peaceful. Slowly, he stretched out his arm and held the flame of the lighter to the flap of the box he had opened. The dry cardboard gave birth to fire.

When they reached the site fifteen seconds later with the extinguishers, there was a fair blaze going, and a good bit of damage done what with the flame, the smoke and the foam.

I am making a citizen's arrest, said Melvin, looking up at the three guards, on suspicion that you have been holding a quantity of a proscribed drug, namely tons of the stuff, with intent to supply.

This is criminal damage, said one of the guards. We've got you on tape. Consider yourself nicked.

After midnight, perhaps, said Melvin, waving his complimentary spliff confidently at them. After midnight, you're captains of industry, serving the demands of the modern consumer. But that's three hours away. Until then, you're merchants of death, aiding and abetting the evil traffic in deadly narcotics.

Well, said the leader of the guards, sitting down next to Melvin. We haven't called anyone about this yet. And since we're not in a hurry, I don't think we're going to for a while. And when we do, that's you saying you broke in here at nine pm. And that's three of us going to tell the police you broke in here after midnight. Wonder who they'll believe? Eh? Three against one! He laughed, so did the other guards, and they stroked their moustaches.

At this time Lester and Leila were lying naked together in the quiet warm lamplight of their bedroom. Lester was bruised and cut and his shaved upper lip was speckled with dots of clotted blood.

They'll be suspicious. They'll think I gave in too easily, said Lester. Especially giving him the code for the door.

Don't worry, baby, said Leila. We'll just say Melvin tortured you. And he did. If you want, I could torture you some more, to make it look extra real.

He tortured me enough, said Lester, touching the red space where his moustache had been.

Now that he's taken your uniform, said Leila, maybe you could get a job doing something else.

Maybe.

And now that he's shaved off your moustache . . .

Oh but Leila. It meant a lot to me.

I know, I know, but baby, baby. Without it, believe me, you're a different man.

After he was sentenced, Melvin re-enrolled in the writing course. One Monday morning, he sat at a PC, lit up a Marin, picked an aggressive font, set it in bold, and wrote:

MANAGEMENT SECRETS OF THE NAZI GENERALS
by Melvin Menimonie

He sat back from the keyboard and took a reflective drag. He switched fonts, and began to type.

Class Action

Manhattan, Wednesday – The number of professional people among the disruptive mentally ill at large in the New York metropolitian area is underestimated by the public, two city agencies said in a joint report released yesterday.

The Association of Special Housing Bureaux and Temporary Hostels, ASHBATH, and the Manhattan Authority for the Interception of Known Urban Risk Groups, MAIKURG, said that the popular image of violent or suicidal mental patients as coming from society's underclass was wrong-headed and prejudiced.

In a single day last month, ASHBATH and MAIKURG said, they had taken into care a writer who made regular contributions to national news magazines, while a lawyer once known as one of the keenest legal minds in America had skipped surveillance at a secure hostel and was last seen screaming obscenities outside the offices of an Iraqi émigré organisation.

It proved impossible to reach ASHBATH or MAIKURG for further comment before this issue went to press. When contact numbers were dialled, a low, undulating, swishing sound could be heard, as if the telephone had been lifted from its cradle and laid on the summit of a high, windy mountain.

East Village Weekly News, 25 April 1999

I thought it was him. I wasn't sure. But at three, the eveningfall of waiters' day within a day, a fault of silence opened across the jingling clinking murmuring space of the bistro Melchior. All chewing jaws happened on the midswing at once, each wondrous thought and pip of gossip hit pause, each perspiring glass of Sauvignon chanced to have its dribbling hips untouched. The arbitrary gap of noiselessness ripped across the chequered hall like white space shot diagonal across a printed page by a freak of typesetting. Before the common rocks of bedlam closed the fault again, a single bar of sound crashed louder than it ever had or would on a trading day lunchtime in Melchior's workspan: ice cubes lurching from a waiter's stainless steel pitcher into a tumbler. The waiter, entranced by the music of the ice chonking into the water, let it run on, overfilling the tumbler and prickling me with drops of cold when it splashed my shirt. I was watching the man standing at the oyster cart. The sound of the ice in the silence caught him and he turned to look at me. I'd been right. He was the man. He was the man who had once been Maurice Mak.

He'd been staring for so long at the oysters that the attendant had stopped asking if he could help. Mak was in a dark blue three-piece, hands in pockets and jacket open. In profile I could see a swell of belly restrained by the waistcoat. That was a mark of change. In the eighties the labour fitness thing'd filled out his image, got men like me and our breadgivers, the commissioning editors, interested. He'd unfolded into the highest value triptych: brilliant professional, establishment hate figure and guru of personal self, individual enough so you didn't have to find three or four more like him to spin it into a new breed. He was 5,000 words with pictures by himself. The shot of him stripped to the waist at the ditch, mouth slightly open, sunred pecs ashine, leaning on the handle of his pick – really leaning on a real pick

– with his cellphone in a stained sweatproof case hung from his neck with a really worn thong – Sony forgive me, some things you can't fake – flew to its *Beau Visage* cover without dissent. Good for my story, but bad as well. If you remember Maurice Mak maybe that's what you remember him for. You remember him as the health guy, not the finance guy, as you should. Labour fitness won him enemies. His credo that working out should be worthwhile communal labour, digging ditches or drawing water or generating electricity on treadmills – jogging, he said, was 'energy masturbation' – got him fascist and communist labels among his old corporate client base. The gym owners and personal trainers were up in arms. They got physios to denounce it as 'a genocide against the musculature of America'. The unions said the last refuge of the honest working man, manual labour, was being bought up by dilettante white collar types. Roads departments started putting up signs saying No MBAs. Mak's own road gang didn't mind him taking pick and shovel work off their hands – most of the heavy stuff was done by machines they operated – but they resented his 7.30 to 8.30 am workshift and the way he showered afterwards, changed into a thousand-dollar suit and drove off in a grey Jaguar. Mak didn't care. It kept him fit, marketed him, got him the personal brand image, rebel against the corporate mind, he needed for the main thing. The main thing being money, as I thought then.

I was on my own in Melchior. I'd been spinning out a coffee with some mail after the guy I was lunching with went back to his desk. I got up and walked over to Mak, reminded him.

He had a politician's memory. Hi Bob, he said, shaking my hand and focusing on my eyes. He was tired and had me lapped aging but there was a transaction in him. It looked like he was about to hawk me a quantity of wisdom he'd optioned. It looked as if it was going to be cheap. What he knew in exchange for being able to ask for help. Even beg. Which was hardly more than a hearing since I was not a helping man. I saw he had white clay under his fingernails.

He said: They reissued my license. I'm legal. I'm practising.

Hey, I said. Back from the dead.

His mouth shrank and his gaze flattened. He was shutting up the shop. Who told you? he said. Have you been talking to the gods?

There are gods now?

There are gods, said Mak. There are many gods. And they have finance.

It hadn't been a deep encounter with Mak before, when he was big. I never got the packaging off him. I had him for half an hour in a hotel suite where he sat like a movie star, taking writers off a conveyor belt. That was as close as you could get in those days. It was the time when he'd frozen corporate America in its tracks with the first deployment of his device, the hostile class bid. He'd turned half a million grossly fat citizens into noble litigants and was about, they thought, to make them joint owners of the fried chicken franchise they were suing. Naturally they loved him. Some thought they'd be rich, some thought they'd be thin, some thought they'd be rich and thin and get free fried chicken for the rest of their life. This company's been making the little guy eat its tainted chicken for thirty years, said Mak. Now the little guy's going to eat the company. Not long after my story was on the newsstands the little guy found out Mak had been dining off him and HappyHen both.

I'd fleshed out the piece with hangers-on and enemies and a public meeting he'd addressed. A thousand obese men and women came to hear him speak. Instead of coughing, the speakers were interrupted by gunlike reports as chairs cracked under pressure. Hipfat merged into solid waves along the intact rows. Love handles meshed like gears while the participants panted with the exertion of sitting upright without the aid of external cushions. Mak stood up with his weathered young face – and because of labor fitness, which only ever really worked for him, his leanness, smartness and rigour didn't mock the balloon people in the audience, it seemed earned, struggled for, not a bought shape like the machined young execs from HappyHen – and told the hall that they weren't the way they were because they'd been too greedy. No way. They were good, honest working people with good, honest working people's appetites. OK. The government and the big corporations said they were extra large cause they ate too much. Ate too much fat. Didn't that sound kind of strange? They started out as regular-sized Americans, they ate something that seemed like tasty food, something that didn't have any warning labels, didn't have any alerts or advisories on, and suddenly – woah! Size fifteen jeans! One moment they were nibbling on a few buffalo wings, the next, couldn't get the bath on over their hips! Could they imagine another manufacturer trying it on? You drank a few beers, the next moment you were blind – the mother of all settlements! You ate your favourite candy and your hair fell out – that wouldn't be litigation, it'd be a courtroom massacre! But when they ate HappyHen fried chicken, and before you could say barbecue sauce their good souls were wrapped up and weighed down by so much sudden flesh that the Lord himself would barely recognise his children, it was their fault! It was like the operators of the Titanic saying to those folks drowning in the ocean what, you mean you didn't want it with the iceberg? Well, he was there to make sure HappyHen didn't get away with it. Sure, they were going to sue the company. Sure, they were going to put whatever hotshot corporate lawyers HappyHen hired on to the griddle and flip 'em till they spat and sizzled and were done, both sides. But they weren't going to settle for money. Mere millions, tens of millions, weren't enough for the hurt they'd suffered. They didn't want a handout from the company. They wanted the company. He, Maurice Mak, was going out to get HappyHen stock for every victim in that hall, and thousands more besides. They were going to take HappyHen over, or see it destroyed. From diners to owners, it'd be an American dream come true. In two years time, they'd be dining at the HappyHen table together – the boardroom table!

After the applause one guy half-raised his hand and asked: If we win, do we still get to eat the chicken?

My friend, said Mak, his voice catching. As long as there is justice in this country, there will always be chicken.

He'd been focused then, and stayed focused right through the case, right through the triumphs in Missouri and on appeal, and then right through his own trial, the Chicken Stock trial, while they laid out his misdemeanours, how he'd begun loan-sharking to his clients on the basis of a successful outcome to the case, how they'd signed away their rights to a share in the spoils when they couldn't keep up the payments, how when Mak won his great victory it was he who ended up taking control of HappyHen, how it turned out he'd been taking kickbacks from Chick-O-Matik all along so's they could buy up their rival on the cheap. They convicted him on a technicality. It was enough to put him out of the game for a long time. When the judge sentenced him Mak looked alert and undefeated, listening carefully, as if the judge was a client explaining a problem to him. His wife, who was very beautiful, was there, leaning forward, intense. Because we're weak we looked at Mak and told ourselves we'd known all along that he was a sleazeball, but we were lying, and when we looked at his wife we could see how badly she still wanted him and how weak we were.

Now Mak had put on weight and the focus was dispersed. He'd been through other things, things I didn't know about. I asked how his wife was.

We split up a long time ago, he said. You remember her name, I know, because of the way she looked. You wouldn't remember her if she'd been plain.

Madeleine, I said, and smiled, which I wouldn't have done if anyone else had been there.

Yeah, Madeleine. I once thought she was fantastic looking too. Since then I met Inanna.

Still doing the labour fitness routine? I asked, understanding that there was a connection between Inanna and Mak's gods and hoping to keep the conversation on the useful side of psychosis.

You can see the answer, he said, patting his stomach. I got a taste for eating clay when I was among the dead and I can't shake it off. He twisted round and fetched a waiter over to check out the dirt of the day. But Melchior wasn't serving clay that day, or any day. Mak sighed and ordered a double espresso.

In a metal vessel, he said.

We talked for a while about some cases we'd taken an interest in. Mak might have looked like a knife gone blunt but he still knew what was going on. He was quick, he was rational, he cut to the main thing. I found out he'd been separated from Madeleine for twelve months and was working mainly for private clients. He was about to file a suit against the federal government. And one of the reasons Madeleine left him was because he'd taken to wearing too much gold. I guess I raised my eyebrows because he undid the second top button of his shirt, pulled it apart and showed a gleam of precious metal, a thin gold breastplate flush against his thorax, embossed with what he said were representations of locusts. He buttoned up and shrugged.

I got used to doing it for the clients, he said. They like to hang out in gold. They're old-fashioned.

What did Mak find out? That I was in demand. That I was working on profiles of some Hollywood players. That I had a new book in the works.

I remember that piece you did about me, said Mak.

Long time ago.

I remember. It must have been good for me to remember.

Most people remember the ones that say bad things about them.

It was good. That thing about me being a triptych. I liked that.

He was lying, I thought, but it was a nice kind of lying that was easy and pleasant to listen to, and I thought I'd let him lie some more.

This federal suit, it's going to be a big deal, the biggest, said Mak.

Oh really?

I was talking to Dave Filipchuk over at *Madding Crowd*. He was interested but I told him how much I liked your stuff. Which was kind of stupid cause I could end up with nobody writing a piece at all.

I smiled. Mak clearly knew the truth about Filipchuk, what a schmuck the guy was, how he'd shouldered his way in between me and Jacko's people when I was two thirds of the way to getting access.

So tell me, I said.

Don't you want to take notes?

Like you said, if it's good, I'll remember.

Mak went pale and he looked to be struggling to swallow something. He shook his head and breathed deeply in and out.

The spasm passed. It'd been fear, but fear he'd learned to live with, like indigestion.

I was at a party when one of the gods appeared in front of me, he said.

Like materialised?

No, I mean he was one of the guests, I was turning away from someone I didn't like and he was standing there, close, watching me, with a glass in his hand. He was young but he looked wise. Seeing him, I don't know why, I got this idea he could be trusted with a secret. You wanted to give him your deepest secret. There was something about him, he was wearing just a jacket and shirt but it seemed to me he was wearing the signs of other people's secrets on him, like honours. That was Enki, Inanna's friend. He told me he and his family had been impressed by my work on HappyHen. They wanted to retain me for a similar project. We went out on to the roof garden and he spelled it out. It was crazy. You won't understand how I stood still and listened. I'd had a couple of Scotches. OK. It wasn't only that. He had a way of speaking that made the world around you turn to a kind of fog, and the people round you to paper. You know what I mean, Bob. You must have met people like that.

Maybe, I said. But they didn't claim to be gods. They had imperfections.

These gods have imperfections, said Mak.

Oh yeah? Like what?

Well, for instance, the male ones suffer from permanent erections. It's painful for them, I think. It's incredible they move so well, considering.

I didn't interrupt Mak again until his story was finished.

Standing on the roof terrace with a glass of Pouilly-Fouissé Enki told Mak he was one of the gods of Mesopotamia. Way

way back one of them, his friend Inanna, had made a move on the afterlife, where the Mesopotamians went when they died, and hung out for eternity, in a dusty twilight. Why she originally wanted control over the afterlife Mak didn't understand but it seemed that the gods had conservative ideas about investment. They kept their holdings in land. They had the title to big properties on the Euphrates and the Tigris but that didn't bring much in the way of income. Anyway, Inanna's first attempt to mount a takeover of the afterlife was a fiasco, a real botched job, which, Mak pointed out, showed what happened when anyone, god or not, tried to do anything serious without a first class legal team behind them.

Lately the Mesopotamian gods had fallen behind. The forward-looking gods had transformed themselves into committees, more subtle and powerful than traditional deities, since their servants, clients and enemies believed the gods were the sums of their human parts, and failed to notice when they began speaking of beings which had no tangible existence: Nato, the god of war, Imf, the god of money, Wto, the god of trade. The Mesopotamians had made feeble attempts in that direction with Inanna, the Iraqi National Non-Nuclear Association, and Enki, some kind of crappy import-export group, but they understood they'd left it too late to gain their old preeminence. They needed a different strategy. They would return to the dead, but this time they would persuade the dead to sue. It would be a class action against world governments and the ruler of the underworld, Ereshkigal, for negligence and abuse of civil rights in failing to give the dead the opportunity to live. Relatives of the dead went to law every day, but, if the dead themselves would testify *en masse*, it would give the Mesopotamian gods leverage. Mak savoured the concept: Inanna and Enki would maul Ereshkigal so badly in the courts that she'd be forced to quit the underworld and let them take over.

And what do the dead get if they win? said Mak.

We sell it to the dead that they get life, said Enki. When we win, we persuade them to settle for something less. I don't know. Stock in a floated underworld. Mineral rights.

They discussed jurisdiction. Enki wanted the suit to go ahead in a US court. Mak was doubtful. Enki dropped a lot of articles and after a while Mak realised that he saw the US as Us, a god in its own right. He asked Enki what Us was god of.

The god of normal people, said Enki. Like in that hymn by David Byrne. *People Like Us*.

Mak looked out at the city to anchor himself. It wasn't the best of anchors and when he tried looking over the edge of the roof garden he saw the ants getting in and out of taxis forty stories below and that didn't do much for his sense of unbelief either. He swallowed and told Enki he'd love to represent him and Inanna. He'd love to count Enki as a friend. (He hadn't intended to say that.) But as an aetheist, he couldn't in all conscience take on a client on the basis that the client was divine.

Enki said: You want proof, I suppose.

It's OK, said Mak, afraid his interlocutor was going to jump off the roof.

You don't think I'm a god. You want me to strike some-one down with lightning, or change that flower tub into a serpent.

I guess. Or conjure up a million bucks in cash for the case.

I can't do that, Maurice, said Enki. Everything needs time. You meet a neurosurgeon at a party, he doesn't have to slice off the top of your wife's cranium with a butterknife to prove he is who he says he is. Look. What I'll do. You're only a mortal, but I'll give you a ride up and show you the way it is where the gods are.

And Enki led Maurice back into the party. The mayor was there, and the state governor, and a dozen celebrities, singers and actors. Charming as he was, a minor former celeb in his own right, Maurice didn't know them. And Enki led Maurice into their circles, and spoke to the stars in such language that they took Maurice as a friend, invited him to their homes, gave him their numbers, offered to share their cocaine with him. When they began writing him cheques, Maurice looked at Enki in fear and wonder and shook his head. Enki smiled. Maurice looked at the movie actress who was trying to persuade him to join her birthday party on a private island, turned to Enki and, pursing his lips, he shrugged and nodded.

One cold ragged sunrise a few days later Mak was at an airfield in New Jersey, boarding a Gulfstream. Enki said he'd borrowed it from Iata, a god of flight. Mak asked where they were going. Enki said they were going to take depositions. Mak asked what he should wear. Enki said he should wear gold. Mak took a Rolex and his wedding ring and packed lightweight suits, shirts and a cashmere sweater. The dawn wind cut through Mak's raincoat when he got out of the limo and stood at the bottom of the steps with Enki.

Don't become her slave, said Enki. We didn't hire you for that. She has plenty.

The door slid out and open and they entered the plane. They joined Inanna in the lounge for takeoff.

Mak was a lawyer, one of the best. He knew as well as anyone how to use the spoken word to make those who were listening see what he wanted them to see. When he spoke he didn't stutter or mutter or forget what he was going to say. He didn't um and ah. He always finished his sentences. He didn't nest parentheses inside his speeches as new thoughts occurred to him. He had a craftsman's love of a well-turned lie. He knew all the tricks of rhetoric, from Plato to Stalin, and all the music of human emotion. He saw the flaws and weaknesses of the powerful and knew how to coax flames of pity in a jury from the meanest tinder. But he became incoherent when he tried to describe Inanna.

She was dark, with deep black eyes, and looked in her mid-twenties. From the moment she took the tongue and clasp of the seatbelt in her long hands, pressed them together over her belly, looked at Mak and smiled, he forgot Enki's advice and became her slave. Nothing else he said about her made sense. He said she was in jeans torn at the knee and a cheap synthetic fleece, and then it was something like a dress-shaped cobweb made of fine gold chain, which made her body shimmer in lines like a city seen from the air at night, and then he had the three of them naked, playing poker for pennies, but the next moment denied that they'd taken their clothes off, ever. There was a layer of heat around her, Mak said, which you could feel when she was close to you. When she spoke she looked into his eyes and her words flew to the things she talked about as if the word and the thing were the same. When she stopped speaking and looked away it was like a death, like a final parting, and he wanted to follow, crawl into her thoughts and wrap himself in them, but couldn't.

They flew eastward all day and dived into the night rushing west. Mak and Inanna played backgammon for points, using little human figures of baked clay which Inanna dug out of a hemp sack by handfuls. She said she was sorry for the way the Babylonians had treated his people two and a half thousand years before. Mak, child of grocers and grandchild of Bolsheviks, wasn't sure what she meant and accepted the apology. Inanna complimented him for keeping in shape. It was purification, she said, an honour to Aba, the American god of law.

Mak asked Inanna what the afterlife was like. Inanna said it was like low tide on the beach without the sea, the sky or the beach. That bitch Ereshkigal hung me on a hook to die, she said. Enki sent people down for me.

Why? said Mak, filled with violent envy towards Enki.

They didn't want to let me go. You'll be all right, though. You're a lawyer. You'll talk your way out.

A steward in a white kaftan brought chicken and rice and wine. They ate and lay down on reclining seats to sleep. The cabin lights went out. Mak lay awake for a long time, listening to the dull keening of the engines, watching the stars. He pressed his forehead against the cold glass of the porthole to look down at cities' and ships' lights. He heard Inanna singing and his guts twisted so fiercely for love that he almost shouted out. The plane dipped and rose in gentle turbulence and somewhere aft he heard a goat bleating.

When he woke, Enki and Inanna were dressed in gold, eating muesli and drinking orange juice.

Inanna asked him if he wanted to play dice, for stakes. Mak said yes.

There's no time, said Enki. He pointed out of the window. Two F-18 fighters were flying alongside them in the clear blue. The land below was brown and crinkled.

Mak asked where they were.

Mesopotamia, said Enki. Those are Us planes. They show us the way.

Mak had put geography to one side as a child but didn't want to say he didn't know where Mesopotamia was. He figured it was somewhere in the Balkans.

Mesopotamia, said Enki. The English speakers have taken to calling it Iraq.

Isn't that where they have like a no-fly zone?

Enki does some business for Pentagon, warlord of Us, said Enki. Here, belt up.

The jets banked, one after the other, and dived down. The Gulfstream followed. The goat bleated.

Is there a goat on board? said Mak.

Don't worry, said Enki. It's tethered. Let's have some tequila. He opened a door on the surface of the table that was fixed within arm's reach of them all and took out three silver cylinders, smoking with frost. They unscrewed in the middle. In one half was the drink, in the other a pile of peeled lime segments thickly encrusted with salt crystals. When Inanna took hers she placed the two containers in brackets next to her seat to leave her hands free. She was pushing the buttons of a Nintendo console.

The F-18s had levelled out. Look, said Enki, and they saw green bombs unlatch from the fighters' wings and drift, rocking, towards the ground. Spears of flame roared from the fighters' engines and they shot away. The Gulfstream was following in the direction of the bombs. The aircraft went into a steep dive and banked round in a tight circle. A river ran through the brown land. Twisted in a knot at a bend in the river was a city.

You'll enjoy this, said Enki.

The tight turn pressed them into their seats. The plane straightened, still diving, and for a moment the weightless salted limes began creeping into the air. The Gulf-stream levelled out a few score feet above the ground. They were flying over the shacks and weedgrown lots and allotments on the margins of the city. At their speed the passing streets and buildings were a clanjamfrie of fragmented details, a door, a dog, a white car skidding off the road in a U-turn, an old man looking up, two running women, a donkey, a line of palms, a gun on a rooftop poking out from sandbags, a row of posters of Saddam Hussein, a grove of drying washing, a neat green plot of maize in the garden of a neat red-roofed bungalow. The air and light changed, a brightness bloomed on either side, fading to the chaos of unripe fire, and the plane shook, every joint creaking, fuselage bumping and scraping the shock waves as the bombs realised their design. Inanna and Enki called out a word in a language unknown to Mak, drained their tequilas and tossed pieces of lime on to their tongues. Mak did as they did. The jet banked again, climbing, and they could see the heaps of broken stone and cloven husks of concrete fuming where buildings had been.

Yeah, the wrath of Us is really something, said Enki.

Maurice, I'm sorry, that wasn't good, said Inanna. Sometimes they can be so accurate. Shall we try another one?

It's time to land, Inanna, said Enki.

Were there people down there? said Mak.

Yes, said Inanna. People drop the bombs on people. But remember we aren't people, Maurice. We're gods. One of the things about being a god is that we don't care about what happens to people unless we need them.

I—

Another of the things about being a god, Maurice, is that we get bored quickly.

I'm not a god, said Mak.

Hey, Maurice, lighten up, said Enki. You're more than just people to us. We've got a contract, haven't we? Have another tequila.

It was a time of new awareness for Mak. He understood that those he was sharing a plane with partook of the law but were not bound by it. He understood that he had met gods before. In his corporate law days he had defended them and sued them and knew them by the fact that, when they lost a case, no matter how grievously, it left no mark on them. And he understood that no matter what Inanna did, he would love her.

They landed just before sunset on an airfield outside the city. The Gulfstream taxied to a round tarmac stand at the opposite end of the airfield from the jagged ruin of a control tower and a row of hangars. Where the line of tarmac ended, cracked, sunbaked clay began, studded with clumps of dry thorn. A few yards from the stand was a bomb crater, furiously green with weeds around a puddle of muddy water at the bottom.

They waited in the plane with the engines running while the steward set up an awning outside, with armchairs, a table covered in a white tablecloth and a brazier. He hammered a peg into the ground, carried the goat down the steps, tethered it and placed a wicker basket of straw and carrots at its feet. Mak and the gods changed into jeans, boots and sweaters and deplaned into the cooling evening. The engines stopped. They sat under the awning without speaking, drinking mint tea. The coals in the brazier crackled and a breeze began to blow. Summer lightning flashed on the horizon. Mak had many questions but after mentioning the fate of people he dared not speak again.

A car approached. They heard it coming before they saw it in the darkness. It had no lights. It was a pick-up truck. It was travelling too fast in low gear and weaving from side to side. It turned sharp in front of the jet and slid to a standstill.

Enki supplies Saddam with a few things he couldn't get any other way, said Enki.

Inanna walked to the truck and opened the driver's door. Mak loved the way she moved: the strength of her arm, and the grace of her stride. She pulled an injured boy out from behind the wheel and carried him back to the awning. His thigh had been slashed by shrapnel, not deeply. She laid him down on a rug, put a silk cushion under his head and washed and dressed his wounds, murmuring to him and stroking his forehead. After he was bandaged and given water, Inanna and Enki helped him to his feet and took him to the back of the pick-up, where a tarpaulin was lashed over a heap of something. Enki threw back the tarpaulin and there was a murmured conversation. Enki called Mak over and shone a flashlight on to the truck's cargo. There were seven blood-caked and dusty corpses, neatly stacked like logs, heads to the rear, although one didn't have much of a head to speak of. Mak put his hand to his mouth and stroked his chin. There were five men in military uniform and two women, one an old woman in black and the other younger, in a blue polka dot dress and what had once been a white headscarf. There wasn't a mark on her that they could see.

That's the boy's mother, said Enki. Remember her face. Her name's Najla. It means beautiful eyes. You may see her in the afterlife. I don't know. Look out for her, and call her by name. She should be easier to engage than the rest. Tell her her son's OK. Tell her she should sue. Get her to sign an affidavit.

Was this the bombs? said Mak.

Sure. The wrath of Us.

Maurice, said Inanna, you have to go now. We'll wait for you here. Are you ready? She put her hand on the back of his neck and pulled his head towards hers for a kiss. Are you ready? she said.

Yeah, said Mak.

They gave him an oilskin coat and a pack with a bottle of water, a knife, a coil of rope and a bundle of yellow legal pads. Inanna gave him something the size, shape and weight of a cereal bar, wrapped in gold leaf, to be eaten in dire extremity. Enki showed him how to slaughter the goat, handed him the leash and patted him on the shoulder. Mak walked off the tarmac and on to the clay.

After a few minutes he looked over his shoulder. The light of the brazier was almost invisible. There was no moon and thickening clouds smothered the stars. On the horizon the shimmering sheet lightning crystallised into forks and he heard thunder. The goat bleated, though it trotted along willingly enough behind him. He walked on. He heard a cry like that of a seabird, only deeper, and a booming like surf. It was utterly dark, save for the lightning, which when it discharged showed a perfectly flat plain, the dry clay veined with fine cracks. His feet and the goat's hooves left no trace. For hours he walked without seeing anything except lightning and without hearing anything except thunder and the pattering of boots and hooves on the clay.

His free hand knocked into something hard. He stopped and felt the obstacle. It was wood, planks nailed together, like the hull of a boat. By the next lightning he saw it, an unvarnished, unpainted boat lying on its shallow keel, with a single bench inside and no oars. He walked around it and moved on. As he walked subsequent flashes showed more boats, of similar size, dotted across the plain, some upright, some keel-up, some smashed.

It began to rain. In seconds the ground was covered with a thin, frictionless layer of mud, and Mak fell on his face, losing hold of the goat's leash. He got to his knees and waved his arms blindly in front of him, seeking the rope. He found the animal by its bleating and wrapped the rope twice around his hand. The rain fell in sheets and Mak felt his feet sinking into the ground. He tried to walk forward. Each time he lifted his boot it became heavier as more mud stuck to it. It took him five minutes to walk twenty yards. By that time the mud was almost coming over the top of his boots and it was becoming harder to drag the goat along with him. The lightning gave just enough light through the rain to see the nearest boat. Mak took the goat leash in his teeth, unlaced his boots, tied them together and hung them round his neck. With the leash in one hand and his filthy sodden socks in the other he waded for the boat, crawling the last few yards, almost swimming, and climbed into it. He hauled the goat up by the collar and sat on the bench.

The rain stopped, and the thunder and lightning, and a crescent moon rose. Mak looked over the side of the boat. The mud still glistened, but it was drying out. He waited. The moonlight showed the flat plain to the horizon, and hundreds of boats. Again, he heard the booming sound, but this time it didn't fade, it strengthened to a continuous rumble, growing louder. Mak saw one horizon shiver, flex and grow, as if the world was curling up at one edge. When the rumble reached a certain intensity, and the sound was overlain by hissing, and the edge of the world grew to a certain height, and Mak could see not only the twisting crest of what was approaching but the white clouds lining its foremost rim, he dropped the goat's leash and stood up. The wall of water came on, a dark streaked swell rising to four, five, six storeys, and as it ate the boats between it and Mak, its smoothness was as terrible as its roar. Mak's legs gave way with awe and dread and he fell, clutching the struggling goat, pressing his face into its warm hide. Inanna, he said, and the wave hit the boat square on the stern, driving it forward, then pitching it over and hammering it into the mud like a nail.

Only the mud proved thin, and the boat shot through it. Mak felt gravity flip, like a swing going over the top, and instead of being pressed down into the mud the boat was shooting up into the air in a spout of water from a hole on the mud's other side.

He, the boat and the goat landed keel down with a slap in a glutinous river in a different place.

Here, it was light, or at least not wholly dark, a light like a foggy day before the sun has risen. The banks of the river were undulating clay littered with stones. There was no vegetation. Flat brown toads croaked a merged, scratchy song. On one side of the river, human forms walked slowly to and fro, squatted in groups or lay on the ground crosswise, eyes to what passed for sky.

Mak's boat drifted to the populated bank. He put his boots on and stepped out, dragging the goat behind him. There were thousands of people in sight. The individuals kept at least twenty feet from each other and the few groups didn't contain more than three people. No-one looked at Mak.

He went up to a couple of men squatting opposite each other. They wore tight-fitting business suits so covered in dust it was impossible to say what colour they were. The tips of their fingers were dark with moist fresh clay. As Mak approached, one of the men dredged his fingers through a fresh scoop in the ground, oozing and green-gray against the white surface, and lifted a dollop of dirt into his mouth, then chewed and swallowed it. The two men weren't speaking to each other. Mak was struck by the absence of hope in their grey faces. He'd never seen anyone so drained of hope before, and for that reason had never understood how it was a primary emotion. It wasn't an optional part of the palette. He realised that when he'd seen people defeated before, the hope had been turned right down, but it'd still been there, like a TV where you could tune out the red or the green but not make them go away completely.

Hi, said Mak.

The men didn't look up.

Hello! Gentlemen! Could I trouble you for just one moment of your time?

No, said the guy on the left.

Look, sir, I'll make it as brief as I can, and then you can go back to your dirt.

We don't have moments of time, said the talkative one. If you have moments, that's fine. I'll take one of your moments. I'll take as many as you can count out.

That's very kind of you, said Mak.

No kindness involved. I need your time. I haven't got any. 'Cause you've just arrived you've got time. You can still reckon in hours, maybe even minutes. You still think the sun's going to rise and set. You still think your watch is going to work. You still think your heart's going to beat, leaves are going to fall off trees in fall and flowers are going to bloom in spring, the moon's going to wax and wane, the tides are going to come in and out, ladies are going to bleed once a month and you're going to guess the hour from horns and bells and the noise of the traffic. None of that happens here. We've got no time. Nothing beats, nothing ticks, nothing changes. You can try counting for a while, clapping your hands, drawing lines in the clay. Over there – the man pointed – there's a place covered a day's walk in any direction with five bar gates scratched in the ground, each stroke a guess, a guess, at a day gone by. And a cross every six gates, for a month, and a star every twelve months, for a year. Then the one that did it lost a star. He doesn't do it any more. And over there is a crowd of maybe fifteen gathered round someone who counts. Just counts numbers out loud. He's up to one billion now.

I can help you, said Mak. I'm a lawyer.

Excellent, said the man. But if you're one of those lawyers that charges by the hour, we'd better start counting. He began to clap his hands together, chanting in rhythm: 10 cents, 20 cents, 30 cents, 40 cents – start talking – 60 cents, 70 cents, 80 cents, 90 cents, a dollar . . .

It's OK, said Mak. No win, no fee.

I was joking, said the man. He picked up a toad sitting next to him and squashed it brutally between his hands. The toad emitted a guttaral wittering as it deflated.

Why did you do that? said Mak.

Laughter, said the man. It's too tiring to laugh ourselves so we crush the toads instead. The sound is similar.

I'm going to go out on a limb here, said Mak. I'm going to guess that you don't like being dead.

The man seized another toad and compressed it with the same ferocity.

I didn't mean to be funny, said Mak.

Oh, I wasn't laughing, said the man. That was anger. He shrugged. None of us can be bothered with emotion any more, so the toads stand in for everything. The toad laughs. The toad cries. The toad gets angry. It's all the same.

He toppled over and lay on the ground, staring at the river.

Have you ever thought about getting back at the people responsible for leaving you in this state? said Mak. Have you ever thought about claiming damages?

La-la-la, sang the man softly, not moving his head. Ba-ba-ba.

Sir?

The man whipped over onto his other side and curled up into a foetal position. He moaned.

Sir?

No name, whispered the man. I lost my name. The names are the first to go. No-one recognises me. Sometimes we play the mirror game. We sit opposite each other and match each other's movements. Sometimes I find a good reflection. I start to recognise myself. But as soon as you start to recognise yourself you begin to fail to reflect your reflection. Then your reflection gets angry and fails to reflect you. You don't recognise yourself any more. You still don't know who you are. Nobody knows who you are, because you lost your name.

I'd need your name for an affidavit, said Mak. He looked along the riverbank and saw Najla sitting at the water's edge, hugging her knees tight to her chest. He went to her and spoke her name. She listened while he made his pitch.

Did you see my son? she said.

Yes.

How was he?

He was good. He had a little bit of shrapnel in his leg. He'll be fine.

I saw the fire after I was already dead, said Najla. I thought he'd be dead too. She pressed her hand to her face and waved it at Mak palm up. Where'll he go without a roof? Who'll cook for him? She lowered her face into her hands and shook it from side to side, and straightened up. Her eyes widened as she spoke to Mak. That world. She pointed her thumb over her shoulder. That world we came from. It was better, wasn't it? It had a good smell. She inhaled and knocked on her chest with her fist. A good smell. And colours. I was cooking. He was out on the street playing football. I put the bread on. There were some herbs. Mint. A few mint leaves, not a handful, enough to pick up between your fingertips. I rinsed them in water from a bowl and shook them and held them to my nose for a second. There was a pain shooting down between my shoulders and along the edge of my jaw and I saw the fire. I saw the fire and I saw my son running and I knew I was already dead. It was a good world, better than this, whatever it is. Now I can't get there and he can't get here, yet, unless the next bomb hits him. I'm glad he's still there in that world. Only I don't know how he'll get by without me. And here I am without him. What use is a mother without her son?

Mak had been nodding all this time. When she finished he asked whether she'd thought about legal redress. About suing. Would she be prepared to give testimony.

I'm dead, said Najla. My son's alive. We're apart. You can't take me back.

Najla, if we're going to work together, there's a few things you have to understand, said Mak. One of them is, I don't like the word can't. Another is this thing about you saying you're dead. My feeling, and at this stage it's only a feeling, is: that isn't going to play well with the jury when we get this case to court. Terms like dead and alive, those are their terms. We don't want to make ourselves prisoners of their terms. We not going to accept this outrageous, offensive division of people into dead and alive. It's an affront to human dignity. As far as we're concerned, you're not dead. You're a victim of, a victim of . . . ISL. Involuntary Separation from Life. Try that for size. Try saying it.

ISL, said Najla.

Good. And what happened to you? I'm not coaching.

The Americans dropped a bomb close to my house and I was killed.

No! No. I'm not coaching here but what we want, I think, is something like: as a result of US negligence I was forcibly separated from life.

As a result of our negligence—

US negligence.

—US negligence I was forcibly separated from life.

And made to endure conditions of appalling discomfort, etc. We can work on your full deposition later.

Can you take me back to my son?

The law is a strange and wonderful country, said Mak. It has many new lands still to discover. It would be wrong of me to promise that I, a humble lawyer, could raise the dead. I mean, resolve ISL cases. But I wouldn't be taking part in this action if I didn't think we were talking about colossal damages. Absolutely colossal.

Damages?

Money.

What can you spend money on here?

Najla, I'm sorry, I'm going to have to slaughter the goat now, said Mak.

He led the goat to a smooth mound of clay a few yards away that gave the highest elevation as far as he could see in any direction. With his hand he dug two scoops in the clay at the foot of the mound and two shallow channels running down to the scoops from the top. Standing on the mound, he took the bottle of water and the coil of rope out of his bag and set them down. He hunkered down next to the goat, which turned its head away, placid and anxious about the lack of vegetation, and bleated.

There now, said Mak. Easy. He stroked its back with slow, firm strokes, murmuring Easy, girl, easy. After he'd stroked for a while he grabbed the beast around the neck, holding it in a tight lock, and with his other arm reached around to enfold its legs and jerk them off the ground. As soon as the flank of the struggling animal hit the clay he pinned it there with the full weight of his body and looped the rope around its ankles. Dust rose off the surface as he pushed his locking hand out from under the goat to finish the knot binding the goat's legs. When it was done, still pinning the animal down, he dragged it, bucking and twisting, so that its head was more or less over the top of the channel. He took out the knife, pulled the goat's head back by the ears, felt for the pulse, and cut its throat. The blood ran free into the channel and flowed down to collect in the scoop. When the animal had stopped moving and there was no more blood Mak stood up, lifted the goat by the legs and flung it to the bottom of the mound. He drank water from his bottle and poured the rest into the second channel.

Within a few seconds a crowd of clay-eaters was mobbing the scoops. Where there had been puddles of blood and water there was a seething tide of scalps and outstretched tongues. The goat was torn to pieces. Its stripped white bones flew out of the scrum in broken lengths, sucked dry of marrow.

Ladies and gentlemen! called Mak, clapping his hands together. Could I have your attention, please. Thank you. My name is Maurice Mak, I'm an attorney, and I've come here to your afterlife today to talk about litigation to ease the difficult conditions you find yourself living in, through no fault of your own. Firstly, my sincere apologies to those who were unable to taste the goat or the water. In the fullness of time, if we are successful, I hope there will be goat and water enough for all of you, as much as you need. That's the very least you deserve.

The crowd peered up at him, silent and attentive. Mak took a legal pad out of his pack and brandished it. In the colourless realm it seemed to shine like a hazy sun.

At the other end of the river, in what they like to call the land of the living, they call you the dead, he said. That's when they call you anything. That's when they don't forget about you. Because they don't like to think about you much, do they? They live their fine lives in the light, with their steak and wine and their beating hearts, and they don't concern themselves with you. If they do, it's for no other reason than to be glad of the distance from here to there. They don't want so-called dead people coming into their homes and their gardens and their shopping malls. They'd do anything to shut you out. They're afraid of you! It's true, isn't it? They're afraid of you. Why is that? Why should they be afraid of you? After all, you used to be where they are now, and chances are they're going to be coming here some day themselves. Wonder why they're afraid? Could it be because they're guilty? Could it be because they know they're walking round in a civilisation built by the people they call dead, and deep down they wonder whether those people aren't going to come back and claim it? Well, maybe they're right to be afraid. Maybe it is time you went and claimed what's properly yours. They call you the dead. But let me ask you this. Was anybody here born dead? I don't think so. Did anybody here ask to be dead? OK, the gentleman at the back, I see you, but you thought you'd end up somewhere better, yes? Yes. My friends, this is a defining moment in the history of dead rights. As long as enough of you are prepared to testify, and you can remember who you are, like Najla here, we are going to pursue our campaign for justice in the very highest courts of the still alive. And believe me, when the dead begin to sue, the living had better run for cover.

Excuse me, said a voice over Mak's shoulder. He turned. A thin, short, bespectacled man in tee-shirt and jeans and sneakers stood hunched there, arms folded, all Adam's apple and no chin.

Yes? said Mak sharply.

Can I see your papers?

What papers?

This is a restricted area, said the man. It's off limits to living people. I need to see your permission.

If you'd just wait while I finish this meeting.

I'm not going to wait, said the man, simpering. I'm Ashbath. One of the servants of Ereshkigal. Now show me your papers.

I don't care who you are, said Mak. Get off this fucking mound and let me talk to these people.

Ashbath laughed for a second, wiped his nose with his finger, took a flick knife out of his pocket, triggered the blade and stabbed Mak through the heart with it. As Mak went down he felt Ashbath gather his hair together in a bunch in his fist and start dragging him along the ground.

Later Mak woke up on a plain of fine, talcy dust littered with sharp pebbles. He was lying on his side outside a trailer home. The only other feature in sight was a rusty iron gibbet with a butcher's hook hanging from it. He felt no pain. When he got up he felt nothing except a sense that he had been simplified. His hands, arms, legs looked and worked the same as before, but if he'd been told he'd been reduced to cardboard, clay and straightened-out coat-hangers, he wouldn't have been surprised.

The door of the trailer creaked open and a woman stepped out, chewing gum and holding a cigarette. She was tall and slim, in a tight black polo neck and black jeans, with a tiny pouty red mouth and her eyes covered by a fringe of curly brown hair. She plucked the gum from between her lips, tossed it into the dust, took a drag of the cigarette and said: You Mak?

Yes.

Come in.

Inside the trailer Mak found the woman sitting behind an almost bare desk, a cheap sheet of veneered chipboard on a trestle. There was a full ashtray and an open bottle of red wine. On the wall was what looked like a calendar and in one corner a muscular black dog dozed.

Hi, said the woman. I'm Erishkigal. I'm in charge here. She leaned over the desk and shook Mak's hand. Mak sat down on a three-legged stool facing her.

So, you're an attorney, said Erishkigal. She took a swig of the wine from the bottle. What brings you to these parts?

Just a little routine legal work, said Mak.

OK. What do you think of our realm?

It's unusual.

I need to see your passport.

I don't have one.

Any ID?

Mak handed her his driving licence. Erishkigal examined it while helping herself to more booze. After a few moments she tossed the licence over her shoulder. The dog sprang into the air, caught the licence in its jaws and slunk back to the corner, chewing.

Hey, said Mak. You have no right to do that.

Don't worry, said Erishkigal. Don't worry! You're so anxious! All these travellers get so anxious about their papers. They're in a strange place, they don't have the right documents, they start to panic, they go to the police, the police start asking questions, the travellers freak out. Like if you don't have the right visa the police are going to take you out and shoot you! She laughed. Mak laughed with her. I mean, said Erishkigal, chortling in a girlish way Mak found attractive, what must these travellers think about the world? Like some bureaucrat is going to destroy you because of some crappy stamp.

Right! laughed Mak.

No, said Erishkigal. No. If someone like yourself, a living person, comes here without my permission, then there's absolutely no problem.

No problem, said Mak.

We cut right through the bureaucracy. We just stab you through the heart, you're not living any more, and you remain here for the rest of eternity among the dead.

Mak clenched his teeth to stop his jaw going slack and clapped his hand to his chest. He felt with his fingers under the brittle clay crust of his shirt and stroked along his ribs. There was a dry slit in his chest over his heart. He fumbled with his fingertips for a pulse in his wrist. He couldn't find one.

You look fairly flummoxed by what I've just said, said Erishkigal. Have yourself a drink. She handed him the bottle.

Mak drank. The wine was profound, majestic and noble, a dark stream seeped through loam, beech-mast and truffles, trickled round venison sepalled with cobwebs.

Good, isn't it? said Erishkigal. That's your blood you're drinking.

Ma'am, I'm a lawyer—

I know who you used to be, said Erishkigal. You're dead now. We don't have courts here. We live pretty much in a general state of injustice, and there's no going back. So you won't be needing your law. Or your reputation. Even your name won't be much good to you after a while.

Mak gathered himself. Listen, he said. Just you listen. He took another swig of his blood. He drained the bottle and licked his lips. I've done my research. Tell me this. Who's better qualified to say whether the courts of the state of New Jersey are going to accept jurisdiction in the afterlife of Mesopotamia – you or me? You want to talk about law? See you in court.

You're dead, Mak, said Erishkigal. Death disqualifies counsel.

Macy versus Tagus, 1927, said Mak. See? You don't know jack.

Erishkigal cocked her head. You shouldn't trust Inanna. Last time my bitch of a sister came here I hung her on that hook out there, dead as you are. She screamed at me to let her down and I pushed her toes and watched her swing. I enjoyed it. What is it with her? Who does she think she is? Why does she want this fucking place? Does it look like fun to you, sitting around eating dirt for ever and ever? She got the looks in the family, she got the lifestyle, it's like, everyone loves Inanna. What's going to happen to Erishkigal? Oh, she's dysfunctional, better give her the afterlife to take care of. Yeah, I'm dysfunctional, I'm running this operation, try counting the number of stiffs out there on the plateau. Try doing an audit. I'll tell you who's fucking dysfunctional. You know how my sister got out of here? She gets one of her big god friends, Enki, to send her food and water to bring her back to life, and she sweet talks me into letting her go as long as she sends me a substitute from among the living. And who does she send? Her husband! She says Erish, while I was away, the bastard was whoring and partying like it was going out of fashion. Dumuzi, his name was. He's still here.

I could find you a substitute, if you'd let me go, said Mak.

Erishkigal laughed. I can't let you go, she said. You're not a god. You're not a hero. You're not even a king.

Eternity, yeah? said Mak. Eternity. OK. I'm going to deal with your points one at a time.

Mak began to argue. He argued in Erishkigal's trailer for thirty-three days and thirty-three nights, or would have if there had been days and nights. Erishkigal's aides, the Anunnaki, and her messengers Ashbath and Maikurg hung on the walls, eavesdropping. Some of the dead even summoned up the interest to try to listen in, greeting the lawyer's sharper thrusts with a great bellow of squeezed toads. Stopping only to eat clay, Mak dredged up precedents going back to the ancient Egyptians, staged Platonic dialogues with imaginary witnesses, expounded on natural justice, fair play and the rights of man. He plucked articles from case law, canon law, commercial law, international law, common law, Roman law and the Code Napoléon. He cited from anthologies of near-death experiences, from Homer, Norse sagas, Pythagoras, Origen, Plotinus, Milton and the *National Enquirer*. On the thirty-third day, Erishkigal banged her fist on the table and told him to shut up.

OK. Leave, she said, folding and unfolding her arms. Go on. Try making it back. Try.

I can go?

Sure.

I can just leave?

Three conditions, said Erishkigal, standing up, stretching and yawning. To get back to the land of the living, you have to be alive. Second, you have to bring me a substitute within seven days, or you get the hook. Third, you have to sleep with me before you go. You're quite good-looking, and I don't get enough of it.

Mak took out the gold cereal bar Inanna had given him and put it in his mouth. Chewing it was like chewing a live mains wire. Rings of shock rippled through him and his heart ground out the futile stutter of a broken starter motor. He forced it down, fell to the floor writhing and screaming, scraped grooves in the floor with his nails and lay still. His head ached. He had a pulse. He smiled and snivelled and looked up at Erishkigal.

Well, she said. You're alive. I don't know whether to be disappointed or excited. Straight to condition three.

Just as Mak had struggled and failed to describe Inanna, so conveying the experience of sex with her sister proved beyond the glib lawyer's mastery of English in all its registers. He groped for modifiers: dry, he said at last. It was dry. Disturbing. Dry and disturbing? No, not that . . . he had never felt so inadequate. So he got no pleasure out of it? No, no, there was pleasure . . . not enough . . . He came too early? Of course, several days early, but it wasn't that . . . It was like you'd lived all your life in a desert, and the biggest stretch of water you could imagine was a pond, and when you thought of the sea you imagined something maybe like the pond, only ten times bigger, and then just before you died you saw the sea, and your whole notion of the scale of water changed, and you understood that what you'd thought was swimming was only paddling, and there was a whole new scale of travelling over water to comprehend – sailing – and you'd been so proud of your paddling . . .

Forty days after Maurice Mak arrived in the afterlife, he stood at the edge of a glassy stretch of desert cleared of the dead, with Ashbath holding him by one hand and Maikurg, a short, powerful man with a Karl Marx-like beard, by the other. They began to walk forward, then to run. Mak's feet left the ground and he floated back like a pennant in the slipstream as Ashbath and Maikurg thundered across the desert, a racehorse in two parts. The ground began to slope away from them. As it sloped steeper the two emissaries ran faster to stop themselves falling. The surface of the desert blurred, turned to a mirror-like finish, and they were running upside down on the underside of it. Mak felt himself turned inside out like a surgical glove carelessly peeled from a doctor's fingers, felt Ashbath and Maikurg's hold on his hands slipping, and curled himself up into a ball, hanging in the void. He hung clenched for an indefinite time, until he heard a dog barking and felt a warm wind on the back of his neck. He lifted up his head and saw an apricot light on the horizon, braiding the folds of thunderheads over an unseen ocean. He wept. Then he thought of Inanna and laughed. To see her again, hear her voice, meet her eyes. That warmth and grace. She was a goddess. But to match stories of the afterlife. They were the only ones who could do that now.

Mak stood up. He was on the airfield he'd left from. The Gulfstream was gone. It was morning. He could see a city in the distance. Not far away, Ashbath and Maikurg were playing volleyball with what looked like a brick.

A small figure emerged from a ruined hangar half a mile away and started walking towards Mak. Shaking his arms to drain out the rush of postponed pain through his muscles, Mak jogged to meet the receptor. His mind arranged the slim dark shape as Inanna and joy and love burst through the agony. A few seconds later he stopped and stood still, waiting. It was the boy, Najla's son.

Where's Inanna? Mak called as the boy approached.

The boy didn't say anything. He walked up to Mak and said: Did you see my mother?

What would you like me to say?

That you saw her.

Well, I saw her.

Is that the truth?

Yes, it's the truth. She asked about you. I said you were fine.

Is she happy there?

Yes. She's very happy. It's peaceful there.

Is that the truth?

Yes. It's peaceful.

And she's happy?

Mak hesitated. Yes, he said. She's very happy.

Good, said the boy. I'll go there tonight.

No, said Mak. She said you were to stay here until it was time for you to go.

Why? If it's so good there, and my mother's there, why should I stay here?

Because some things are better for you here.

What? When there's no work, and we don't have enough to eat, and we can't travel anywhere, and between the bombers and the police and getting called up and the Mafia you don't know who to be more afraid of?

You're alive, said Mak. Your heart keeps time, the sun rises and sets, the wind blows, the seasons change, and you can feel it all. If there's just a piece of bread, you can smell it and taste it. People care. Even if they hate you, it means you matter. Even if they don't care, you can try to make them. You can shout. You can laugh.

So when you said my mother was happy, you were lying?

Yes, said Mak. That was a lie.

How am I supposed to live now?

I don't know.

The boy took a letter out of his shirt, gave it to Mak and walked away.

I'm sorry, said Mak.

The boy didn't look back.

The letter was printed out. It was on Enki-headed paper, pp Enki, no signature.

Dear Maurice,

We waited for you for several weeks. We were prepared to wait for you indefinitely. However something happened which upset Inanna so much that she insisted we leave. A fall of blood-red hailstones the size of oranges in the city of Mosul signified that you had exceeded your brief in the afterlife. Soon afterwards this was confirmed when we learned that you had attempted sexual congress with Inanna's sister, Erishkigal. Maurice, that was very wrong of you. No doubt she told you that this was the only way you could escape to the land of the living. We feel that it would have been loyal of you to resist, and, like other courageous lawyers in similar situations, found another way to escape from the afterlife, no matter how long or painful. After all, we hired you to take on Erishkigal and her attorneys in the courtroom, not to sleep with her.

I warned you against becoming Inanna's slave. You chose to ignore that warning. I noticed how you felt about Inanna, of course, and decided to let it pass. She noticed it too. But having become her slave, neither of us can understand how you could then disgrace her so blatantly by having sex with her sister. Have you no sense of decency or honour? I am very disappointed.

Erishkigal is a vile serpent, and our sworn enemy. At the same time she is one of us, a god. It would have been bad enough if you had sullied your worship of Inanna by having intercourse with one of your own. But to lie with a god suggests you had ideas incompatible with your status. It suggests that you dared to dream – I can barely bring myself to dictate these words – of a carnal match with Inanna herself. Shame!

Inanna's first intention was to wait for you nonetheless and slay you on the spot. I persuaded her against it. Please consider our contract rendered void by your actions. I hope your sojourn in the afterlife, your disgraceful behaviour aside, was not too upsetting. I realise that, as a US citizen without papers present on an Iraqi military facility without any rational explanation, you may experience difficulties returning to New York. I wish you luck.

Maurice, we gods are rich, attractive, clever beings with time on our hands, little interest in ordinary people and a passion for social codes and breeding. In short, we are snobs. Inanna looks down on you, and so do I. We're better than you are. You won't be seen in our circles again. Goodbye. You're alive. Be grateful.

Sir? said the waiter. We'll begin serving dinner in a few minutes. Would you like to see a menu?

I blinked and looked out towards the street. The glass had darkened. The lights were on.

What do you say? said Maurice.

I saw it. I saw the beautiful worked-through logic of his psychosis, like a simple maze, and I saw how I was going to step through the maze to the way out and leave the restaurant without upsetting him, and carry off with me to dinner at Lee's a marvellous story of Mak's downfall to set against the missed meeting and calls of the lost afternoon.

I get it, I said. They blew you off. There's no lawsuit, right? The dead aren't going to sue. The story's not the case. It's what you've just told me.

No! said Mak, laughing and shaking his head. No no. Not the dead. Me! I'm going to sue.

The walls of the maze telescoped upwards, shutting off the exit. I narrowed my eyes.

What?

I'm going to sue the federal government! For negligence! Is it my fault Inanna won't love me? Am I responsible for the way I am, for the way I look, for the way I talk?

Right, I said.

Rejected lovers. I'm telling you, Bob, this is the case to end all cases. It's not just me. This is going to be the greatest class action suit since the universe was formed. And I'm going to be the plaintiff, and the head lawyer, leading that lovers' army into battle. We will not be fobbed off with money or phoney dismissals. We will demand that the court grant us the love we have been unjustly denied.

Sorry, I said. I got to my feet. My apologies. I understood you wrong. There was me thinking it was the dead who were going to sue.

That would have been a nice article. That would have been prov-
ocative. That would have been an excellent feature. Now you're telling me the government's going to be sued by disappointed lovers.
Maurice, that's not credible. It won't play. It's the wrong format.

Where are you going? said Mak.

Got an appointment.

Wait a second. Listen. If I gave you a real exclusive, would
you take it?

Come on, Maurice, we've been here all afternoon.

How about if I gave you a chance to visit the afterlife?

Sure, I said. Sure. I'd love to go. Call me tomorrow.

You'd love to go?

Can't think of anything better.

You're absolutely sure now?

Absolutely. I'll see—

Because I don't have to call you. They're going to take you.
Ashbath and Maikurg. They're waiting at the door.

He pointed. I looked over at the doorway. There were two
guys loitering there with their hands in their pockets, a thin,
spotty one with no chin and a stocky character with a bushy
beard like Karl Marx. They looked like social workers. They
probably were social workers.

OK, I said. Maurice, great to see you.

Goodbye, Bob, said Maurice, shaking my hand. He started
to cry. I'm sorry.

Maurice, the main thing is not to worry. You'll be OK, I said,
putting my hand on his shoulder. You can find your way home,
can't you? He nodded.

I said goodbye and made for the door. The social workers
moved towards me.

Hi, said the beard. I wonder if I could ask what you were
discussing with Mr Mak?

That's private, I said. Excuse me, I'm in a hurry.

Sir, said the beard, we're empowered by the city authorities to question anyone who comes in contact with Mr Mak.

I don't think so, I said.

The two men took out plastic wallets and showed me their IDs. Maikurg, said the beard. Ashbath, said chinless. Sir! Sir! Please don't attempt to leave! We're going to have to restrain you, sir. Sir!

The Return of the Godlike Narrator

He limped to the beach one evening in spring. The limp was from a sporting accident in a dark hall. That morning, when he examined the injury, he'd rinsed the bandage in a dogbowl-sized basin in a guesthouse room, rubbing it with a pale green arrowhead of soap and chafing the folds together against the smell of smoke and old banknotes which'd impregnated the cloth. He'd sat cross legged on the bed, wearing just his vest, looking at the wet cotton strip smoothed out and flat on the bedcover in front of him, and read the brown shape left there by his blood.

Blasphemy, he'd said, and bent his body to lick the wound with his tongue. But his belly airbagged out to prevent him.

The beach was clean, flat, finegrained sand, on a bay stockaded by an even wall of sandy soil where the land dropped ten feet to the backshore. He'd known the tide'd be low before he saw it. He'd laboured so long and hard on the beach he could feel the moon's hauling on the water of the bay, when he lay awake on beds and floors, when the stormy surface of the blood and water mass inside his body settled and cooled. He'd see the tiny eddies and kinks on the surface of the deep curl like singed hairs and the knifesharp shadow of a single bird move over it, passing between his blood and the dulling shine of his setting heart, his inner sea stopped. At that time the moon beat a tremendous blow and his blood shivered, the artery walls flattened to a bowl. The moon shook his blood from side to side, heaving it till it rose and fell in steep waves, stroking the inside top of his skull with foam and breaking down through his body. It tipped his blood up until it ran shallow and puckered across his bones, filling fleshscoops with billowing pools, gushing latticed through sinewy channels, in a navel-shape a hundred miles across, a crimson delta lazily shored by skin.

The causeway was there as he'd built it twenty years before, a bridge to nowhere, stretching out three hundred yards into the sea from its anchor, a concrete military obstacle sunk in the sand, once a cube, now a pyramid. The wood, almost white with sap when he'd nailed and lashed it together, was black now or, as he got closer, a dark grey-green, as if the powder left when the ocean dried was not salt, but ash. The first joints he'd made, once he'd rehearsed a few scenes of carpentry, were heavy, earnest and time-consuming. He'd worked over them again and again, dovetails mostly for the right angles, and diagonal support struts, not just hammered in for strength, but modelled for elegance, so they fitted flush with the round vertical posts pounded deep into the sand which carried the weight of the structure and prevented it being blown away in the storms. The planks on the boardwalk were planed smooth and flat and fitted together so snug that if you lay under them on a midsummer's noon you'd hardly have light enough to read by. He ran his fingertips down one of the posts. He'd still been inspired then, mad to get at what he'd seen out on the bay. All the same, it'd seemed important to make the causeway perfect. He'd gone back to those first few timbers a hundred times, ripped them out and made bonfires of them and started again, when he could have gone ahead and built the causeway more quickly. After all, he'd known where he was going: he was building a bridge to what he'd seen. Now he wondered if he hadn't had doubts from the time he hammered in the first post. It'd been easier to linger on the beginning of the causeway, tinkering with it, prising out nails, taking an hour to plane a millimetre-thick curl of wood off the narrow edge of a plank, than to hare on into the sea, sacrificing craftsmanship for speed, not because it was harder working below the high watermark, but because beginnings were always easier. Yeah, looking down towards the surf line, he could see how in the end he'd forced himself to charge seawards, lurching out a dozen yards at a time in forty-eight hour frenzies of labour, lips crimping cold nailheads, left thumb beaten black, slave to the sledgehammer, how in the last stretch he'd given up the nails and lashed it together with ship's rope, up to his waist, inventing knots and bracing the timbers against each other, against all engineering intuition. He was a fool. The idiot in him had stolen up on the wise man one night and eaten his brains. Only a victim of duty would finish a structure like the causeway. The other one, the smart one, he'd known what he was about, tackling the beginning from every angle, always meaning to go on and finish it, but never doing it, just making the beginning more and more perfect. A beautiful beginning was something you could take with you happy to the grave, it was inexhaustible, it was immortal. Only failures never left before the end.

Once he'd finished it, he astonished himself with his patience. He waited for the exact weather, light and time of day when he'd first caught sight of what he'd seen out on the bay. After two weeks he judged it right. He climbed the steps and walked along the causeway to the end. The bare boards became thinner and looser under his feet as he walked but they were well-fixed and strong enough. He reached the end and stood at the edge, looking at the sea. Whatever it was he'd seen that he'd wanted to reach with the causeway, it wasn't there any more, and never had been. He watched the waves, the rocks and the clouds for an hour and walked back to the beach. He brought petrol in a canister and threw it over the causeway and tried to set fire to it, but the petrol sank into the sand and his matches blew out in the wind. It started to rain. He fetched an axe and got ready to swing into one of the middle posts. The rising tide unrolled around his feet. He put the axe down. At first he felt sorry for his labour, then he realised that, now it was built, the causeway had nothing to do with him any more. He slung the axe over his shoulder and walked away.

On the evening of his return he limped towards the ladder, climbed up and set off along it. There was a small girl sitting out on the end, where at lowest tide the causeway ran about ten yards into the water. She was sitting with her feet dangling over the edge, her back to the shore, looking at the horizon. She heard him coming when he was about ten yards away, looked round, stared at him for a couple of seconds, and went back to the horizon.

What happened to your leg? she asked, when he reached the end and was standing next to her, leaning on one of the two shoulder-high posts which marked the causeway's end.

Sporting accident, he said.

What sport?

Snooker. I was supposed to lose the game. I won. I didn't mean to.

The girl nodded, not looking at him. Men outside her family were generic, numerous but remote and hard to tell apart, like stars, and you might watch them, but you wouldn't talk to them, and you wouldn't expect them to talk back. It wasn't the limp so much that'd opened her mouth as the way he'd approached, as if he was on his way somewhere, and the end of the wood and the beginning of the water had confused him.

What are you doing here? he said.

Just sitting and watching, she said.

Seen anything?

Nothing special.

So why are you sitting here?

It's the pier, she said. It's good to go out to the end and sit there.

He became angry. It's not a pier! he said. It's a causeway. I built it.

She looked at him with her eyes saying she wasn't such a fool as all that.

It's a causeway, he said sullenly. I was walking along the beach and I saw something out there in the bay, out at sea, that was – you're too young to even think you've been in love.

The girl shrugged.

You haven't, he said. But suppose you had. Think about how it might have felt. And think about how it would be if your life and your memories and your imagination weren't real, if they were cheap substitutes, but you didn't realise it, and thought everything was fine, until one day you were walking along the beach and you saw something out there that reminded you of your real life, the one you didn't know you'd had.

I think I know what you mean, said the girl.

You'd have to have it, wouldn't you? So I built the causeway to try to reach it, even though I didn't know what it was, even though the closer I got to where I thought I'd seen it, the clearer it became that it'd never been there. By the time I got to the end I hated the causeway because, even though it turned out the false life was my real one, it wasn't worth as much as it'd been before I'd started building. I should have made more of an effort to burn it. It would have burned nicely. I'm sorry.

You may not have got what you were looking for but you left a good pier behind.

I don't care, he said. I don't like it. I shouldn't have come back. He turned and limped off towards the shore.

The girl turned her head and watched him go. I like it, she said, not sure whether he could hear her or not. She saw him raise his left arm and wave his hand in the air with a contemptuous downward sweep. She laughed, turned back to the sea, sat on her hands and swung her legs.

I like it, she said to the wind. It's a good pier.

The
Club
of Men

These Lovers

Gordon's son Kenneth was coming round for dinner with his new girlfriend. The bell rang at eight. Gordon went to get it. He had a glass of Grouse with ice in his hand. He was wearing white slacks and a scarlet v-neck with a white poloneck underneath. He opened the door and Kenneth and the girl were there.

Fucking hell, said Gordon.

Eh? said Kenneth.

Good to meet you, said Gordon, stretching his hand towards the girl.

Did you swear just now? said Kenneth, standing there in a purple linen suit and green silk shirt buttoned up to the neck.

Good to see you, said Gordon.

Hi, said the girl, grinning. She was – You jammy bastard, his own son. His own flesh and blood. Was there not a law, if your own son had a woman in his legal father's house and his legal father lawfully wanted to take her upstairs. Those legs, the black dress, the breasts on her, it was unfair, it was so unfair after all these years. The boy had no right.

This is Julie, said Kenneth.

Hi, said Julie, grinning and bending her head forward a bit. She was tall!

How old, said Gordon, and took a shot of the whisky, not taking his eyes off Julie, his hand still somewhere out there in her direction.

What's old? said Kenneth.

How old is it. How old it is, said Gordon, looking at him and frowning. Come in.

Have you been on that stuff all afternoon? Kenneth was nudging his dad back down the hall and Gordon was trying to stay where he was, letting his son go on in so's to be able to touch Julie. Kenneth shuffled round and eased Julie in, keeping his body between her and Gordon, so for a moment the three of them were wedged in to the hall together. Julie giggled and jumped for freedom. Stiletto heels! No, no, no. He'd given birth to a monster.

Mary appeared in the hall. Julie! she said in a long low voice with a grin fixed to her face, chin tucked into her chest, fingers locked together, earrings trembling.

Mrs Stanefield.

Mary. Julie!

Mary clamped her hands on Julie's shoulders and touched cheeks. Julie. Mmuh! Mary shook her and held her stiff at arm's length, staring and grinning like she was miming the Snow Queen at the mirror.

You must be frozen in that dress, Julie, said Mary. My goodness Kenneth's a lucky man, eh Gordon.

Aye.

What's wrong with you? Come on and get the young ones a drink. Where was it Kenneth said you were from, Julie?

Darlington.

Darlington! The north of England. It's not so grey and industrial now, is it.

They went into the lounge and sat down in separate puce

leather suite items. Gordon went for the big settee but Julie sat by herself in an armchair. By God that boy of his had her on a short leash. There was a law. The right of seniority, it was called. It'd be to be found in the library.

Drinks, said Mary.

Ah come on Smithie.

Mary got up, leaned over close to Gordon and murmured in his ear. If you call me that one more time in front of your future daughter in law I swear I'll have you committed. Get the drinks. She whiplashed back, locked her nails together and smiled at Julie.

There were two ways Gordon could deal with the situation. One was to shoot off to his local, lean against the bar, ask for a pint of the usual, shake his head at Jimmy the barman and say These lovers, eh. Only he'd never had a local. There was only the golf club and it was a different young lad behind the bar each time. They didn't get lassies any more. He didn't have a usual either. He liked trying the different German lager beers.

Mary had a gin and tonic. Kenneth had a Perrier because he was driving. Julie had a glass of white wine. Gordon sank down into the settee, leaned forward with a squeak of his slacks against the leather, took a drink of Grouse and feasted in silence on Julie's thighs.

I'm dying to know how you two met, said Mary.

It was the conference centre, you know, Mum, said Kenneth, looking down into the bubbles. We're both on long-term contracts now. It was environmental consultants.

No Kenny, it was fast food franchises.

It was environmental consultants, Jul. Not remember that guy who got electrocuted by the model rainforest.

It was fast food franchises, Mrs Stanefield, said Julie. I remember cause they had their own catering, tacos and root beer and buffalo wings and stuff. The environmental consultants had a bulk order of Liebfraumilch.

That's one of the German lager beers, said Gordon.

It's wine, said Mary.

It's beer.

It is wine, Dad, said Kenneth. It is German, though. The name means young girl's milk.

There was silence for a time.

Where'd you leave you car? said Gordon.

In the street outside the house.

It won't be safe there. Folk've had their tyres slashed.

This is a neighbourhood watch area, isn't it? All these bungalows with burglar alarms on them.

That's just what attracts them.

How come you've got one then?

And there's joyriders.

They'll not get much joy out of a 1.3 litre Vectra, said Kenneth. Different next month when I get the Puma, eh Jul. Out on the old autobahn.

Maybe you should take it up into the drive if it's not safe, said Julie, turning to look at him and fidgeting with her wineglass. She glanced at Gordon, crossed her legs and stretched the hem of her skirt towards her knees. She let it go and Gordon gazed at the elastic material as it crept back, millimetre by millimetre.

It's the first thing I've heard about slashing, said Mary. You sometimes leave your car out there.

I've not told your mother everything that goes on in this neck of the woods, said Gordon. He put his whisky down on the coffee table and got up. I'll just go and check everything's OK.

I'll go myself, said Kenneth.

Och, just relax. You've come a long way.

What, from Barnton?

Relax, said Gordon. He turned and smiled at Julie's thighs and went out of the lounge, closing the door. He went into the cupboard under the stairs and hauled out a cardboard box marked Windward Islands Bananas. He plunged in his hand and groped among the squirming nails and screws and hinges till he felt the fat smooth handle of the Stanley knife in his palm. He pulled it out and put it in his pocket. He took a hand drill off one of the shelves and went upstairs, stepping on the sides of the stairs so's the creaking ones wouldn't be heard. He went into Kenneth's old room and put the drill down on the carpet next to the skirting board on the wall going through to the guest bedroom. He went back downstairs and out into the night.

What a grand smell that was, that November smell of burned leaves on a frosty night. He'd need to burn some leaves. He'd go down the garden centre tomorrow for a big bag of them, the proper autumn leaves. They had them by the shovelfull in big barrels. Serve yourself. He couldn't remember how you stopped them falling through the holes in the shopping trolley. His daughter in law! See even Mary understood the point of law. She understood things. That was the way it was with your pals. That November smell, mind how they used to buy a big box of fireworks when they were wee and the two of them. What was it they used to do. The Catherine wheel, what a racket it made, and so bright. Him and Smithie.

He opened the gate and stepped out into the street. Kenneth's car was right there. He squatted down by the first wheel and slid the blade of the knife out by two notches. He put his left hand on the tyre and leaned on it to steady himself and pressed the point of the blade into the rubber. The blade bent and made no impression. Gordon sniffed, shifted his feet, wiped his nose with the back of his left hand and moved round so he was side-on to the wheel. He took hold of it again and drew the knife firmly towards him from the far side of the tyre, pulling and pressing in at the same time. The blade scored smoothly into the rubber and dived deep inside. Air sighed out into the night. He waddled over to the next wheel and did the same thing. The Cavalier settled comfortably down against the kerb. Fuck, there were some kids coming. Willman's sprogs, the specky ones.

Look, that's Mr Stanefield slashing a man's tyres, said the older boy.

Evening lads, said Gordon. Out late, eh.

We've come from scouts, said the wee one.

Scouts, eh, said Gordon. Was there not some child abuse scandal up there recently?

What're you doing? said the elder boy.

What, don't tell me your dad's never let you help him let the summer air out of his tyres? When it gets to winter, like now, you see, frosty, you have to let the warm air that's been gathering in there all spring and summer escape. Otherwise the tyres would just explode. Pfoo! Come on round here, you can give us a hand. Come on.

They went round together to the other side of the car. Scrunty little spies that they were, everyone was out to betray you in this street.

He held the knife out to them. The wee one snatched it from him and his brother fought him for it and won.

Here! That's enough now, said Gordon. There's a tyre each, you can both have a shot. And mind that knife, it's not a toy. Come on down here. They squatted down together.

Watch your breeks, said Gordon. I don't want your father

on at me for ruining your trousers. And don't be too long or you'll catch your death. He took the boy's small cold hand in his own, eased the blade out, guided it onto the rubber and began the cut. Gordon let go, stood up and watched him digging away. They were good lads.

I'm away inside, he said. Bring the knife back when you've finished. Don't be too long and mind and give your wee brother a go.

Gordon returned to the lounge. Mary was talking. She stopped and they all looked up at him.

Looks like you'll have to spend the night here, said Gordon. They're out there now, slashing your tyres. He sat down and took a sip of Grouse.

Eh? The fuck they are, said Kenneth. He jumped up and went to the bay window. He pulled the gold velvet-effect curtains aside a few inches and pressed his face against the double glazing.

You'll not see anything from there, said Gordon. There's the hedge.

I'm calling the police, said Mary, getting up.

Kenneth stood looking out for a bit. He turned round and undid the top button of his shirt. I'll sort them out, he said, taking off his jacket, folding it carefully and laying it on the back of a chair. Julie got up and took it from him.

Let the police handle it, Kenny, she said. Have you got a hanger for this? she asked Gordon.

Gordon got up and moved towards her. Come on upstairs, there's a wardrobe free, he said.

Kenneth moved between them. How many of them are there? he said to Gordon.

Couple. Local youths, I think.

Fuck's sake, bungalow psychos, they're the worst.

They had identical jumpers on and they were wearing these kerchiefs.

Jesus, radge casual bastards in gang colours. Have to put the old thinking cap on here. Don't want to go piling in too soon.

The doorbell went.

That'll be them, said Gordon.

Oh my God, said Julie. She grabbed Kenneth's forearm. Gordon knocked back the whisky sharply and stared at her fingers pressed into his son's flesh. It'd been different in the old days, when you'd had the power of life and death over your kids. If you didn't like your son, or he was being a pain in the arse, they'd take him away. There was a bit of paperwork and you were free. Smithie'd never had kids. Only Smithie was still around, was he not? Ach, he was married to her. So what was Kenneth all about, eh, turning up on your doorstep and nabbing all the lassies? There were things it was hard to tie together. The autumn leaves and the shopping trolleys, for one.

Don't answer it, Kenny, said Julie. They'll leave. The police'll come.

How old would you say they were? said Kenneth.

One was about 12, the other was a wee bit younger, said Gordon. Are you OK? You've an awful sweat on you.

12, said Kenneth, nodding, and began inhaling and exhaling deeply. 12. 12. He raised his forearms, clenched his fists, closed and opened his eyes, ran out of the lounge and down the hall and pulled the front door open. Gordon was reaching out to take hold of Julie's bare shoulders when Mary came back in and said the police were on their way.

They heard children screaming and Kenneth shouting from the front door. Oh God, said Julie, putting her hand over her mouth and looking at Gordon and Mary. The sounds moved outside for a few seconds, then the door slammed and Kenneth tramped back into the lounge, grinning and wiping his troubles off the palms of his hands.

What a fright you gave us, said Mary, hand on chest. Daft laddie. Did you give them a battering?

Julie went and hugged him and stepped back, looking at him, holding her throat with one hand, stroking him with the other, biting her lip.

Don't think they'll be coming down this street again in a hurry, said Kenneth. He reached into his trouser pocket and took out the Stanley knife. That's a handy piece of equipment, eh.

Julie put her hand on her mouth and invoked God again. Gordon took the knife from him. Kenneth's hand was shaking. Gordon wiped the knife carefully with a paper napkin and gave it back to Kenneth.

Here, he said. Souvenir for you. Kenneth grinned and put it back in his pocket.

Might as well have something stronger than water, eh, said Gordon, pouring him a big tumbler of Grouse and handing it over.

Might as well, said Kenneth. He sat down and Julie clung to him.

Is that blood on your hand? said Julie.

Kenneth looked at his knuckles. Ah, must've been where I hit the boy's glasses.

What if he was HIV? said Julie, moving so there was half an inch of air between her and Kenneth all the way down.

It's my blood, said Kenneth. I'm not sure they were old enough. I mean of course they were old enough but they didn't look like poofs or junkies is what I mean. But the menace of them, Jul, the sheer menace. You know you see it on the videos when they come for someone that's defenceless and they enjoy it, don't they, they drag it out and they taunt him cause they know he can't get away. I opened the door and there's this boy with specs – they weren't real specs, you understand that, they just wear them with plain glass in, it's a fashion – and he's holding out the knife towards me and he says Finished. Like that. Finished. It was a kind of low voice, low and soft at the same time. Low and soft and like cold.

You'd best all come and get your dinner, said Mary.

They went through to the dining room and ate smoked salmon. Mary cleared the plates away and brought out a casserole and the police came. Gordon went to the door. It was two constables, a man and a woman. He invited them through to the lounge.

We were just having dinner, he said.

Your wife called us, said the man constable.

You must know my brother Bruce, said Gordon. Bruce Stanefield. He's CID.

It's all under investigation, said the woman constable. We can't say anything just now. I'm sure he'll be back at work soon enough.

He's on full pay while he's suspended, said Gordon.

I never knew him personally, said the man.

I wondered whether maybe the lads were getting together some kind of support fund for his family while he's suspended, said Gordon. I'd like to contribute. He pulled a folded 50-pound note out of his pocket and held it in the air between the three of them. Nobody said anything for a bit.

Kind of support fund, said Gordon again.

We're from the uniform branch, said the man. You should

go to plain clothes directly. He glanced at the woman. Right Wendy?

Aye. You're best going to them, Mr Stanefield. See we're not supposed to carry messages from the general public. I know the DI's your brother and that but there's all sorts of rules about us taking money, eh Lindsay.

Fair enough then, said Gordon, putting the note away. Was it my son you were wanting to see? It was his car got its tyres slashed.

Aye. Aye, said Lindsay. Only we got another call from your neighbours up the road, the Willmans, saying your son beat up their kids. They came home with their faces all bruised. And the kids say it was you that slashed the tyres.

It's awful cold out tonight. I'm not a young man. I'm a pensioner. Where's the motive, eh, son? Where's my motive?

You understand we had to ask, Mr Stanefield, said Wendy. You know the things kids'll say.

Och yes but we had to ask, said Lindsay.

That's OK, said Gordon. I went out to check my son's car was OK and I saw these two shadowy figures slashing the tyres and I went back inside.

Could you give us a description?

No. They were like I said shadowy. But I remember there was this strong smell of burning leaves.

You don't think your son'd mind popping down to the station with us for a chat?

It's not the best time but what can you do? I'll go and fetch him.

He's never been known to be violent, has he? Aggressive?

Kenneth? Our Kenneth? Aggressive? The boy couldn't punch his way out of a meringue cake.

Right.

That's maybe why he carries a knife in his pocket. Self-defence, I suppose.

A hunting knife?

No, nothing like that. One of those DIY tools, what's it called, a Henley knife. I mean when you've had a bit to drink like he has tonight you can lower your guard maybe and then you need some extra protection, right.

The constables stood up and put their hats on. If you'd just fetch him, said Lindsay.

Gordon went back to the dinner table. They want you to nip down the station with them, he said to Kenneth.

You what? I just about got fucking killed back there.

Language, Kenneth, said Mary.

I can't help it, Mum, you know that, when I feel strongly about something. I haven't even started on the casserole. They should be out chasing the psychopaths that slashed my tyres.

They'll be wanting a statement, I suppose, said Mary. You remember how your uncle Bruce used to operate.

Christ if Uncle Bruce had anything to do with it I'd need a crash helmet before I went down there.

That's no way to speak about your uncle. He's twice the brains his brother has and it's not his fault about the alkie.

Can I go with him? said Julie.

Best not, said Gordon. They'll bring him back soon enough.

I'm not budging, said Kenneth.

Don't worry, we'll look after Julie, said Gordon. You'd both best spend the night here, you can have the spare room.

Maybe they could interview you here, said Mary.

I'm not going anywhere, said Kenneth. He started cutting up a piece of meat on his plate.

They'd think you were hiding something if you didn't go, said Gordon. That's what I'd think.

It's really delicious this, Mum, said Kenneth.

Might affect your insurance, said Gordon.

OKAY! shouted Kenneth, throwing his knife and fork on the floor. OKAY! I'LL GO, RIGHT? Keep your bloody shirts on. He stomped out. They followed him. The police were waiting in the hall. Their blue lights flashed through the glass in the door.

Mr Stanefield? said Lindsay.

OK, I'm coming, I'm coming, said Kenneth. This'd better not take long.

Gordon caught Wendy's eye and made a gesture. It'll be all right, he said. That shouting was completely out of character. He didn't think, the wee brat'd never been able to hold his drink. God if his brother'd been on duty he'd have been on the phone, out with the balaclavas and teach his nephew the difference between a boy and a man and not to poach his elders' and betters' women.

You'll bring him back, won't you? said Julie to Wendy.

Of course, said Wendy. It's all routine. They went out to the police car and drove away.

I'll get a taxi home, said Julie.

You will not, said Gordon. You'll stay here with us till Kenneth gets back. We can't have you sitting at home on your own worrying about him.

I should have gone with him.

Gordon's right, love, said Mary, looking at Gordon and narrowing her eyes. Come on and we'll have some Bailey's and coffee. We've got some Amaretto if you want.

Gordon yawned and stretched. I'm off to bed, he said.

At ten o'clock? said Mary.

It's been a long day.

You didn't get up till half nine this morning.

I've been to work.

You haven't been to work. You haven't got any work. You're retired. Never mind him, Julie, let's go through and get a drink.

Night night, said Gordon.

Night, said Julie, looking over her shoulder at him and smiling. Gordon went upstairs to the room where he'd left the drill, picked a spot at eye level and began drilling a hole in the wall. The work went well. In a minute he'd penetrated the first layer of plaster. He got stuck in a bit of timber. Christ why did they not just make walls with holes in so folk could watch each other? They did it with doors. He moved a few inches and started on another hole. This was the one. Straight through.

What the hell are you doing to my walls? said Mary.

Oh fucking shite Smithie, can you no leave me alone even for a minute? said Gordon, stopping the drilling, leaving the bit stuck in the plaster.

I'm not Smithie. I'm Mary, your wife. Smithie's dead. D'you not remember? He stuck a shotgun in his mouth and blew his head off. Mary came over and took the drill out of the wall.

These lovers, eh, said Gordon, putting his hands in his pockets and looking at her, puckering his lips. How'd she crept up on him like that? Jungle training she had. Moving without the snap of a twig. She'd been practising. While he'd been out on the golf course she'd been practising moving silently round the house. It wasn't fair.

You won't get a glimpse of Julie's knickers that way, said Mary, leaning against the doorframe and toying with the drill. It's all fitted wardrobes on the other side.

Gordon sat down on the chair at Kenneth's old desk. There was still that Iron Maiden poster hung up over it. The boy'd never had a poster of a lassie hung up there and he got a Julie. The injustice of it was so terrible Gordon felt like greeting.

These lovers, eh, he said, turning to Mary. How old it is.

Pure

Gordon woke up. There'd been a dream with a white and mint-fresh-green plastic cover for a domestic appliance with an insect stuck in a crevice inside which he'd been trying to get out with the end of a spoon handle. That'd gone on too long. Mary was up and moving about. It was barely light. Gordon just opened his eyes so's he'd be able to see but they'd still look shut. Mary was lying on the floor on her back, holding her knees in her hands and pulling them down towards her. She pulled and grunted with the effort and rocked back and forth for a second and let the knees go. She did it again. She could have put a tracksuit on. The thighs on her.

Give us a break, eh, said Gordon.

It's my back, said Mary. I can't sleep, I have to do my exercises.

What's the time?

Half seven.

Jesus.

I've told you, it's bloody sore. You've never had back problems.

I have so.

There's no justice. You haven't got piles or heart disease or arthritis and you're the biggest bastard I know.

I get headaches.

Aye, you know what that is? That's your brain stotting against your skull, trying to escape.

I was dreaming.

Oh aye. What about?

Plastic.

Mary pulled her knees tightly down towards her chest and grunted through clenched teeth.

There's been no word from Kenneth, she said.

Eh?

Kenneth, your son Kenneth.

There was something good in this, a prize, something that came before the plastic. What was it? Gordon turned over and put his arm out onto the quilt.

He should've called. They're allowed a phone call.

Who? Gordon had something hell of a good coming to him but what form it was there was no remembering. He sat up in bed and rubbed his eyes with his fingertips.

Kenneth. That's nine hours he's been down there now. Julie'll be worried sick.

Gordon swung out of the quilt, stood up and made a run for the door. When he got there Mary was already leaning against it with her arms folded.

She'll be wanting her breakfast, said Gordon.

You can't even open a yoghurt carton.

I can.

Aye, I've seen you. With your teeth. From the bottom. Why can't you leave her alone? She's not for you. You won't get in to see her, she's locked in. Get dressed and come down.

Where's the key?

Mary shook her head, put on an acrylic dressing gown with pictures of pagodas on it and went out of the room. Gordon put on blue jeans and a cream polo shirt and a light blue Lacoste cardigan and went to the door of Julie's room. He turned the doorhandle and pushed. It was locked. He knocked.

Julie! he said.

Hello, said Julie from far away, like she was half under the covers still, like he'd woken her.

Can I get you something?

No, I'll come down.

Kenneth's on the phone.

Right, she said, I'll take it here. Sure enough there was a phone in the room, the planning of it was meticulous from beginning to end. He was in the hands of a master. What was the use. He started off downstairs, hearing her pick the phone up and say hello and hello and put it down and call out to him that they must have been cut off, she'd come down. He shook his head and laughed and kicked the skirting board with the toe of his slipper as he came round into the hall.

In the kitchen Mary was putting orange halves onto a machine which was making them into juice.

Can I have a shot? said Gordon.

Your paper's on the table. What d'you want to eat?

Kippers. Gordon sat down and picked up the paper.

Kippers. Mary laughed. I'll make you some bacon and eggs.

Julie's greeting and screaming upstairs cause you locked her in. Where's the key?

Screaming is she, said Mary, clenching her teeth as she pressed the fruit onto the growling spindle.

Give us the key, eh, I'll go up and let her out.

D'you want juice?

No. Gordon found the obituaries column in the paper. He grinned. Hey Smithie, he said, mind that old cunt used to teach us Latin?

Mary turned round with a gouged-out half-orange in her hand. Looking at Gordon she took hold of the lapel of her dressing gown, put the orange down, reached in and took out her left breast. The broad puckered brown nipple stared at Gordon.

I'm not Smithie, Gordon, Mary said. He was a man. He didn't have any of these. D'you see that? D'you understand what I'm saying?

I'd forgotten you had them on you, said Gordon.

I know you did, said Mary, tucking her breast in and going back to the oranges. You forget too much. People who've forgotten a good sight less than you are bouncing round the Royal Ed. And I won't have you using words like cunt in my kitchen either.

How—

And you don't speak a word of Latin.

I do: Friends, Romans, countrymen. Listen if Smithie had a shotgun how come he never gave me a shot?

Julie came in. Has Kenneth not called back? she said.

How did you get out? said Gordon.

Out of what? said Julie.

Your door was locked.

I'm sorry. It's a habit from hotels. I always lock the door. I can't sleep otherwise.

Might have been a fire, said Gordon. Here, come and sit down. He grabbed a chair and pulled it close to him, patting the seat. Julie glanced at Mary and took another chair at the far corner of the table. Mary put a glass of orange juice and a toast rack in front of her.

Julie, I should have said, borrow some of my clothes, said Mary. You don't want to be wearing that nice dress two days running.

She does, said Gordon.

Shut up, said Mary. Just go up to our room, my clothes are in the units on the left, and help yourself. Pair of jeans probably for a Sunday.

Thanks Mrs Stanefield.

Mary.

I'll go and help, said Gordon, getting up and lunging forward. Mary pulled a knife from a mahogany block on the sideboard and flung it at the floor. It landed upright in the parquet tiles just in front of Gordon's foot and quivered there, the blade imbedded half an inch into the wood. The three of them looked down at it.

Slipped out of my hand, I'm sorry, said Mary. Away you go upstairs, Julie. Gordon stood and watched his wife while she came over, tugged the knife out and put it back in its place. She'd been practising. Well then, if that was the way of it, two could play at that game. Once he found out what game it was he'd be onto them like he used to be. But did she have to take those legs away? They were so long and smooth. One wee stroke was all he'd been after. He sat down and opened the paper.

Need to go up the garden centre again, he said.

What for?

What not for!

How about Kenneth?

Ah, he'll not want to come.

He's at the police station still. D'you not think they should have let him out by now? I'll take the car and go round there with Julie.

I'll take her.

Mary didn't say anything. She broke eggs into the frying pan. After a while she said: I'll put any money on those refugees for the ones slashed Kenneth's tyres.

Gordon was reading the livestock prices. What a bargain a sheep was! So much cheaper to buy a whole one at the auctions than get it in penny packets at the superstore. They knew how to screw the punters right enough. Maybe there was some angle in there for a middleman with a bit of capital.

Andrew said he'd see they never got permission to put them there, said Mary. And then look. Outvoted on the committee. We'll all be murdered in our beds. What's his name that Shiltie calls himself a Christian minister and he fills our church hall with foreigners. If folk want to be refugees they can do it in their own country. We never got German refugees coming over here during the war.

She put bacon rashers into the pan and they sprayed out fat loudly. Gordon looked up.

You'd be better buying a whole one, he said.

A whole what, said Mary. Here's your coffee.

Julie came in and sat down. She was wearing a pair of Mary's jeans and one of her black handknitted jumpers that looked liked it'd been caught on the barbed wire trying to get away. Gordon glanced at her and looked back to the paper. The jeans and the jumper were baggy on her. It wasn't the same Julie as it'd been with the legs and the dress and the breasts and the lips and the arse on her. It was a different lassie. It was a skinny girl with her hair out of place not knowing where she was or what she wanted. How could Smithie take that Julie with the legs away without her being dead and without there being two of them, it was like there was only one of them at the heart of it all but they'd gone off on different roads, the Julie of the black dress on one by herself without Gordon, to a place he couldn't go, and the Julie of the baggy jeans with Gordon and Mary, getting older and more vulnerable to attack with every passing day. It was awful quiet in the kitchen, why was that? He coughed.

See eh, see they're wasting our money on the river, he said, flicking a story in the paper with his fingernail. Literally throwing it down the river. Stopping folk dumping stuff in it.

Is there a river here? said Julie.

It's the only thing that keeps this part of town clean. Imagine if you couldn't dump stuff there, eh Smithie, eh – Mary. All the dead dogs and cats and the old prams and mattresses and household appliances piling up in folk's gardens. And now they're looking to put up signs against it with our money. Literally throwing it down the river.

It's not easy to clean a river once it's polluted, said Julie. We had one in our town. The council spent tons of money on it and it's really pure now. It's great. It's amazing, you can catch salmon.

Never. Really? said Mary.

Yeah, it's true. The man who caught it got fined because he didn't have a licence to fish there but the magistrate said it was a bonus for the community.

Gordon put an old fridge in our river.

I never, said Gordon.

I was with you, said Mary. You heaved it off the bridge at one o'clock in the morning.

You're imagining things. I wouldn't have done that. It's good to have a river that's pure.

He's havering, Julie, said Mary. He doesn't know what purity is.

I do so. I do so know what purity is.

What is it then?

Purity, it's when all the germs are killed.

Mary took Julie to the police station in the car and told Gordon to wait till they got back. After they'd gone Gordon went upstairs and into the guest room. Julie had made the bed.

Gordon pulled back the covers, pressed his face into the sheets and inhaled. It smelled the same as their own sheets when they'd been washed. He looked around for the black dress. He couldn't find it. He went downstairs and found the washing machine already working. He knelt down and looked at the dress slapping against the glass as the drum churned it round. How small it was with the water on it. He put the palm of his hand on the warm door and felt the humming and sloshing of the water. It was incredible. All that time Smithie had a shotgun and not once had he given Gordon a shot. What had he killed himself for? Who was he living with if it wasn't Smithie anyway? Ah, the woman Mary. Left-footer by the sound of it. And now the jungle warfare. He didn't much fancy the idea of sticking a gun barrel in your mouth. The metallic taste of it on your tongue. Or were you supposed to put your tongue inside it? What if you threw up before it went off, eh, from the fear. Ach Smithie. He was a good pal till that boy came on the scene, the wee fucker. And he'd seemed a nice enough lad, like those Willman sprogs. Eager to please. They betrayed you in the end.

Gordon put on his waxed jacket and a tartan scarf and a cap and went out. Kenneth's car still sat deflated at the kerb. Gordon grinned. He ran the toe of his shoe round the rim of the exhaust pipe. Better not, eh. Too dirty and a hell of a lot bigger calibre. He turned and headed up towards the river.

At the stone bridge he leaned over the rails and looked down at the black and yellow scum-flecked torrent slipping through the rocks and branches and household appliances. Looked like a washing machine down there. Money you could save putting the machine in the river and just putting the clothes in and leaving the doors open. He heard a sound behind him and looked round. A boy about Kenneth's age was trying to climb over the rails.

Hey! shouted Gordon. There's salmon in that river! He ran

across the road and grabbed the boy's black leather jacket just when the balance of his weight was tipping over the edge. The boy didn't resist, he sat there on his arse with his legs dangling over the edge, like a mealbag, swinging whichever way Gordon pulled him. He had half a mind just to push the lad off anyway to see what would come of it but letting the river fill up with suicides wasn't going to impress Julie of the legs if she ever came back, especially suicides that hadn't washed, like this one by the look of him.

Fuck off, said the boy, like Kenneth, the pansy.

None of that cheek. Get back on the pavement, said Gordon. That river's designated for purification and it's good so you keep out of it.

The boy laughed like a brightly-plumaged bird of the rainforest and fell backwards off the railings onto the pavement. Gordon let him fall and the boy lay there cackling. He had a plastic carrier bag containing something square and heavy fastened to his neck with a piece of clothesline and some elaborate knots. He stopped laughing and looked at Gordon seriously.

I'm very clean, he said. I have a shower every morning and every evening and sometimes in the middle of the day if I'm at home. I change my underwear every day. It's important to be clean if you're going to show that the white race is superior. He narrowed his eyes.

Get up, said Gordon.

Think I'm ashamed? – 'cause I amn't, said the boy, getting up. He loosened the cords round his throat, took off the rope and opened the carrier bag. There were leaflets inside. He took one out and handed it to Gordon. Here, he said. Support the master race! He laughed.

Gordon looked at the leaflet. It was a single piece of paper folded in half. On the front was a Xeroxed sketch of a boy lying on the ground stripped to the waist with something like blood pouring from him and a group of men standing round grinning. One of the men had a turban on. At the top in big letters it said ENOUGH! WE MUST DEFEND OUR PEOPLE! On the other side there were several columns of small dense print and a picture of a row of young lads wearing dark shirts and swastika armbands and holding knives above their heads.

Aye, said Gordon. Did you draw this yourself?

Of course I fucking didn't. It comes from the general staff.

Here, said Gordon. I'm warning you, I won't tolerate that kind of language from folk your age.

It's about how white people like us are getting murdered and AIDS-infected and our women raped by pakis, yids, chinks and niggers. The boy took a sharp step back and lifted his hand in front of his face and ducked his head like he thought Gordon was going to hit him and then giggled like a lassie.

Gordon looked at the leaflet again and sure enough one of the grinning men had huge lips and a bone through his nose. Right, said Gordon. We do get a lot of that round here. He nodded and handed the leaflet back to the boy, who flinched again, blinked several times and snatched it out of his hand.

Eh? said the boy.

Niggers, said Gordon. There's refugees in the church hall.

The boy's mouth pinched together. You're Special Branch, aren't you? he said.

My brother wanted to get in but it's all stitched up with Oxbridge, isn't it? So is this what you do, son, hand out leaflets? Must be very boring work. That's why you were jumping off the bridge, eh?

The boy put his hand on the parapet and looked out over the edge. He turned back. His lower lip was trembling. What was it about young folk these days? Christ it was hard not to laugh.

The boy sniffed and tears came out his eyes. My girlfriend said I was a fascist prick, he said.

Is that right? said Gordon. He looked at his watch. He'd never get to the garden centre at this rate.

And she calls up the commander and tells him it was me tipped off the plods about the petrol bombs, and how I was working for the Bangladeshi secret service, and now they've put my picture in last week's newsletter saying I'm a traitor.

It's terrible what they'll do to you. I know. They're like – you know what they are? They're fascists. Wee Hitlers the lot of them. They'll sell you down the river. Look, seeing as you're interested in the ethnic business I'll walk you down the road. It's on my way. OK?

What's the point?

You've got to keep up your interests.

It's not worth it. There's nothing but injustice wherever you go. The boy wiped the tears off his face.

You're right, said Gordon. You're right to trust no-one. I don't. But where's the guarantee it's going to be any better after you're dead? Two young lads, right, two young lads. One of them's a miserable jessie with a daft haircut and so's the other one, in fact, but one of them's alive and the other one's lying drowned face down in the river. Along comes this wee smasher with fantastic tits. Maybe she won't fancy either of the young lads, she wouldn't if she had any sense, she'd go for an older man with some money and an understanding of the world, but supposing she's thick and fancies one of these boys. Which one's it going to be? The one still talking and breathing, or the cold one in the river? Eh? She's not going to go down there and start shagging the corpse, is she? It's a question of chances. Even when you're alive you've got virtually no chance of getting off with a lassie like that but when you're dead you've got no chance at all.

Not that you know of.

Not that anyone knows of. You'll get to try being dead in the end. Everyone gets a shot. In the meantime you've just got to try to entertain yourself in the queue.

What about faith? said the boy.

Listen, I've got to get up to the garden centre, said Gordon. I'll walk you down the road, and then if you still want to jump off the bridge you can come back. It's only a few minutes. OK?

The boy wiped the tears off his face and they went off together.

There's a hell of a lot of foreigners, right enough, said Gordon. You think there's too many of them here, you should try going abroad. I went to Bangkok once. Just don't tell Smithie, eh, if she found out there'd be hell to pay. Ach ye bugger Smithie was with me, was he not, so who was it not to tell? The left-footer, the jungle fighter, what was her name, Mary. With breasts, she cooked breakfast for him not half an hour ago, and they slept in the same bed. Have to pick up some of those twigs while he was about it. How did it come about that they were sleeping in the same bed. Marriage, that was the one. Marriage. And old Smithie, he knew better than that, he knew to steer clear of the organisations, the fascists, they shot you in the back of the head the moment you stopped even to take a breath. Mind you what was he about, shooting himself? It wasn't Gordon's fault the wee one was a bit slow on his feet in the traffic.

The boy with the leaflets was holding forth about the militias in America.

My brother had some books on the Ku Klux Klan, said Gordon. He said we needed something like that here only there weren't enough negroes in Scotland and it'd have to be for the Catholics instead.

The door to the church hall was open. They went into the

lobby and passed through a narrow way cleared between two great piles of boots and shoes and coats and through another set of doors into the hall. It was hot and bright and filled with chattering and shouting in a language which was not English. Women were sorting blankets and sleeping bags and trying to make spaces for their families among the others and the grannies were sitting stunned on the floor and kids were hurtling up and down and playing soldiers on the stage and the men were standing up in groups, smoking and talking and waving their arms at each other.

Gordon went up to the nearest group. D'you speak English? he said to a man with his hands in the pockets of a brown leather jacket.

Yes, said the man.

We're looking for the refugees.

We are the refugees.

Gordon looked round the hall. I mean the other folk, you know, the Africans, he said.

The man shook his head and looked round like he wasn't sure himself. There aren't any Africans here, he said. Maybe we look like Africans to you but that's the fucking Serbs' fault, excuse me. He spoke a few words to his pals in his language and they laughed.

Gordon told the suicide boy to hang on for a couple of minutes and went outside to look for Shiltie. The minister was in an office round the back of the church. Nice little number. Free house, no work to speak of, tax exemptions all over the shop. Maybe work an angle.

Shiltie was clacking away at the old computer. When Gordon came in he swivelled round on a chair and took his glasses off and didn't get up.

Good morning, he said.

Aye, morning, said Gordon. Here I thought you were supposed to be getting refugees for your church hall. Did you know the place was full of hundreds of folk standing around smoking and chatting and dossing, kids and grannies and everything?

Those are the refugees, said Shiltie.

Oh, is that them, is it? I thought they were going to be more coloured.

They're from Yugoslavia.

Right, there's a war on there, isn't there, right enough.

Shiltie sighed. You would have thought God would have singed him across the chops just for that sighing, one of his own. What do you want? he said. We've got permission. They're not doing anyone any harm.

I found this boy trying to jump off the bridge, and you know they're trying to keep the river clean, said Gordon. He was depressed about the eh, racial . . . ethnic . . .

Ethnic cleansing, said Shiltie.

Aye. That was the phrase he used. It was just I was on my way to the garden centre, right, and I thought if I dropped him off here in passing seeing as he was interested in darkies, and you with the refugees.

You make me sick, said Shiltie, getting up. He was trembling. I can turn the cheek with every other old bigot in the parish but there's something about you that makes me want to commit violence.

Nancy boy. The feeling was mutual. Wait till he got to heaven and had to work his ticket in front of God. That'd be funny, watching the minister crawling round in the clouds looking for his specs and God saying I'm sorry, did you lose your specs? Oh look Gabriel, I'm standing on them. I'm awful sorry, Shittie, they're broken. D'you see that, Gabriel, I've broken Shittie's specs. And I was wanting to ask him to read off the sizes on the soles of our boots. And Gabriel and all the angels would laugh and hitch up their rainments and piss in a bucket and Shiltie'd have to drink it while they did the slow handclap. Could you rely on angel piss not to taste good, though? It was going to be no joke up there till you got in close with the chief. Need to have a word with the bank about it. Christ, the minister was still havering away.

I think it's quite encouraging – who cares what you think? – that the attitudes of some members of your generation haven't infected all young people, said Shiltie, getting up. And I think – Christ, there he was, thinking again, he had to tell you each time – it's terribly sad that boys like this have been so disillusioned by the legacy of greed and hatred you've left them in the world that they're ready to kill themselves. The West bears a heavy share of responsibility for the tragedy in the former Yugoslavia. I suppose it's to your credit that you stopped him jumping. Where's the young lad now?

They went to the hall and found the boy standing bent double, weeping with laughter in the middle of a group of young male refugees. They were all laughing. One tapped the boy on the shoulder to make him look up and mimed a gesture of cutting something between his legs and stuffing it into his mouth. He made his cheeks bulge out and his eyes pop. They all roared. One of the refugees saw Shiltie.

Oh! Mr Shiltie! he shouted, putting his hand round the boy's shoulder. Why didn't you tell us before there were such people in your country? He kissed the boy on the cheek.

Is this him? said Shiltie to Gordon.

Aye, said Gordon. You seem to have cheered up a wee bit.

Are you homeless? said Shiltie to the boy.

No, I live with my mum and dad in Portobello.

You seem to be getting on famously with our guests from the Balkans.

He's one of us! said the refugee, squeezing the boy's shoulders. He's a patriot. He's not a communist like you, Mr Shiltie. If everyone here was like Julian you never would have lost your empire.

Julian grinned.

Maybe you should go home, said Shiltie.

No! shouted the refugees. Let him stay! We'll teach him how to fight, then we'll all go and fuck the Serbs together, eh?

Julian grinned.

Now just hold on, said Shiltie.

That's me away to the garden centre, said Gordon.

Wait, said Shiltie.

Gordon walked over to the door. Before he walked out he looked back and saw Shiltie picking up one of Julian's leaflets and frowning. Julian was lying prone on the floor, squinting down the length of a broom handle while one of the refugees instructed him in the art of sniping.

And the Days Grow Shorter

Gordon hadn't been to the garden centre on foot before. It was a fair haul across the car park to the entrance and coming on to rain too. What was he doing letting Smithie go off with the car like that, it was his, he'd paid for it. These wee laddies with their fancy motors, red Jap Dinky boxes-on-wheels for folk who never learned to tie their laces and wore slip-ons, there should be a law that they had to stop for their elders and let them take the wheel. I'm sorry son, I'm going to have to take this vehicle off you for a few days, looks like we're in for a wet spell. I understand, sir, you've earned the right, here are the keys. Spot on, son. Cheerio!

He went in, released a trolley and cruised the aisles. He put in a power drill, a baseball cap saying Team Bosch and a shiny steel tool in a fold-out case with forty different attachments. He didn't know what it was for but it looked like you could have fun with it. Christ, look at that fountain. You just plugged in the hose and it started burbling away. Classy. Could have it in the front room, run the pipe under the rug. Marble-effect plastic. An absolute miracle, a gem. Probably from China right enough but who was it bought it, eh? Who had the taste and the spending power? Not old Charlie Chan, that was for sure.

Could buy one for Smithie. Ach, not Smithie, the other one, with the breasts. How did she know Smithie was dead? They never told you anything. One thing was sure: Smithie would've wanted his pal Gordon to have the shotgun. That was agenda item number one at the next meeting.

Past the sun loungers again, that was the third time. There was a boy in a white shirt and black breeks and a badge with his name on in case he forgot who he was in the midst of a transaction. They had it easy, there'd been times when Gordon could have done with one of them, quick glance in the window to get the reflection and read it off, but he'd always had to wing it.

I'm looking for autumn leaves, said Gordon.

Eh? said the boy, pushing his face into Gordon's.

Autumn leaves, said Gordon, you know, for scattering round the garden, and bonfires.

Aw we don't do them mate, sorry. Need to try somewhere else. He was turning away.

You always used to do them. There were big wooden barrels and you'd lift them out with tongs and sell them by the pound.

The boy narrowed his eyes and scratched his head. His name was Mr Campbell Ferrier. No, he said. I've worked here two years and we've never done autumn leaves. He was beginning to have his doubts though.

I've been coming here all my life and you could always get autumn leaves, said Gordon. Heaps of them. They're in season just now. It's autumn.

I think most folk just gather their own, sir, really, said Mr Campbell Ferrier. I'm sure you'd get some from the council. Anyhow this place only opened two years ago.

You should ask your supervisor, said Gordon.

Honestly sir, he'd say the same as me.

You'll be telling me next you don't do twigs.

No, we don't do twigs. What kind of twigs? Plastic twigs like?

What would I want with plastic twigs? Real twigs! The kind that snap when someone steps on them.

Campbell! Another man came up. He looked exactly like Mr Campbell Ferrier except his moustache looked real and his badge said Mr Fairlie Cochrane. They're needing more shrubs in area 10.

Do we do autumn leaves and twigs? said Mr Campbell Ferrier.

What kind of twigs? said Mr Fairlie Cochrane.

The kind that snap when you step on them.

So you can hear when someone's coming, said Gordon. You used to sell them in packs of ten.

Mr Fairlie Cochrane gazed at Gordon and his trolley for a while with his jaw jutting out and his mouth just slightly open. He put his hand on Gordon's shoulder and pointed to the far end of the warehouse. See up there where it says Home Security? he said softly. You can try up there for the twigs. I can't promise, mind you. If you've no luck there try going through that wee door at the back. OK?

Home security had a ring to it right enough, but no twigs. Gordon went up the back and rammed the door open with his trolley. Raw November air rushed in. Gordon passed through. There was a stretch of tarmac, some rolls of green twine, a van and sacks of fertiliser. The tarmac was surrounded by a high barbed wire fence and the open gate had a fibreglass bothy watching over it. Beyond the gate there was a road and fields and farm buildings.

Gordon pushed the trolley up to the gate and peered through the window of the bothy. It was empty. He went out the gate and up the road towards the farm buildings. The racket the trolley made on the road, you'd think they'd have got round to tiling it and roofing it over by now. That was a grand smell of dung, though. Gordon breathed in the damp grey air with the sweet smell of cow shite. He'd been shopping here a long time.

He found the place after about fifteen minutes. There was no sign hung over it. Nothing to hang a sign from except the sky and the trees themselves. The trees were the same trees. What were they beech trees, aye? After all this time you'd think they would have got more modern trees, in keeping with the rest of the garden centre. A fire would be good. The smell of burning leaves and the smell of dung. The corbies looked like flakes of charred paper coming off a bonfire just started, the way they rose and fell like that. The trees came down both sides of the road, an avenue, and a little way into the fields on one side. Between the copse and the field was a stone dyke. There were cows in the field.

Gordon dragged the trolley on to the verge and walked in among the trees. He picked up handfuls of wet beech leaves and put them in the trolley. Sure enough, some of them slipped through the mesh. It was a bad business and a hard life. Gordon wandered away towards the dyke. Snap! Christ, there you were. Would you have to pay for the twigs you used? They shouldn't leave them lying in the dirt like that. He bent down and picked up a few lengths of twig. A crow called and the tops of the trees rustled. Gordon looked up. The trees were so much bigger than he was. Supposing they fell? It was a cold, wild, unloving place. Gordon looked over his shoulder. A feeling like waking up from a nightmare in the darkness touched him. If anyone had been there to ask him what it was, he would have held on to them and asked them if he wasn't a burglar who'd broken into his own mind and found it was a terrible fearful place but that he couldn't get out or do anything about it.

Gordon reached the dyke and stood with his hands in his pockets looking at the half-dozen cows in the field. One of them was lying on the ground, not like they usually did, but on its side, like it was drunk. While he watched, another one started to keel over, just as there was the sound of a shotgun going off. The cow tottered forward a few paces, shook its head from side to side, and buckled. The remaining animals shifted their ground and made faint mooing sounds and looked at the woods nervously out of the corners of their eyes.

Gordon walked along the wall and saw a farmer slotting cartridges into a broken shotgun. The farmer snapped it shut, took aim with his elbows resting on the top of the dyke and fired. A third cow toppled. Gordon broke into a trot and called out: Give's a shot, eh!

The farmer looked round, shook his head, and let off the second barrel.

Ach, now look what you've away gone and done, he said. Blown its fucking nose off. He began to reload as the cow galloped around the meadow, screaming. Gordon had never heard a cow scream before. It was a bad sound.

Sorry, he said. Let us do it, eh. Go on.

Ever used one of these before? said the farmer, locking the gun shut.

National Service!

The farmer hesitated and frowned. No, he said. It's my gun and they're my cows. He let loose with both barrels and the screaming stopped.

Ah, I remember you, said Gordon. Mind how we used to come and build dens here and kick seven kinds of shite out of the teuchters?

Aye, I mind very well. I was one of the teuchters. You were one of the snotty heathens from Heriot's.

It wasn't Heriot's, said Gordon. Give's a shot, eh.

No. The farmer broke the gun and crooked it in his arm. He leaned on the dyke with his free hand. As far as I remember it was us used to do the kicking.

How come you're shooting all your cows?

BSE.

What, are they all mad, then?

I don't really know, said the farmer. I get compensation though.

Shame, eh.

Aye.

Give's a shot, go on.

No. You might be from the cruelty people for all I know.

Fair point, said Gordon. I'm not though.

Mad farmer's disease, that's what it is, said the farmer. I was daft not to have got rid of the livestock years ago and move on to setaside. You know what the clever money is in these days? Ostriches. That's where they say the future is.

Ostriches? said Gordon. For the feathers?

The meat. The meat's very tasty, they say.

Aye but how could you even get one in the oven.

That's a good question, said the farmer. Another point is precipitation. If you compare African scrubland and Central Scotland bogland, there's a world of difference.

You're right there.

The ostrich is going to notice, isn't he?

Uhuh. They stopped talking for a while. The ostrich in the rain. And the snow, and the wind. Blinking. Greeting. Unable even to complain.

If it's ostriches they're wanting, said Gordon, why not pandas? They're always saying how short they are of pandas.

The farmer wrinkled his nose. They can never get them to breed, he said.

That's because they never give the pandas enough choice, said Gordon. Put yourself in the panda's situation. You're sitting in some wee room and suddenly this door opens and you go scampering through because there's nothing else to do and there's this naked female sitting there eating bamboo shoots. And you're expected to jump on her and give her a poke. Only she's not some dolly bird, she's old and fat and horrible and besides she's not into it. And they don't give you any choice, it's her or nothing. And they're surprised when nothing happens.

Bollocks, said the farmer. They deserve to be extinct if they take that kind of an attitude towards breeding. I'm telling you, I'd give her one, if there was no-one else, whatever she looked like. You think the way the youngsters do today.

I do not!

Aye you do. If you can't have a skinny young lassie, you'd be better not having a hump at all, or abusing yourself. That's what everyone thinks. That's why the sperm count's going down, if you ask me. They blame farmers. They blame fertilisers. You know what it's really all about? Too many pictures of perfect skinny lassies all over the place, in TV and the magazines and the adverts. If it goes on like this we'll all die out like pandas cause we're too fucking choosy.

Gordon leaned back against the wall. The wind was getting up and the great black bare trees waved like kelp in a spring tide, hissing.

Are they set to roof this area over, then? he said. It's a bit rough on the trolleys out here.

Haven't heard anything, said the farmer.

I mind when that garden centre wasn't roofed over either, said Gordon. They didn't have trolleys or checkouts. There was just stuff growing in a field. You helped yourself. There was dirt and thistles and sometimes they got hedgehogs in, and eggs.

The farmer followed his eyes to the corrugated hangar, painted grey and scarlet. It's an eyesore, right enough, he said. It's a shame. And they paid me almost nothing for the land.

How much do you want for the gun?

The farmer held out the gun and spun it slowly in his hands, pursing his lip. Not for sale, he murmured.

I'll give you 200 for it.

Cash?

Uhuh. With the cartridges, that is.

Gordon gave the farmer the money and clasped the heavy gun in his hands. He placed it in the trolley and stuffed the cartridges the farmer gave him into his pocket.

You'll need the cover, said the farmer.

It's OK, said Gordon. I'll come and fetch it later. They'll give me a bag at the checkout. He shook the farmer's hand and forced the trolley back onto the tarmac. The castors squealed and shook down the road back to the building. Gordon went through the same back door and rolled up to the till.

The lassie at the checkout held the laser poised in the air in her right hand and pulled the mesh of the trolley towards her with her slender white fingers, shiny crimson nails like blades. She peered down into the layers of damp leaves and twigs. Her name was Miss Caitlin Fernie.

Where's the packaging? she said.

There's no packaging. They're sold by the pound, said Gordon.

They've got to have a barcode on them, else they won't go through. What is it?

There's autumn leaves, and twigs.

The girl leaned into a microphone and her voice calling for help echoed through the building.

I'll just take this for you in the meantime, she said, reaching for the gun. She gripped the barrel and lifted it out of the trolley, frowning and wrinkling her nose with the effort. She held it with the butt resting on the conveyor and swivelled it, stroking it with the laser.

I paid for it already, said Gordon.

Oh right, said Miss Caitlin Fernie. What department?

Back there where the trees are.

I'll just need to check. She swung the weapon back into the trolley and rang up his other items. She clasped her hands with the laser on her lap and looked around impatiently. Gordon started packing his purchases into plastic bags. He found a good big bag for the gun and wrapped it up while the girl was looking the other way. A supervisor called Mr Forbes Cameron sloped up.

There's no barcode on these assorted leaves and twigs, said the girl.

Ach, they're selling them loose again, said Mr Forbes Cameron in disgust. Just enter it like compost.

How much though? The customer says they're selling it by the pound.

They never tell us anything. Enter it like a two-kilo bag. I'm sorry, sir, it's the reorganisation, it's just chaos.

Chaos, said Gordon. He nodded. Mr Forbes Cameron walked away and Miss Caitlin Fernie rang up a two-kilo bag of compost while Gordon stuffed the twigs and leaves into a bag. He put it on Visa and strolled out through the automatic doors. The sky had darkened and the storm was throwing rain horizontally across the car park.

All right Gordon, said Charlie Sturrock, coming out the garden centre after him with two petrol canisters and a coil of thin clear plastic tubing. How you doing? Good, eh? Fine with me too. Couldn't be better, aye. Turnover aye, got to watch the turnover, don't want to be in a cash negative situation, no worries, no worries. Aye terrible weather, eh, terrible weather. No, it's fine, really, great. You eh, you eh, haven't seen you down the club house for a wee while, you eh, everything all right? All right? Aye? Good 'cause you don't want to let these things get you down do you, no, they happen, and they say his books were in a terrible state.

All right Charlie, said Gordon. How's it going with you?

Oh, it's great, fantastic, cash positive, cash positive. In the black every time. Up on every deal, uhuh. Uhuh. It's a shame to take their money from them but it's their lookout if they don't know what to do with it. No we're feeling really good about it, expanding soon, got to put some of the profits back, you know.

We? said Gordon. I thought it was just you.

Just me? Oh there's a massive payroll, there's Liz and the office manager and the accountant and the bar staff and the bouncers. It's a big operation, Gordon, and the spondulicks keep rolling in, you can't stop them. It's like, you've heard of these cash mountains, that's what it's like. A cash mountain.

I'd like to get to the top of that mountain, said Gordon. Any chance of a lift?

Not got the car? No problem. The company limo's standing by.

Got a new car?

Only a Jag.

You always had a Jag.

It's not the car, it's the running costs, said Charlie. Any flash arsehole can buy a new Jaguar but you need to be loaded to run a vintage one.

Gordon put his goods in the boot and settled down in the worn leather seats. The rain slashed across the windows and drummed on the roof. The car even creaked a little in the wind. Vintage. Another word for old. Vintage wine. Vintage fish heads. Vintage men. Gordon and Charlie and the farmer, vintage men. Vintage bastards. Vintage fools.

Look at that poor lassie from the garden centre running out into the rain, said Charlie, watching in the rear mirror as the Jag moved away. Some poor bastard must have gone off without paying. Bad news for the boss, eh? The cash flow is paramount.

Weather, said Gordon, shaking his head. Never get a fire going for the leaves at this rate.

I don't know, said Charlie. Depends where you light it. He cleared his throat and put his foot down.

The Club of Men

Park here, said Gordon. I don't want them seeing you. I'll be two seconds. Wee recce.

Don't be long, said Charlie. Just get the eh, get the girls on the blower, eh. Up for it? Up for it? That's my man. He winked and his big thumb foraged daintily for numbers on his mobile keypad.

Gordon got out of the car and walked over to the house. The rain had stopped. He unlatched the gate as quietly as he could and went into the garden. He bent over, scurried to the lounge window, bobbed his head up and keeked inside. Darkness and stillness. He stood up straight. No fire. Water drops hung from the leaves of the hedge. Gordon walked to the hedge and put both hands in among the leaves. He ran his wet palms over his face. Was it good for you? That was dew. Dew for lassies, rain for men. It had acid in it, cleaned out your pores maybe. That was what it reminded him of! That drop hanging there off the end of that wee leaf, it was like that time Smithie started greeting in Bangkok. He'd sat there shaking and the tears pouring out of his eyes like leaky guttering in a storm and Gordon'd stared at him. And a drop hanging off the end of his nose. It'd been a roasting day and he wondered if it was cooling Smithie down.

In fact he'd asked him whether his tears were hot or cold and that was when Smithie'd walked away from him and lost him, the shit. Aye and having to fly back on his own and trying to make them stop the plane because he'd left something behind. He had, too, if only he'd known what it was, but if he'd known, he wouldn't have left it. They never did stop. It'd been a 747. Hard to turn round, right enough.

Gordon ducked down again and ran at a crouch round the house to the kitchen side. He knelt under the window ledge and raised his head. There they were, the schemers. Kenneth in Gordon's chair with a big tumbler of Scotch, laying down the law with a vertical finger stabbing the upholstery and a silent mouth snapping away like a lizard after midges. That was an impressive growth he had on him, he'd look better with a beard, and it didn't look like he'd slept too well. And Julie was back! Julie of the legs! For a second he was about to jump up and collar his neck with the double glazing and scream Treachery! Whore! when he realised she just had her head on his son's lap and wasn't moving. Smithie, ach what d'you mean, Mary, was moving up and down the carpet, doing the karate moves. She had the gear on for it, the white pyjamas, and it was a one, a two with the hands like axe blades and then hup! you beauty, the leg above the head and the flying kick. That was Gordon's jaw, no doubt about it, spinning up into the air in slow motion like the bone in *2001: A Space Odyssey*, and him standing there chinless, stunned.

He laughed. Oh – too loud. Smithery snapped her head round and Julie was up like a bloodhound and Kenneth, he was rising out of the chair, they'd heard him. He ran back round the house and was out the gate and into the Jag. Charlie was gabbing away on the mobile.

Let's get going, said Gordon urgently, shrinking down into the seat and checking the wing mirror. Come on.

Right, fine hen, tattie bye, see you there, aye, best behaviour now, guide's honour, remember we're respectable men, Charlie said into the phone, nodding and winking and grinning at Gordon.

Come on, said Gordon. In the mirror he saw Kenneth poking his head out from behind the hedge, still holding the glass. Kenneth stepped out onto the pavement and stood there looking at the Jag, one hand in his pocket. He raised the glass and emptied it slowly, rinsed the whisky round his mouth, swallowed, drew in breath between his teeth, put the glass down on the ground, hitched up his trousers and began to move towards the car with a thoughtful expression on his face.

Charlie, it's time to go, said Gordon. I've been spending too much time with the family lately. Could you not talk and drive at the same time, eh?

Kenneth was trotting towards them now. Charlie started the car and pulled away, still havering to the lassie on the phone. Aye, I know you're respectable too, I know that, uhuh, but eh, not too respectable, eh? Oh that's a lovely laugh you've got, aye, no, really, absolutely sincerely, I've never heard anyone laugh like that. I didn't mean that, of course I've heard you laugh before, I have, aye, uhuh. No no. No no no. Never. Not with the clients, hen, never with the clients, I don't know who's been saying that to you, they're too young, they're just wee lassies, that'd be bad business, conflict of interest, aye. No, that's not true, not true, I couldn't. Who's been telling you that? I couldn't. No hen, I don't mean couldn't like that, I could, I've had offers, don't get me wrong, of course I've had offers, I mean I couldn't take advantage of them, they're too young, aye, aye. They're not like us, d'you understand what I'm saying, not like us, aye. It's not different ages it's different speeds, different speeds hen, we just walk, right, see what I mean, we just breathe like normal people, but they don't, they move awful slow sometimes, awful slow, aye, for the ambient, it's too slow for me, and they move awful fast when the techno's on, it's terrible, terrible, like a tape that's gone wonky, slow, fast, asleep, double time, slow, fast, asleep, triple time. It's the drugs. No of course not, of course not, drugs, aye, you can't stop them coming in, they're awful small, oh yes, yes, awful small, you can't search everyone, I'm telling you you can't. OK. OK. Aye. Of course. Of course. Me too. Me neither. Aye. Run and get your knickers on hen else we'll still be talking and I'll already be there. Aye. Me too. Bye.

The Jaguar slipped without friction through the black wet afternoon. Gordon settled back. Kenneth running in the mirror was far behind. Maybe he was still running. Running was good. Gordon'd done a lot of running when he was wee, running for the sake of running. Look at all those poor drenched folk walking and looking in shop windows. Don't walk: don't look – run! Run! Run back! Run back and find the thing you left before they take it!

So how's eh, how's eh, how's Kenneth? said Charlie.

Not so good. Had a run in with the boys in blue.

Never! He never did. What the eh, the police, aye? Never.

Assault.

Tsh. That's terrible. Was there, I mean, was there no way your eh, your eh, brother could he maybe sort something out, keep it quiet, aye, 'cause when it's family and all that you need to don't you, as long as it wasn't serious, the law's the law, aye, right enough.

Right enough.

Aye, right, right enough.

Gordon fidgeted with the ventilation and heating controls. He said: Do you ever feel like you've broken into your own mind to try and steal something and then you find it's a terrible place, but you can't get out of it?

Sounds a bit deep, Gordon m'man, said Charlie.

Deep. Gordon didn't want to be deep. Deep was when your feet didn't touch the bottom and you were treading water and getting tired. Shallow wasn't good either. That was you standing there like a prat with the water lapping round your knees and the wee kids flapping round you with their water wings. Gordon wasn't deep or shallow. He was in it just up to his neck.

They pulled up in a side street on the edge of the zone parking area. Charlie led him to a place called Muriel's Tea Shop. In the window were chintz curtains and two white-haired old women practising octogenarian fellatio with slices of cake.

Always one for the high life, eh, Charlie, said Gordon as they went inside. A bell tinkled when they opened the door and Gordon had to duck his head.

Not to worry, not to worry, your Charlie man's got the old flask, aye, the magic flask, and eh the crumpet you sometimes see in here, the crumpet it's something else, you'd be amazed Gordon, and I'm not meaning the eh the cakes with butter on, no. There they are.

One of the women looked hellish familiar. She was in black. A black dress and a serious face even though she was smiling. The other one he didn't know at all. She was a looker in an old kind of way. Better than the one in black, who couldn't be his wife, the wifeness was elsewhere, and his mother died a long while back. She'd been better looking.

Hi Gordon, said the one in black, smiling but looking as if she was about to greet. Haven't seen you since the funeral.

Aye, said Gordon, sitting down opposite her. Gordon Stanefield. He put out his hand. The woman took it in her dry smooth palm and squeezed it. I know, she said, I know who you are. Gordon opened his mouth in wonder. It was like the harder she squeezed his hand, the more tears fell from her eyes, like juice from a lemon. Better to stop.

Here now, here now, come on, let's not have this, said Charlie. No tears, hen, come on, we're all friends, aye, it's eh, it's right you're upset but it's happened now, it's all over, you've got to move on, move on and look forward, it's what he would have wanted.

It's good to cry, said the other woman.

Aye Betty but not all the time, eh.

Smithie grat, said Gordon.

Part of him he didn't control came up with the solution: he remembered.

Smithie. Your brother. Jean.

Yes, he did cry, said Jean. More after he came back from that trip to Bangkok with you. Thought his heart was broken. She sniffed and touched her face with a hankie clenched in her fist. I don't understand.

The heat was too much for him, said Gordon. Lot of spicy food out there. Chillis. Make your eyes water.

My brother loved a curry, said Jean.

Look now, let's eh, let's eh, draw a line, said Charlie. Aye, a line. Here's your tea and we'll have a toast. Toast everyone. There you go. He poured whisky into their cups. Here's to Cedric Smith. Lovely man, great golfer, top salesman, Jean's favourite wee brother, our friend, liked a drink and a laugh. Here's to him. They drank. Charlie aaaahed and winked at Betty. Life's short, hen, he said.

I hope you're not short, said Betty.

No, I'm not short. I'm not short at all. He drawled. I'm longgggg.

Betty laughed. Getting longer, she said.

Could be, said Charlie, getting up. The two of them shuffled off through a set of curtains. A door opened and closed.

Jean sniffed and smiled, looked over the way they'd gone and looked back at Gordon. She folded her arms on the table and leaned forward. You men, eh, she said.

What men?

All you men, Gordon, said Jean. She took one of his hands in hers and laid it palm up on the table. She traced his life line with the blade of her index fingernail.

Aye, all us men, said Gordon. What men are we? Jean was writing circles on his palm. Her hands were cool like the inside of a fresh bed. What men were they. It was the club he belonged to, the club of men, only he was forgetting the rules, and there were rules. It was men only, that was for sure. He couldn't remember when he'd last had a good night out at the club of men. Aye he could. That Asian lassie. She'd punched his ticket. What'd been good was she'd been the rules. No need to know the book by heart, or even find where it was kept. The Thai girl'd been the regulations come to life. When she'd taken him by the hand and led him into another shape of light and sat him down and released his flies and begun to suck, he hadn't had to do anything: he was only entering the rules of the club of men. He was deep inside the clubhouse and the other men were all around, glad, deserving and taken care of. Then it turned out Smithie'd never known the rules at all and hadn't been a member of the club of men. He'd been sneaking in all that time and never paid his subs, never got his card. Like he was trying to get Gordon kicked out as well. Like he knew Gordon was already getting lost in the club, not knowing anyone there any more. Here was Smithie's sister working the same plan, stroking his hand, saying You and Mary, you were never swingers, were you. Jean wasn't like the Thai girl. She was a hell of a lot older for a start. She had him by the hand and was wanting to drag him out of the club of men where he was lost already and into some more difficult world. When she was doing the gypsy doodling on his palm the tearoom sharpened, grew and brightened. The stainless steel teapot shone like chrome at noon and the white china teacups were surely about to melt, the sugar lumps took on the span of sea defences, every stalk and seed in the bunches of dried flowers pinned to the walls could be numbered. Jean's eyes, they were terrible, finding him in the peaceful murk of himself like sun intruding on a midnight room. He knew fine he couldn't find his way any more, he'd lost the measure of other beings and all the scales of life, but he didn't want to be found by her, he didn't want to be found by anyone. Best to doze in the shadows. Except to be fetched by Thai girls and Julie for a session in the club of men under red lampshades, with romps on velvety wall seats.

You've got a long line of life, Gordon, said Jean. Still stroking his hand she looked over her shoulder at the curtains. They've been gone a while, eh. She giggled. Wonder what they're up to.

Must be penetration, said Gordon.

Jean opened her mouth, boggled eyes at him and bowed into the table in mute heaves of laughter. You're the devil.

I am not.

We've got to spend less time thinking about Cedric, bless'm.

Did Smithie have a long line of life?

I never did my brother's fortune.

Did he?

Yeah, I think he did.

What happened to him?

You know what happened. He shot himself.

Aye, I forgot.

How could you forget, said Jean, eyebrows sliding all over the place. You were the first there after the police. They had to stop you putting your fingers in the blood. You were asking if you could have the gun since he wouldn't be needing it any more. You were in shock, Gordon.

It's OK now, said Gordon.

I know.

I bought one up at the garden centre.

Jean took a packet of Benson & Hedges out of her bag and lit up. She flooded her bronchi with smoke, touched her hair.

How are things at home? she said.

Fine.

How's Mary?

I couldn't tell you.

That doesn't surprise me, Gordon, said Jean. She folded her left arm under her bosom and leaned forward, cigarette standing to attention in her other hand. You've been through a hard time what with your best friend, and your brother, and your Kenneth, and Mary's not helped you, has she? She smiled, blinking, put her hand on Gordon's and squeezed it. I haven't helped you either. I'm sorry I was suspicious. Would you look at me when I'm talking to you?

Eh? said Gordon, still staring at the cigarette. If it was a cigarette and not the chalk of a cartoon artist, drawing Jean, drawing her badly, struggling with her fingertips, about to crumple up the sketch and throw it away. Cartoon ideas: there's this old woman and this old man, she's always trying to catch him, but no dynamite, no mallets, no irons involved, so not a good idea.

Hey, said Jean, clicking her fingers, stubbing out the cigarette.

The artist, said Gordon, reaching for the fag and holding himself back.

What artist?

You looked like you were being drawn by this.

Mmm. Jean took Gordon's face in her hands and shook it from side to side. She brought him very close to her sunbed tan, the dark spots on her skin, the dryness of lips under the crimson. I was never sure if you were a boy or a poet or out of your head. She let him go. But you are the devil.

I am not.

I'm not talking about evil, Gordon. Evil is not on. I don't fancy it. Dangerous is another matter. And loose. You've come loose from all the things they'd like you to be fixed to. Being nice. Being tolerant. Being a good shopper. You're nasty, greedy, selfish and lonely, and maybe so am I. How's about we make something of it.

Make what?

L. O. V. E. whispered Jean. Love. By which I mean S. E. X. You and me. Like Betty and Charlie.

You're too old for me, said Gordon. I couldn't with a woman with as many wrinkles as you. What I like is girls in their late teens.

Jean's lower lip started to beat up and down and her shoulders shook. She folded up, bowing towards the table. She lifted her face with eyes red raw as picked scabs.

I suppose you'd fuck my granddaughter, she said.

I'd have to take a look at her first, said Gordon.

Jean hunched in and pawed fags and lipstick for hankies. There was a scuffling and shouting from behind the curtains and Charlie came through them backwards as if he'd been pushed. Betty came out after him and shoved him in the middle of the chest. There was no blood in her face at all. She screamed at Charlie that he was a liar. A solid scream, half a mile's worth, with rasping lowlights.

I don't agree with what you're saying, hen, said Charlie. I can't eh, I can't, aye, it's nothing to do with anyone else, no, I know, I know, you've got to, eh, you've got to eh give it time, no, it's not cause I'm seeing anyone else, men my age have their days and they have their days, no there's no need to be striking me.

Betty screamed that she deserved to be treated with respect, and that Charlie was a cunt. Charlie glanced at Gordon, who got up and moved towards the door.

Just you sit down, love, aye, sit with Jean a while, she looks, eh, looks, eh, maybe wee bit of cake went down the wrong way. The walnuts here can be murder. Charlie's away to get you a good proper drink, aye that's right, there you go. That's right.

Gordon slipped out of the door and waited by the car. In a moment Charlie strode out of the tearoom. They got in and drove off. Charlie shook his head a few times and blew breath noisily from his lips.

Aye, he said. I got, eh, got distracted for a moment, fatal, aye. Betty feels me getting, eh, getting soft, and there's no sympathy at all. None, uhuh. She knows a man my age can't be turning, eh, can't be putting in, eh, gold medal performances every day of the week, and she's eh, she's eh, making all these accusations, aye, she is, about me having used it once today already, on someone else. Not saying, Gordon, between eh, between you and me, might not have done that other days, but no way today, not this time. Just, eh, just got distracted. Started thinking about the golf.

I birdied the twelfth last week, said Gordon.

Aye? Did you now? I holed it in one once, aye, I did. Best day of my, eh, best day of my life, uhuh, it was. What was up with Jean?

Who?

Jean. Smithie's sister. The woman opposite you.

They weren't drawing her properly, said Gordon.

Aye? Is that right? said Charlie, sucking in air through his teeth, shaking his head, thinking about the swing, the impact, the flight and the gentle falling into the lap of the green.

Waterland

Charlie parked at the back of Waterland, on a narrow shining stretch of cobbles, black and flexed like patent crocodile hide restored to the living crocodile. Rain scratches swarmed about a lamp above the door. Charlie creaked in his seat and flicked the chrome leaping salmon keychain swinging from the ignition. He sighed and made a remark about the weather. He took a cheap cigar out of a tin, offered Gordon one, and lit up. Gordon took his and put it in his pocket.

Almost lost the house with one of these, I did, aye, said Charlie. He opened the window a few inches to let the smoke go. Fell asleep on the settee. Poor quality materials. Burned patch that wide and a filthy smell when I woke up. You're eh, you're surrounded with risk, everywhere. Death traps in the home and work. Bad electrics in the club, for instance. Could eh, could eh, could go any time. Doesn't matter what you do, the old health and safety, uhuh, get out of bed in the morning, might as well be setting off up the Amazon in a canoe.

It starts in bed, said Gordon.

Does it, aye, for you?

You've got no control over who's in there with you.

Well eh Gordon my man I know what you mean but, eh,

I don't in fact. There's eh, there's the old Mary, is there not?

That's it. You've got no control.

She's your wife, Gordon. You thinking of giving her the old big E, the old widescreen Divorcerama, aye, 'cause that's an awful dear business, it is, uhuh, did it once myself, if you mind that, Gordon. D'you, eh, d'you mind that?

The bed's the most dangerous place, said Gordon. That's when you have to get closest to Smithie.

Smithie?

Mary.

Who's in your bed?

Smithie.

What's your wife's name?

I could murder a drink, said Gordon.

I'm wondering if eh, I mean, if you weren't in danger of kind of losing the old place, Gordon.

There's an old one in the bed with me, said Gordon. An old one I know. Mary. Smithie. The names slide off them. The names slide off when they get old. I want a new one.

Charlie took the flask out, drank from it and handed it to Gordon, who held it open without drinking. Whisky incubi flew from the mouth of the flask and wormed into his sinuses. Charlie said he knew what Gordon meant. He said: In the old seventies, they'd come to Waterland, mind Gordon, over-21s only, it was a discotheque, it was a meatmarket, uhuh, and when I say meatmarket I don't mean in a disgusting way, mind eh, it was all totally stylish, sophisticated folk, beautiful underage girls and groomed, aye, groomed lads in their twenties with their first wages and first jackets trying to get them drunk. It was kind of like the place to go. On the playground, uhuh, and the shopfloor and the old office, where were you going? Waterland.

Seven nights a week, regular hours and the DJ he was he was he was just staff, aye, just staff. Used to, eh, spin the old discs myself of a once in a while. Uhuh. Now there's no Waterland at all, no. There's all kinds of clubs at Waterland. You can be *at* Waterland, aye, but not *be* Waterland. The boys, and the eh the old lassies, it's like in the daytime they're in their bedrooms dreaming new clubs, aye, they've hooked the rhythm into their ears and a bit of a sherbert fizz in the veins from the old self-medication, and by evening the club has a name on a thousand bits of paper. Last week you had Soma, Deep Wide, Halo Labz, Santiago and Made. The clubs come and go and change in a night, they're only people and a DJ and a few records, and they're more real than Waterland is. On Thursday they say Going to Soma? and on Friday they say Going down Deep Wide the night? and they're two different places in the same place 'cause Waterland is just the cold dead venue and the club, the club, the club's the only thing that gives it life. Aye. So. I reckon I'll just have to go and burn the cunt down.

Charlie's eyes gave Gordon a quick stroke with the edge of vision.

It's that time of year, sure enough, said Gordon. Bonfires.

Jesting, Gordon my man, jesting, said Charlie. Not like the eh, the insurance is eh, not like I was needing that kind of instant cash flow. No worries, no, no. Not if I win the old lottery anyway, heh, aye, heh. Mm. Can you wait a minute?

Charlie got out of the car. Gordon watched him stand for a moment in the rain with his hands in his pockets, looking up and down the street. Charlie sucked half an inch from his cigar, let it fall and twisted it out on the road. He went to the boot. Gordon saw the boot lid rise in the mirror. Charlie was out of view for a few minutes. When he slammed the boot down he had a canister in his hand. Him and Gordon were looking at each other. Gordon couldn't tell whether Charlie was staring at the back of his head or meeting his eyes boxed in the rear-view. Whatever it was he was adding something up. Boy'd always been adding something up. That time he'd bought out his partner in the massage game after he hired an actor to make it like he was from the income tax and given the daft idiot a stroke. The partner'd hardly been able to sign his name after that. Charlie'd always brought him flowers and fruit and sat with him, talking away while his old partner sat there and shook a bit. What happened to that one? They say he got better but he never got his stake in the massage place back, did he? and Charlie selling it on to those developers a few weeks later like he'd known from day one. What was that partner's name?

Charlie came to Gordon's side of the car. Gordon lowered the window. What's with the eh, what's with the leaves? said Charlie.

Autumn leaves, said Gordon. Assortment. Pick and mix. For a bonfire.

Uhuh. A fire. D'you not think it's a bit on the old wet side? Maybe best to have the bonfire indoors, aye.

There's twigs in there as well, said Gordon. What happened to that daft partner of yours who had the stroke? What was he called?

Ah Gordon. Oh, Gordon. Charlie shook his head and swung the canister gently from side to side, making the liquid glug. There was a smell of petrol. How many, I mean, eh, how many times, it was a long time back, aye, we were younger then, how many times can I say I'm eh I'm eh I'm eh, aye, sorry? I wasn't expecting your heart to eh do. To be. To do. You were all of 35. You've made a full recovery, uhuh, full, aye. Your career didn't suffer.

Right but what was his name? said Gordon.

Charlie stopped swinging the canister, squatted down and looked into Gordon's eyes. He held up fingers.

How many fingers am I holding up? Tell me five things you own. Who are you married to?

Gordon stared at the. Try to count the. He turned to the pouring, gathering in the, dammed by the. Remember the. And the little, the sweet, and the fuckable, the tasty and the warm, the neat and the new, the green and the plastic. It was all there, only the names were not.

Smithie, he said. Smithie's the one. When we landed there was clapping, there was clapping all around us, and Smithie looks at me and says: welcome to fantasyland.

Are you a wee bit tired, Gordon my man? said Charlie. Weary? With the old life thing, I mean? He waited for Gordon to answer. Gordon took a drink and said nothing. Charlie watched him for a while and went to the boot to fetch something else. He opened Gordon's door, took the flask from him gently and put it away. He was wearing gloves now. He took Gordon's arm and eased him out of the car.

Come on, Gordon, he said. I'll show you where you can make your, eh, bonfire.

Charlie led Gordon to the door of Waterland. He gave Gordon a crowbar and showed him how to use it to bust the padlock. Gordon tore the lock off and kicked the door open. A set of CCTV screens inside glowed blue. Charlie switched on the lights, opened the CCTV bothy with a key, took out the video recording events at the back door and left that machine empty. He handed Gordon the petrol canister and the twigs and leaves and pointed to a set of stairs up.

You want to go on to the big dancefloor, he said. Uhuh. Build your fire in the middle of it. There you go, I'll put the lights on for you. Plenty of the old gasolene on the parquet, aye, use a coupla chairs if you fancy. Should be a lovely blaze. I'll eh join you later, got to eh got to aye. Bring some baking potatoes in the old silver foil.

Wait, said Gordon. He put the stuff down and went out to the car. He opened the boot, took out the rest of his shopping from the garden centre and brought it inside.

Got everything? said Charlie. Here's your matches. Off you pop. Mind and give the cameras a wave. He patted Gordon on the shoulder. See you later.

Gordon walked up the stairs. Charlie called after him: Gordon! Maybe! Just maybe! Eh? and pulled the entrance door hard shut with a rattle of the exit bar. Gordon heard the Jaguar tyres hurt the road like a shriek cut off by a muffling hand.

Gordon walked on to the dancefloor of Waterland, an oval auditorium with seating booths on two sides, a shuttered bar at one end and a wall of speakers, topped with a dual turntable, at the other. The wooden floor was stained and scored under the dilute white house lights and splinters were starting to rise out of it. Flaps of cloth hung off seats oozing crumbling foam. Gordon emptied out the leaves in the centre of the floor and organized them into a neat mound. They were dry and crisp. He set a few twigs aside for the house and laid the rest on top of the leaves. Good kindling. He only needed solid timber to have embers for the baked tatties later. There were a few barstools with thick wooden legs and struts and padded leatherette seats. Gordon laid a couple on the fire and set a couple more on either side of it. The slatted steel shutter sealing off the bar was fixed with a padlock. Gordon loaded the shotgun, stepped up to the bar and let the padlock have it with both barrels at point-blank range. The lock snapped open and the shutter furled itself. Gordon helped himself to a sextuple Grouse, lit the fire, reloaded the gun, held it broken in the crook of his arm, sat on the barstool and sipped his whisky, inhaling the lines of smoke and watching the maggoty wriggles of red gnaw at the leaves and hatch into yellow flame. Gordon tossed a little whisky onto the fire and it blazed blue.

The lights went out. A drum break shot from the wall of speakers, birthing a dogged, body-resonant thump of bass and a string section which first whined, then moved to the edge of panic. The drums cleared a fresh path and the voice of a woman, sad, petulant and vengeful, Sixties-reedy, sang:

> *I won't love you any more*
> *I won't love you any more*
> *Sorry*
> *Sorry*
> *You made me think I loved you so*
> *The tricks you used were only low*
> *I guess now I see*
> *That you're wrong for me*
> *Our love is awry hope you understand why*
> *I won't love you any more*

A red strobe began to flash and lasers started up. A pair of bare legs jerked into the strobe field, smooth, slender and strong, dancing to the music in white shoes with two-inch pointed heels. The legs, mythically long, stretched far up towards the roof, with only a vast, twisting structure in between preventing them reaching it. The curved structure was tightly sheathed in white fabric, printed with large overlapping circles. It moved from side to side in time to the music and was attached to the legs. Two bare arms of fantastic length were fixed to the structure and at the peak an immense head tossed to and fro, short blonde hair, heavy black circles of eyeliner and mascara, and pale lipstick. She was a lovely young girl in a minidress. She was Gordon's kind of lassie, young and bonny, not bony. She looked like Julie. Only Julie was ear-high to Gordon and this one had to be seven feet easy. Maybe eight. And everything built to scale. Her dance steps made the building tremble.

The record stopped, the strobes and the lasers came off and a gentler, dappled light sequence coloured them the colours of the rainbow in succession. The giant approached the fireside.

It's members only, she said. Are you a member?

No, said Gordon. But I'm armed and the boss is a friend.

I'm the boss tonight, said the girl. She had a deep voice. It travelled a long way to reach her mouth. Gropey Charlie owns the venue but the event is mine. This is White Sugar. Northern Soul till the early hours. It's called White Sugar because I am white, and because I'm sweet, like sugar. You've set fire to the dancefloor.

It's that time of year, said Gordon.

D'you like Northern Soul?

I don't know.

Listen to this. She climbed up to the decks and played more tracks.

I never got the bar open before, she said. I'll give you free membership for that. That's you the first member. Just for tonight, mind.

They went to the bar. Gordon left the gun by the fire and strolled beside the giant girl while she tacked forward in tiny steps and swayed to the sound of The Ellusions, mouthing the words, air boxing and tossing her hair. She picked Gordon up, lifted him over the bar and set him down on the other side. He fetched her a Red Bull and gave himself more whisky.

Her name was Sheena and still at school she'd gone on a pilgrimage to Wigan to the shrines of Northern Soul. She'd got a basketball scholarship to Detroit University but came home because her American wasn't good enough and the clubs of the city no longer paid anything but token, exploitative homage to the lost true souls of soul, to the genius of their pre-funk forefathers. She wanted a job but it was hard to find one. It was hard to find a bed that fitted. It was hard to get clothes. Or friends. The ceilings in her parents' house were low, the walls close together, and you got tired of sitting with your knees up against your face. Sheena started to inhabit the many clubs of Waterland. She fell foul of some door policies and others sought her out. She didn't dance to anything post-1980 and mostly hung at the edge of the lights, stooping to the dwarfish punters with Walkman earphones in her hand, offering Northern Soul, trying and failing to make converts. Some of the punters, particularly those who'd been tripping heavily, were terrified when the face of the beautiful giant loomed down into their plastic consciousness. They chatted about the Northern Soul Monster with dread and anticipation in the queues. The door policies got tougher and Sheena took to hiding in the club after it closed. There was a big roof space she'd roam with her Walkman. She had candles up there for reading. When the club was shut she'd come down and play the decks. Sometimes she'd be inside for 48 hours at a time, living off leftover beer and drugs and sweets and napping in the booths.

You want to find yourself a nice lad your own size, said Gordon.

I don't want someone my own size, said Sheena. I had a boyfriend, five nine, very slim and good-looking. I was happy with him, even though he wasn't into the music. I dumped him 'cause he always made me go round his mum's house on my knees. She was half-blind and he didn't want her to know I was so much taller than him.

Charlie should be here with the potatoes, said Gordon.

What's wrong with you? said Sheena.

Nothing wrong with me. Careful.

There is. When you listen to enough soul music you learn soul-searching. I can search your soul.

Do I have one?

Yes. At the moment you're empty, but there's a lost soul inside you. A soul without a club. Without a club your soul is like a punter wandering through the empty venue of the man, without music to dance to or people to dance with. You need a club. The creed of White Sugar is my creed. There has to be music. The music has to have four beats to the bar. And you should never, never, betray anyone you love.

I'm in a club, said Gordon. The club of men.

I don't know that club.

It's a good one. But it's not been the same since Smithie left.

I don't know who Smithie is.

We were in Bangkok. Welcome to fantasyland, he said. And then I couldn't find him. I heard a peacock screaming.

Gordon heard a peacock screaming in the garden outside the window. He got off the bed and watched the lustrous blue creature promenading across the lawn. The grass had just been watered. In the centre of the garden was a tree with a broad, sinewed black trunk and millions of tiny shining leaves. Smithie hadn't woken him. Bangkok had turned cold. Gordon pulled the white bathrobe tighter and fetched a mini-Teacher's from the fridge. A maid arrived and offered to do something to the bed.

Go ahead, said Gordon. Is it morning or afternoon? She was fine.

It's six o'clock in the evening, said the maid. You just arrive?

She laughed and tore at the bedlinen with thin, powerful arms.

It's freezing, said Gordon. Cold.

Air conditioning, said the maid. She leaned over the bed, smoothing down fresh sheets. You can change it. She finished the bed and showed him the dial. It's too low. What you want, 25? She turned it so the arrow pointed to 25. Gordon moved towards her. She took a step away. Gordon loosened the cord of the bathrobe, dropped the minibottle into his pocket and took out a folded wad of banknotes.

Is sex with the maids included, or is it extra? he asked.

No sex, said the maid, holding her arms tensed in front of her, crossed at the wrist, palms outward. She backed towards the half-open door and opened it wide with her heel. No sex. All the maids are married. I'm not a maid, I'm the housekeeper, and I'm married too. You want to go to the red light district. Yeah, red light. Plenty of girls there for foreign men.

Gordon sat on the bed and suckled the bottle for the last drops. A boy in polyester blue with a six-hair moustache and an angry frown came to take away the things the housekeeper had left. He watched Gordon the whole time.

You look like my son, said Gordon. Although he's a white man, of course. Where's the red light district?

You take a cab, the boy said, and went out swiftly.

Gordon called Smithie's room. There was no answer. It was getting dark. Gordon put on a cerise polo shirt, beige slacks and black moccasins and went out. He padded along the corridor to where Smithie was staying and knocked on his door, saying Smithie's name, then shouting it. He drummed on the door with the knuckles of both fists. No Smithie. Gone off to find a drinking place. The drinking was the one, the one before the taxi, before the tarts. Only you had to be sure you drank together otherwise where were you, you were heavily outnumbered by foreigners. They were small and polite and once your back was turned they'd come at you with their knives. It was a wonder Smithie'd ever done business with the Bangkokies. Said he'd played golf with them. Dodgy business. You had the advantage of height and weight, of course, but what was that when all you had in your bag was irons and the Bangkokie had his knife. Soon as they sensed the power of your swing they'd steer you into the rough and rush you. Bamboo stakes in the bunkers. Miserable.

He came to a door that led to the outside, to a path between hard glossy bushes, lit by globes of light, leading to the reception building. The door was pulled open as he was approached by a Bangkokie in a coffee-coloured uniform, like a policeman, only without a gun. The policeman smiled and nodded at him and saluted. Oh, they were polite. The heat closed around Gordon like the numbness brought on by certain pills and gases, irreversible once swallowed. He stopped and turned, moved his hands to catch a cooler pool of air, and the heat was everywhere.

You OK, sir? said the policeman.

Open a window, said Gordon. It's stuffy.

You're outside.

It's cold inside, said Gordon. Open the windows and it'll even things up.

Sir, reception is straight ahead.

Gordon went to the reception desk and asked about Smithie. He'd left his room key and gone. No message.

He came here on a business trip once before, said Gordon. D'you know where he used to go?

Don't know, said the girl at reception. She was fine. Maybe he went for a drink in hotel bar?

Gordon looked at her. She smiled. He asked her if sex with

reception clerks was included, or if it was extra. She lowered her head, shaking it violently, and began rearranging papers and pens on the desk behind the counter.

You want red light district, she said.

A woman in a black dress was singing in the bar, a Bangkokie with hair down to her waist, shoulders bare and a big voice. She was singing *I've Got a Crush on You*. Men dressed like Gordon were sitting alone with drinks, tapping one or two fingers on the table, nodding their heads and wagging their moccasins in leaden time. The singer had one hand on her mike and one hand resting on the lid of a grand piano. She turned to Gordon, sang: Sweetypie, and winked at him. Over 30. Too old. Gordon walked away, parted the doors onto the car park and crossed over again into the warm electric dark outside.

They were digging up the pavement on the big street, toiling with picks and drills in the night. The road was heavy with Japanese cars. Tired Bangkokies were leaning out of the glassless windows of a square old bus caught in the grind, pillowing their chins on the crooks of their arms and staring into the private spaces of the motorists. White shirts of streams of lean students and office folk flickered in the railings of a pedestrian footbridge straddling the traffic. Higher up overhead the sky was concrete, a V-bottomed causeway raised on monumental pillars, roofing the street. They kept themselves awful busy, the Bangkokies. What were they up to? It wasn't till you went abroad that you realised just how many foreigners there were, and how busy they'd been while there was no-one to keep an eye on them. Working away, building away, more than likely swotting in their spare time. And still they couldn't spell cock.

Outside a shopping centre steps led down to street level. Folk were sitting on the steps, groups of Bangkokie students with folders in their hands, laughing, and groups of Europeans. Gordon stood in the middle of the steps with his hands in his pockets and surveyed the flow for Smithie. There were two white people sitting at his feet. There was a boy with a shaven scalp, dark glasses wrapped round his head and trousers with pockets down the sides, and a girl with a tally of silver rings on the rim of her ear, like a sheep of one flock, her wispy blonde hair bound tight with an etched leather clasp at the back. Maybe you could tell the age by counting the rings. They were resting the weight of broad satchels they were carrying on straps slung across their chests.

D'you know where the red light district is? said Gordon.

The couple turned round, looked up at him, and looked at each other.

Do you know? said the girl to the boy.

No, he said shaking his head and turning away.

I'm a tourist, said Gordon. Supposed to be here with a friend of mine but he's gone awol.

We're not tourists, said the girl. We're travellers. What is it tourists do, Harry?

Sights, said Harry.

That's it, said the girl. Seen the sights?

Sights? said Gordon. He checked the high windows overlooking the steps. Glint of a gunbarrel. Crosshairs on the man in cerise. That's him, the one with the wad. Take him out. Hands grasping him by the moccasins, dragging him away into the shopping centre, head bumping on the steps, stripped naked in seconds, Mary and the runt collecting on the life policy. Too much to bear.

You haven't got a camera, the girl said.

Too true, said Gordon. It'd hardly be worth their while.

Whose while?

The Bangkokians.

The girl laughed. Bangkokians. So what've you been doing.

Gordon said: I came to get my hole, basically. I was hoping to get sucked off by one of the young Thai girls. The trouble is you can't enjoy buying a girl at home any more, they're too bony and depressed, and you can't talk about it with your pals. Whereas here they're really into it.

God, you're disgusting, said the girl.

Smithie! shouted Gordon, trotting down the steps. It was him! In the cream-coloured suit, moving comfortably in the crowds on the far side of the street, carrying a shopping bag, looking back over his shoulder. Gordon stood on the edge of the traffic and shouted Smithie's name. Bangkokites looked at him quickly and looked away. The jam had freed up and the traffic was moving. Smithie! The man had an echo in the mob. Another moving thing was moving with him. When Smithie's jacket slipped out of sight behind delicate swinging arms in teeshirts, the other thing vanished, and when the linen number emerged, paused darker against the food platters in the window of a noodle shop, a shrunken shadow stood still beside him. Smithie looked down at the shadow, his lips moved. The shadow looked up, it shook its head, Smithie moved on, and the shadow followed. Smithie! Over here! Gordon jogged to the footbridge and peered across the street again. He saw Smithie stop at a turning, by a postcard carousel, and the shadow stop too. It was a boy, maybe 13 or 14. A boy in a striped teeshirt and shorts. Smithie pointed at something in the shop behind the postcards. The boy nodded. Smithie went in and came out a few seconds later with a package. The boy reached out his hand. Smithie laughed in the way Gordon knew, in the way Gordon remembered, even though he couldn't hear it, he could hear it, the laugh of having the advantage and loving it, that time he'd had the cream doughnuts and Gordon had wanted a bit, he'd had the air gun and Gordon had wanted a shot, he'd had that lovely wee lassie from Manchester and Gordon'd wanted a go. Smithie always gave and Gordon always got but only after he'd followed and waited. Over by the souvenir shop Smithie laughed and walked around the corner into the side street, out of sight. The boy waited for a second and went after him.

Gordon ran up the stairs of the footbridge. He lost his wind halfway up. He leaned back against the railings, gripping the metal with his hands, the sweat dribbling over him, letting his head settle. He crossed the bridge slowly, keeping one hand on the rail. He paused halfway and looked down at the hosts of cars changing their grounds in the populous night world. They moved in a kind of tunnel, made by the tarmac under their wheels, the causeway overhead and the heavy hanging signs in gold and dull paint and neon, in English and Bangkokish letters. Gordon came down off the bridge and looked in the window of the noodle shop. There were a couple of dozen bowls in rows in the window with plastic samples of dishes, fanned hands of sliced meat and dumplings and greens on beds of noodles. Gordon was hungry. He could smell a twisted braid of food scents, a sharp green herb, dark gamey meat, limes, something sweet and the essence of fish. He walked away and entered the McDonald's on the next block for a quarterpounder with cheese, large fries and a cup of tea. You could feel it going down into you square, marked and filling the space, like the falling bricks in the Tetris game Kenneth used to kill time with. The poor old Bangkoksters, they must have been grateful when Mr McDonald came along with good dry, solid, guaranteed rounds of bread and meat, food that wasn't slippery, wasn't bobbing up and down and wasn't festering with spice. It was enough to bring tears to your eyes, if you were a poof that is, otherwise you took the grief of things and you stowed it away in that space just about where your stomach was, if you were a man. Gordon always had a lot of grief stored in there. But that was the thing about grief, it didn't take up space, it was space. It was tricky carrying all that empty space around inside you without losing your balance. That was the advantage of quarterpounders. They dropped right into the space. Mr McDonald knew there was nothing else you could do with that grief, you either let it out and had everyone thinking you were a soft case, or else you filled it with something heavy, bulky and cheap, i.e. the quarterpounder. Gordon ordered another one.

Outside the McDonald's two policemen stood by their motor-cycles. They had white crash helmets with raised black visors, skintight grey uniforms and tight-fitting jackboots. They were lean and fit like deer and everything shone in the lamplight, the helmets, their badges and buckles, the chrome on their bikes.

Which way to the red light district? said Gordon.

The policemen watched him. They were still. They stared and their faces didn't move. They blinked, but seldom.

Which way to the red light district? said Gordon.

One of the policemen turned on his heel and stepped into the road. He raised his arm and held it stiff in the air. With his other white-gloved hand he took a shining whistle and blew a single note. A taxi stopped. The policeman leaned in to speak to the driver.

Good lads, said Gordon.

You go where driver takes you, right? Don't go running around. He'll take you to a nice place.

Gordon settled into the cool yielding interior of the cab and closed the door. The car murmured up to speed.

When they slowed down Gordon saw lights of many colours in the windows. In the doorways the girls' white teeshirts and stockings and dresses reflected ultraviolet. The driver pointed

Gordon towards a place with a front made of black glass and a vertical blue neon sign saying 4-U-2 Knight Klub. A grey light washed the doorway. A man in dark clothes sat astride a wooden chair outside, chairback between his legs. He held the chairback in his hands and rocked backwards and forwards, softly singing a country and western song in Bangkokian. There were two girls behind him, one in a pale green sleeveless dress coming down to her ankles and the other in a tight white sports bra and leggings. The man called to the driver while Gordon was getting out and the driver said something back. Gordon approached the club. The man on the chair grinned and nodded and waved him past, chairlegs beating his Loretta Bangkok Lynn time on the pavement. The two girls bobbed and pressed their hands together and bowed their heads and smiled and held out their fragile arms to the interior. Gordon went inside.

The scent he entered was thick, blurred and promising, dried whisky, oversweet perfume, cigarettes, grass, incense and a chemical palette to stop the lower forms of life multiplying without discouraging the higher ones: disinfectant, air freshener, incense, nail varnish, mothballs, mosquito coils, shampoo, roach syrup. Gordon couldn't make the music fit together, but he understood it was music. Short fanfares, repeated, like warning sirens that the place was about to explode, and a steady battering, a pneumatic drill in slow motion. It was good music. It put clothes on words that were best not spoken bare. It was a grand place, with a bar, and young Bangkokie lassies in short skirts and tight tops dancing with steel poles, and a few couples in the tables in the shadows, and ceiling fans two yards across.

A Bangkokite woman in a tight black dress and patent leather ankle boots left the bar and took Gordon's arm. She asked if he'd like a drink.

Aye, said Gordon. Scotch'd be very nice, Grouse if you have

it, with a fair measure of water. I can't stay long though, I'm on my way to the red light district.

Oh! said the woman, laughing. Funny. On your way!

Have you seen a man in a cream-coloured suit? Friend of mine? Mr Smith?

Mr Smith? Mr Smith! The woman pulled in her shoulders, leaned her head back and laughed, slapping Gordon gently on the chest. You're funny.

Was there one in a cream-coloured suit? Sly-looking?

If he comes, we take care of him. What's your name? Gordon. I'm Cindi. You not going to buy me a drink? Oh, very kind of you. Cheers! American? Ohhh!!! *Scot*land!!!!!!

Gordon drank. He asked how come the lassies were dancing with the poles. Were there not enough men in Bangkok.

You like them? said Cindi. She looked pleased. Which one you like? Tell me.

Gordon pointed to a girl in a checked pleated miniskirt and a denim jacket, open to show a black bra. She was wearing a silver wig.

Girl with silver hair? said Cindi. She's called Donna. Oh, she is very nice. You like her?

She's got a good arse, said Gordon.

Cindi went over to fetch Donna and left them. Gordon bought Donna a Coke. Donna had sprinkled glitter on her body. She smiled at him without saying anything, swivelling on one stiletto, and let the rim of the glass slide over her teeth. She started stroking Gordon's chest with her fingertips. Gordon stared down at her sparkling breasts. Donna looked up at Gordon from under her eyelashes and traced her fingernails over his crotch. She asked him if he wanted to fuck.

As long as it doesn't take too long, said Gordon. I'm trying to reach the red light district.

We be quick, said Donna. She took Gordon's hand and led him through a bead curtain to a narrow corridor with doors placed close together. In the corridor the light was red. This was how it should be. This was how life should be. When you just walked into a place and the lassies were available. You didn't have to go with them, you didn't have to buy them flowers, you didn't have to talk to them. There was nothing about love, clothes or children. When it was over, you walked away without saying anything. Heaven had to be along the lines of golf interspersed with bouts of oral sex.

Donna put her ear to one of the doors, tapped on it with a single knuckle and opened it. She led Gordon inside. The room had no windows and was lit by a dim yellow bulb in a scorched lampshade drooping from the wall. A fan on a stand scanned the room jerkily from a corner. There was a bed neither single nor double covered in a white sheet, a bedside cupboard, a wicker basket, a fridge, a plain wooden chair and a basin. A box of tissues waited on the cupboard. Gordon sat on the bed.

You want a beer? said Donna.

No, said Gordon.

You want a talk?

No.

It's good, said Donna, taking off her jacket. Oh, the moment.

Wait, said Gordon.

What?

Do that again.

OK, said Donna. She lifted the jacket off the chair where she'd draped it, put it on, and shucked it off, slower this time.

Again?

Gordon nodded.

Like a video, said Donna. Rewind!

Gordon watched her take off the jacket and put it on about

twenty times. Each time he saw her bare arms and shoulders emerge to frame her breasts it seemed new for an instant, and then lost forever.

Maybe that's enough now, said Donna.

No, said Gordon. Do it some more. I like it.

You want a make a video? We can make a video, said Donna.

Gordon shook his head. Donna did the jacket thing a dozen times more. Then she left it on the chair and came over to sit beside Gordon. Gordon stroked the place where her breasts met the stitching of her bra, where the flesh was squeezed a little. His fingers delved inside the fabric and his knuckles rubbed against her nipples. He tugged at the bra and Donna unfastened it behind with a rapid move of her wrist. Gordon covered her warm breasts with his hands. To see and feel perfect smooth skin between his mottled hands, where the white skin was scored and rumpled and ridged with veins. It was no more than he deserved, no less than he wanted, which was the same thing. He was deep, deep inside the club of men, rooms and corridors and doors and passwords and signs away from the breasts of Mary and from girls who wouldn't.

Donna pulled down his flies and rummaged for his cock. She fished it out, soft as an unbaked bap, and went down on it. Gordon stroked her bare back, lifted up her skirt, put his hand inside her panties and fingered her cleft.

Good lassie, he said. It's a shame you're an oriental cause you could teach the girls at home a few things about the right way to behave when it comes to their elders. Where I come from they keep the lassies at school too long and teach them not to touch men. Normal men, I'm talking about. It's no wonder the country's full of perverts and child molestors when the girls don't want to do the business with anyone over fifty. They end up with someone like my son.

Donna sat up, tossed back her hair, gave Gordon's fingers a hard clench, closed her eyes, moaned, smiled and began pulling off his ghost of a hard-on.

You have a son? she said. She kept panting and making moans all the while she talked. She was brilliant.

I do have a son, said Gordon. But he's a wanker.

What is that?

It means he's kind of disabled.

Oh! Donna shut her eyes and squeezed Gordon's fingers so tight he felt them go numb. She opened her eyes. Disabled. I am sorry for you. I know this. She relaxed her grip, stood up and let her skirt fall away. She began taking off Gordon's clothes. My family in Laos has same problem. Where we live American bombers came before I was born. Everywhere was bomb bomb bomb, and my mother, my father, they were small and hid in shelters. Then they marry and start having children. In whole village it's same. First child, it's me, OK. Second child very weak, dies after few weeks. Third child bit stronger, maybe few years. Fourth child disabled. My brother. Born – no arms, big head, like a melon. Hates the sun.

Aye, those bombers did an amazing job, right enough, said Gordon.

Father fixed that I come here and send money home to help my brother. And learn English. Think maybe when I'm fifteen I look for another job. Foreigners don't like it when we get old.

You want to watch out for foreigners, said Gordon. Bangkok's full of them.

Maybe they let me go next year when I'm fifteen. Maybe not. Depends on money. Few thousand dollars is enough.

You'd be better staying here, said Gordon. You get off with

all these men. Must be nice for you. Probably a tab behind the bar too, and your tea. Out there are all the young guys, that's the trouble. Then you get old.

I get tired, said Donna. Three, four, maybe six men a night. Some they don't treat me so well. Last night a foreigner, he was fat and hairy, like a big monkey, he was sick on back of my head while I had him in my mouth. Made me finish.

Donna laid naked Gordon down on the bed, took off her panties and straddled him. She began tugging at his cock again. Is it serious, if you are a wanker? she said. Is it like our problem in village? Your son got a big head?

Yes, said Gordon. He's got a big head all right. And this growth on his upper lip. And whenever you see him he's this purple colour.

Oh! said Donna, biting her lip and bending down to kiss Gordon's cock in sympathy, it's same with my brother. He lies on a bed in the back of the house, he can't move, his head is in a what, harness. Father wrote to say brother is blind now, head grown too big for eyes to see. He just lies there and listens. Sometimes he screams. Sometimes it's hard to keep the chickens off him. You getting nice and hard now. Donna fitted Gordon with a condom and eased herself onto him. She tossed her hair back, clamped his half-erection bravely with her inside muscles and began to toil.

Poor mister, said Donna, I do my best for you. Relax. I know you want to forget about your son for a few minutes. I know.

And my wife, said Gordon.

Oh! said Donna. Poor mister. Your wife as well! You a very good man. Your son a wanker, and your wife a wanker, and you look after them both. Donna's eyes became moist and she summoned all her skill. It took half an hour to bring Gordon to climax. Gordon smiled as he remembered how easy and right it was to be happy and victorious. He opened his eyes and gazed at Donna, the sweat and glitter shining on her little belly as the muscles there quivered with the sudden rest, her mouth open, her breasts rising and falling with her quick breathing. To think they could all be this way if they wanted, and happiness would be on tap.

OK? said Donna.

Gordon opened his mouth to say she was fine, and a good lassie, and he was ready to help her out again, although next time he'd like to try a different girl, maybe two together, when he felt the blade of a spear rise out of his stomach into his oesophagus and lodge there, radiating pain and suffocation. Mr McDonald's acid revenge clawed his chest and he slapped his breast with both hands, opening his mouth and drawing in deep draughts of air. His head spun.

It hurts, said Gordon, screwing up his eyes.

What's wrong? said Donna, dismounting and putting her hand on his forehead. You OK?

My heart, said Gordon. I need Gaviscon.

Oh, mister, don't do this, said Donna. Don't have a heart attack, please, mister. Already lost one that way and they don't pay me for two months afterwards.

Gaviscon, said Gordon. The heart. McDonald's.

Gaviscon not here. That your son? Don't worry. You be OK. Oh dear, mister. I go and call ambulance. Why they come here, fat and old and not used to the heat, I don't know. Donna ran out of the room.

Heartburn, said Gordon. The second quarterpounder must've landed on its side. Should've had a third one for a solid foundation. Another grappling hook landed in his chest. Maybe it wasn't the burgers, maybe it was the smell of the Bangkokian cooking.

Wrapping itself into the beef as it sizzled, invisibly foreign, an acid bomb. Drops of Gaviscon'd fix it. Ayah.

Donna came in with Cindi and they talked to each other very fast in Bangkokish. +++ ++++ ++++ ++ disabled +++ ++ ++++ +++ ++++ +++ Gaviscon ++++++ McDonald ++++ + +++ +++, said Donna.

Cindi shook her head. She was angry. +++ ++ ++++ ++ +++ + +++ + dollars + ++ ++++ + + +++ McDonald + +++ ++ +++++ ++ +++ Scotland, she said.

The two women dressed Gordon roughly. Cindi took Gordon's pulse and peered into his eye. Gordon looked back at her eye. Cindi smiled. How you feeling, sir? she said.

Fine, said Gordon. Heartburn. Quarterpounders. Gaviscon'd sort it out.

Cindi stroked Gordon's forehead and smiled. She shook her head. Gaviscon isn't here, she said. He's at home in Scotland. Don't worry. We see you back to your hotel. You be fine. Take it easy. You use too much energy. Maybe next time older girl for you.

++++ ++ +++ ++, said Donna. Cindi turned to her and shouted something.

The ambulance came. They made Gordon lie on a stretcher, carried him into the back of the van and laid him down on a bunk. A doctor was sitting opposite. He asked Gordon if he had any insurance.

Gordon sat up. I'm fine, he said. Heartburn, it was. If you had some Gaviscon that'd be all I need. He looked out of the back window. The ambulance was moving. Cindi and Donna were standing outside the club. The two of them began pushing and shoving each other. The guy sitting on the chair got up and hit Donna across the face, grabbed her by the arm and started dragging her back inside the bar. Cindi came behind, kicking the two of them in the leg in turns with her steep stilettos. It was cool inside the ambulance. The heartburn had passed. Gordon lay down on the stretcher, yawned, pulled a blanket over himself, rolled onto his side and went to sleep.

The hotel was on night regime when they dropped him off. A single receptionist on the desk, the piano shut up, the bar deserted, no policeman to open doors for him. Gordon went to Smithie's room. He'd hung his Do Not Disturb chit on the doorknob. Gordon would disturb him. He needed disturbing. He needed a hammering for leaving Gordon on his own. Only Gordon couldn't do that. He couldn't hit Smithie, cause Smithie was not to be hit. He was too close. It'd be like punching your own chin. It'd be like mugging yourself. Gordon'd left things with Smithie over the years, piled them up cause there was lots of space there, and never thought about getting them back cause he could always get them if he wanted and he never did, and now. Now what. He couldn't get them back. He couldn't even remember what they were.

Gordon knocked gently on the door with one knuckle and waited. Smithie, he said. Smithie. He pressed his ear to the cool slippery hardwood. Listening to the silence he looked towards the doorjamb and saw a line of darkness along its length, quarter of an inch wide. He touched it with his fingers. It was space. He placed his palm on the centre of the door and pushed. The half-sprung tongue of the lock snapped out and the door swung inwards. Gordon padded forward, his feet whispering over the carpet, into the lurking area between the bathroom and the wardrobe. The door closed behind him. He stopped, put his hand on the wall, and put his head round the corner to look into the body of the room. A little light leaked in from the moon around the edges of the curtain and from the bottom of the door. There was a figure lying on the bed.

Smithie, said Gordon quietly. He stepped forward into the

room, found a light switch and turned it on. Dark eyes blinked and stared at him, bright and deepseeing and afraid, the eyes of a fierce maternal being uncovered on a nest, with itself and something else to protect. The boy was awake and Smithie was asleep, his white belly lazily belted by the boy's skinny brown arms. They were naked, the sheet rolled and shifted into a lyre shape around them. Smithie was smiling. His hands were clasped together against his chest. He whimpered in his sleep, passed one hand clumsily across his face, like a cat moistening its paw, and wriggled his toes. The boy stared into Gordon's eyes.

It wasn't right of Smithie to kit himself out with something Gordon didn't want and still not offer Gordon a shot. Double treachery, he didn't want a boy and he hadn't been offered a boy. It was wrong. It was against the rules of the club of men. The club of boys was different. Two boys could lie naked in the grass by the river in the sun, chest to chest, cock to cock, thigh in thigh. Two boys had. When they grew into the club of men, the situation changed. They stuck together, they helped each other out, they shared the lassies. Or they could try not to. That wasn't on, but it wasn't against the rules. This was Smithie in a different club altogether, and Gordon wanted to go in and see him and talk to him about getting off with the Bangkokian lassie, he just wanted to talk to Smithie, he just wanted to be with Smithie for a bit, and he could go in if he wanted, but he was fucked if he was going in that place, and Smithie knew he wouldn't go in, and he went in anyway.

Gordon beckoned to the boy. The boy stared, blinking, not moving. Gordon took out his wad of notes, thumbed it loose and waved it. He tapped it with one finger and pointed to the boy. The boy stared. Then he slid his arms off Smithie, sat up and put on his shorts and teeshirt. He reached down behind the bed and fetched a shoebox marked with the Nike swoosh. He took a pair of new white trainers out of their tissue paper, put them on his bare feet and began lacing them up. It took him five minutes before he was ready to follow Gordon out of the room. Gordon swept out of the hotel with the boy trotting to keep up. Gordon asked his name.

Billy, said the boy.

I knew a Billy, said Gordon. He was a solicitor. Or maybe it was General Accident he was working for. Or was it not the Billy that had the restraining order put on him for drinking the rainwater from his ex-wife's guttering? D'you remember that? That wasn't you, was it?

No, said Billy. I'm from Khon Kaen province.

Oh, said Gordon. Is there a lot of arse banditry in those parts?

Don't know, said Billy.

If I was your father, I'd throw you out on the street.

No father. Mother throw me out.

Gordon led into less bright streets, the lamps further apart and feebler, single fast cars, a pedal rickshaw and a motor trike with two old women in the back dressed in European mourning black. The road was lined with shops selling Buddhas of all sizes and colours, but mainly gold. Failure glimmered in ten thousand gilt faces behind security grilles, where the artisans had tried to render the Buddha serene, and had only made him smug. Billy began to lag and yawn.

You a friend of Cedric? said Billy, running up to Gordon. He's kind man. I like him. He tries not to hurt me too much. Do you know a place where we can go?

Your laces are undone, said Gordon. He knelt down. Here. Did no-one ever teach you to tie a proper bow?

No.

At 4-U-2 Knight Klub they were nervous and suspicious when Gordon appeared, then relieved. They asked if he was OK, said they didn't want trouble, told him to be careful. Cindi nodded and smiled and let Donna go with him. But this time, she said, and rubbed her thumb against her fingers. You understand?

The three of them sat in the back, Gordon in the middle. They cruised the city for an hour. The children fell asleep with their foreheads against the windows. Gordon rested his hand on Donna's knee. He found a pulse there. He couldn't tell if it was hers or his own but the beat matched the pace of the broken white lines being eaten by the taxi as it wound the night road in. He woke the children at a coffee bar at the foot of a motorway ramp and took them inside. He bought them ice cream. Billy stroked his with the bowl of his spoon and wrote a sign on it with the tip. He asked for a whisky and Gordon ordered him one. The waiter crimped his lips when he brought it and placed it down slowly, looking at Gordon with eyes of stone. Donna, her jacket buttoned up to her neck, ate her ice cream fast, scraping tracks in the oozy remnants on the walls of the glass. She asked for another one. Billy pushed his over to her. They began to speak to each other quietly, not looking at each other, with quick low glances. Donna smiled and laughed once. Billy hung tough, forearms flat on the table, taking his drink in a couple of gulps.

Gordon looked out the window at the cars accelerating up the ramp. He turned to the children. How could Smithie go for the scrawny laddie and not a lassie the like of Donna, who was so bonny? Had the wee pervert put something in his drink?

You're a wicked wee lad, said Gordon. You can't be fourteen and you're away corrupting a respectable Scottish businessman, getting his morals all arse over tit, making him think it's fine to be in bed with you and God knows what else.

He paid me, said Billy. He said I was the best thing happened to him ever. He's good. He wants to adopt me. I think maybe I should go back now.

Look at Donna, said Gordon. She's the same age as you, and she's lovely, and she knows the right way to behave.

Billy shrugged and looked at Donna. He grinned.

She does, said Gordon. She respects her elders and betters. She knows how to treat us. She behaves beautifully and, when she's a bit older, she – when she's older – ah, for Christ's sake, Donna, don't get old, don't do it, avoid it any way you can, it's terrible what happens. And you, you boy, you'd don't know your place at all. You don't have a place. You're a mockery. Smithie, right, he's my pal, we go back, way back, we're one, and we came here for the girls, and there'll be no boys in his bed, there'll be no boys in his time, no boys anywhere near him. I was a boy when he was a boy, we were boys together, and we did all the things together that boys do together, and now we're men together, we're in the club of men, and we're busy with Donna, and you're out, and Mary's out, and Kenneth's out, and all the poofs and fascists and niggers and chinks and cunts from the schemes are out in the heat and the rain and me and Smithie, we're in there, we're in there, we're in there in the cool with Donna, you fucking wee princess, eh.

Donna was biting her lip. She had her hands folded tightly in her lap and was staring into the ice cream bowls. Billy fidgeted with his empty glass.

You know something, he said. Me and Mr Smith, we met last year. We spent two weeks together on Ko Samui. Together all time, every day.

Gordon turned away to watch the cars accelerating up the

ramp. They were fast, right enough, and the cars got sleeker as the night went on, swifter and sharper in the nose.

Maybe you want watch, said Donna.

Eh? said Gordon.

Maybe you want watch. Donna nodded at Billy and tapped her finger on her chest.

Gordon shook his head. He put his hand in his pocket and put a wad of hundred dollar bills on the table.

Here's 3,000 dollars, he said. He flicked through a corner of the wad to confirm its thickness. Let's have a race instead. You're both young and fast. See that road out there? Over there, on the far side, there's a Coke can. D'you see it? Just lying there on its side against the barrier.

Donna and Billy were looking at it.

This is what we're going to do. You two stand at the side of the road, and when I say the word, you run to try to get the Coke can. Whoever brings it back first gets the 3,000 dollars.

For a while they stared at the notes, unbending from the fold like wings from a chrysalis. Then Gordon lifted the money and got up. He paid the bill and the children followed him out into the night, to the edge of the road.

The ramp was straight and three lanes wide and the cars were coming up it at about seventy, increasing speed as they kicked off the confining city streets for the fast highways. They passed Gordon and the children in a hiss and a blur, leaving the flavour of concussion.

The children began talking to each other in Bangkokian, Donna first, quietly, persuading, looking down at the ground but turning her head in his direction, the boy replying with single words, not listening. He shook his arms out, trod in his Nikes, untied and retied the laces, took deep breaths and spat in the gutter.

Hey, said Gordon. No divvying up in advance. There's only going to be the one winner.

Donna looked at him with her eyes narrowed and her mouth full of molten words, burning but to be kept inside for money, and made her tongue lie still to receive and keep the scars. She took off her shoes and laid them side by side on the pavement, toes outward. It made her smaller by two inches. She pinched her bra straps under the jacket, worked her shoulders and nodded at Gordon.

OK, she said.

On your marks, said Gordon. When I clap my hands and shout. Down the ramp there were four sets of headlights, one coming up fast and close on the far lane, two further away on the centre and near lane, roughtly parallel. The far lane lights belonged to a Toyota minibus, the others were a Nissan saloon and a Mitsubishi off-roader. There was something else behind the Toyota, something massive, but Gordon couldn't make it out. There weren't more than six yards to the far side of the road but they'd have to get up to speed first. The Toyota was closing at a good lick. It was a truck close behind. Gordon raised his hands, brought them hard together and yelled: Go! Billy was off his blocks like a born sprinter, he was going straight to the target. Donna was off sharp too, a grunt of effort as her bare sole connected with the warm tarmac of the road, but she was too conscious of the cars coming towards them, she was running at a slant. Billy ran true towards the Coke can, drawing hornblasts from the Mitsubishi and the Nissan as he passed in front of them. The Toyota had no time for a horn. As Billy's foot entered the edge of the far lane, the Toyota was passing ahead of him. Billy's body flew past the back of the Toyota, through the narrow seventy mile an hour space between the minibus and the truck. The space he jumped through was so brief that his left side was lit red by the Toyota's rear lights and his right side turned white in the full-beam blaze of the truck. He was there, he was at the can, reaching for it. Donna'd been beaten. She'd crossed the Mitsubishi and the Nissan fast, with her legs longer than Billy's, but she ran at a risky diagonal. Her slanting track took her to the edge of the far lane with the Toyota already passed and Billy ahead and to her right, disappearing between the Toyota and the truck. Donna looked like she was about to follow but she'd lost momentum and the instant passed and she was left shrinking, eyes closed, legs pressed together and arms hugging her body while the truck passed inches from her face. When the truck was gone she ran towards Billy and lunged for the Coke can he was holding high in the air. Billy laughed and held it out of reach. Donna took his arm and tried to use her weight to topple him. Gordon started cheering Donna on. He yelled at her to kick Billy in the balls. Donna pincered Billy's legs in her own and gripped his hand with hers, prising his fingers off the can. Billy punched her in the chest with his free hand and Donna staggered back, winded. She dropped to her knees, head down. Billy stood for a moment looking at her. He wiped his nose with the back of his hand, spat, hitched his shorts and walked back towards Gordon with the can.

Jammy wee runt, said Gordon.

Billy stopped in the middle of the centre lane. He watched Gordon. He looked into Gordon's eyes. He smiled.

I win anyway, he said.

He turned round and called to Donna in Bangkokian. Donna stood up. Billy threw the can to Donna and she caught it. Billy grinned and clapped his hands above his head.

Billy, said Gordon, pointing. Laces.

Billy looked down at the white cords streaming behind his trainers and frowned. He knelt down and began tying them, looking over to check the next rush of cars coming towards him after the lull. Donna ran back to Gordon, gave him the can and put her shoes back on. She took the money from him and started to count it.

Billy was having trouble with his laces. He'd managed one bow but the second was tougher. The cars were closing. Billy looked at the growing lights and carefully went about untangling a granny knot and retying the second lace. Gordon scratched his chin and folded his arms. The centre lane car, a Landcruiser, was a few heartbeats away and it hadn't seen the boy hunkered down on the tarmac. Billy finished the second bow, stood up, turned his head into the lights, grinned at Gordon and launched himself towards safety, millisecond perfect, the timing of a star. When he began the sprint the ornate flower of the first bow burst silently and his foot slid half out of the trainer. Billy lost his balance and twisted round but was struck by the bull bars of the Landcruiser before he could fall. The blow rang dull in the hollow of Billy's chest over the roar of the car horn and the tearing of the tyres against the road. The boy's body broke and burst inside on impact, he spun up and over the bonnet, hit the corner of the roof and bounced away, falling on to the ground shoulder down, dislocated limbs laid out butcher-flat on the grey hardtop. The car didn't stop.

At the sound of the collision Donna looked up from counting her money and drew in breath as if she had been stabbed. She cried out in Bangkokese and ran in clipped stiletto steps to Billy's body. She knelt down and put her hand on his forehead. She looked at Gordon.

Hey, said Gordon. Get off the road. You might get hurt.

Billy's dead, said Donna.

Ach, he'll be fine, leave him alone. There's cars coming.

He's dead! said Donna.

Clicking his tongue Gordon marched over to the boy, took him under the armpits and dragged him to the pavement. A bubble of blood sealing Billy's half-open mouth burst and more of it flowed from the corner, risking Gordon's polo shirt, and you could be sure you'd pay dearly for getting the hotel to tackle that kind of difficult stain. The boy's arms waggled in their elbow sockets as they swung. Gordon propped him up against the barrier. Donna toreadored a bus, skidding on her heels, to get Billy's lost Nike, which had come off his foot and sat still pure white, coolly sole down, toes to the motorway, in the middle of the ramp. She handled the shoe like something unclean, holding it from her between thumb and forefinger, but put it carefully back onto the boy's bare foot and tied it properly.

You know him? Donna said.

Gordon shrugged.

Maybe he has family.

No idea.

His real name was Vatha, said Donna. You should go. Maybe police won't like it.

Come on, then, said Gordon.

Donna was squatting next to Vatha, stroking his forehead and cheek with the back of her fingers, brushing the hair back. He let me win, she said. He gave me the money.

I gave you the money, said Gordon.

He wanted to win. After he won he wanted to make you angry. He didn't like you.

I didn't care for him.

Why do foreign men hate us?

I'm not foreign, said Gordon. I'm from Scotland.

Why do you hate us?

Hate. Gordon tasted the word. Hate was what you put between you and the enemy. Hate was a tricky business though and Gordon could never abide tricky businesses. 'Cause there were so many enemies out to get you and you couldn't be hating them all the time because you needed them for so many things; like sex and meals and drinking with. Hate was what you went for when they were about to turn on you and there was nowhere you could hide.

I think, said Donna, when you come so far, you fly so many thousand miles to come and fuck us, and then you fly straight back again, you must really hate us.

Well, we pay.

Donna took out the wad of dollars and flexed it between her fingers. I must burn them, she said. I should burn your dollars. But I need them.

She looked up at Gordon. You should go, she said.

I'll take you back to your club.

Donna shook her head. Go now, she said. Gordon walked away. At the foot of the ramp he looked back. She'd gone, and the corpse of Smithie's boy sat alone at the barrier.

In the morning Gordon waited for Smithie to find him at breakfast. He sat at a table under an umbrella by the pool and got coffee and toast and butter near-liquid in the heat. They brought a bowl of fresh pineapple, banana and mango. Gordon pushed it to one side. Smithie came seeking towards the pool in swimming shorts, flip flops and a tee-shirt, saw Gordon and slowly, stiff from the night, sat down opposite. He hadn't shaved and his eyes were red. He rubbed his eyes with the heels of his hands and looked round, blinking.

Came looking for you last night, said Gordon.

I know, I'm sorry, got lost, said Smithie.

Gordon took a bite of toast and offered some to Smithie.

No, I'll just have a coffee Gordon, said Smithie. What did you get up to?

You missed yourself, said Gordon. Picked up this lovely young lassie in a bar – have you lost something? – and gave her a real seeing to. Didn't even have to pay. How come you keep looking round?

It's nothing, said Smithie.

If you're looking for your laddie, he's dead. He got run over last night.

Billy?

Aye.

Smithie stared at Gordon chewing toast. Smithie's eyes filmed over, his mouth trembled, his nostrils flared and the tears came. His shoulders shook and he was biting his lip to stop the sobs coming out. Teardrops swung on his chin and fell on his belly. Nice in the heat. Good if you could switch the tears on when it was too hot, rinse down your face, clean it and cool it at the same time, as long as you had something to wipe it off with. Gordon couldn't switch on the tears. In fact the tear device went faulty a long time ago. It didn't work at all and sometimes his eyes itched with the dryness. Ach, you put up with it.

A waiter came and asked Smithie if he'd like any breakfast. Smithie turned to him, held it back for a moment, shook his head, said no thanks and broke again, squeezing his eyes shut, shaking his head and letting the sound of his misery out in bellows of sound. How do you know? he said to Gordon.

I saw. I came into your room last night and the boy came with me. We went for a walk. He was hit by a car. A bloody great Landcruiser with bull bars on the front.

Where is he?

I don't know, said Gordon. Didn't you pick him up on the street?

Yes.

Well, that's where I left him.

Smithie lifted his tearblind head. I loved him. I know it was wrong. He was so kind to me.

You had to pay him.

I loved him. I loved him. He didn't have any money. I didn't care. I know it was wrong. I wanted to take him home. I was going to adopt him.

You've got to go for a lassie, said Gordon. You're a man and that's what we need. Forget the wee poof and we'll go to that bar together tonight. You can't be dipping your wick in boys. You'd be right out of Rotary for a start, and I'm not even talking about the Lodge. You've got to put the perversion out of your mind with a 14-year-old girl. They're lovely and cheap and gagging for it.

I can't help it. I loved him. I think he loved me. He left his sandals behind in my room.

Loved. What they believed in now instead of whatever it was before, the gods who never turned up. Mary had an interest in other people's love, star love and royal love and children love, but'd had the sense not to try to convert Gordon, who didn't require it. He had the pal, Smithie, and now a place they could practise together the thing they didn't get enough of at home, didn't get any of at home, sex with young girls. They always had their own corner in the club of men, you just went in and you got shown to your seat, opposite Smithie's seat. Smithie just needed a wee bit of help with the membership committee and he'd be fine.

So what d'you fancy doing for lunch? said Gordon.

Smithie went on weeping and shaking and nodding his head. He whispered: I want Billy.

No you don't.

I do. I loved him.

Gordon wrinkled his nose and fidgeted with the bowl of fruit. He said: Sweltering, eh, right enough.

It's Thailand, whispered Smithie.

Oh, said Gordon. Is that where this is. It's good because the other folk, they can't spell cock, can they?

I'm going to find him. Maybe he didn't die.

See those tears, said Gordon. Are they actually cooling you down?

Smithie took a napkin from the table and wiped his face dry. He looked at Gordon with an expression Gordon hadn't seen before, like a rogue bouncer smitten by the revelation that the thing to do is not to stop them getting into the club but to stop them getting out.

Smithie got up. I'm leaving, he said. Make your own way home. Goodbye, Gordon.

Northern Soul

Gordon finished his story and struck the optic with his glass to win another whisky. The bottle was empty. Out there beyond the bar it was no longer possible to tell where the bonfire ended and the dance floor began. The flames snapped at the varnished wood, mottled dark with heelprints. Cankerous rises of black smoke confounded the lasers. The beautiful giant walked through the smoke, coughing, Gordon's gun in one hand and a stack of vinyl in the other. She laid the records down carefully and moved towards Gordon, pointing the gun at him. There was a sound of horns, trumpets and a thumping bass line.

That's my gun, said Gordon.

Come out from there, said Sheena the Northern Soul Monster, grabbing him by the collar and hoisting him into the air. She boosted him into an arc and he flew over the bar, into the fire. He landed on his side, on a spar of charred barstool leg, felt the pain of the impact bark through his ribs and understood that the bright spirits which ran to dance on his jumper were flames. He cried out and rolled away, smothering the burning wool, and crawled to the foot of the bar. He sat there with his back against it and started to taste the agony of his burns with his skin.

Give me the gun back, said Gordon. Leave me alone. I'm an

old man. He looked up at the girl's legs rising high above him, smooth and honey coloured, scattered with tiny golden hairs. If only she was Gordon's size. She was too young to have such beauty and such strength to control men older and wiser and more desperate than she was. He reached out his fingers to touch her and Sheena kicked him in the kidneys hard enough to flip him over. He lay on his back on the ground, knees up, hands protecting his face, keeking through his fingers at the giant's face far above him, haloed with smoke. Closer, the nostrils of the shotgun quivered, pointed at his head.

Careful, hen, he said. I've seen that gun do terrible things to beasts today.

I let you join my club, said Sheena's deep distant voice, and I explained the rules to you. There were only three of them, and you broke one. The last one.

I'm a guest, said Gordon, and a pensioner.

Everyone's a guest, said Sheena. Some leave of their own accord and some get asked to leave.

I'll go. Your club's burning.

Clubs don't burn. Only venues burn.

I've got friends.

You're lying. You haven't got any friends.

How did she know? She knew. Who'd told her? The giant had clearly been at the centre of it all along, the only question being how she'd kept herself hidden. She was working with the wife-creature and the son-creature, she was working in Gordon's mind to blur the names of things, she was, hardest to bear, it was scooping him out inside, she was the prize disguised as Julie and Donna, the youngness girldom he'd only wanted to press his erect fear inside, and all the while the young girls had been powerful giants.

With the boy it was an accident, he said. Cocky wee chap.

You made it happen, said Sheena. Now I'm going to make it happen. She pulled the hammers back on the shotgun.

She started lifting the gun to her shoulder. As it rose it moved more slowly, and froze midway. The giant was swaying. She had a coughing fit. Her eyes shut in the smoke. Water streamed from them. She dropped the gun and fainted, falling straight to the floor without bending, like a tree. The building trembled.

The fire was spreading handily. The way Gordon came in was blocked. Curtains of smoke furled up the walls. His throat was stinging and from the far end of the room he began to hear an intermittent roar, like gusts of wind.

He dragged the giant over to the floor by the bar, furthest from the flames, and fetched the bag from the garden centre. He put on the baseball cap saying Team Bosch, took out the power drill, selected the fattest bit, locked it and plugged the tool into a socket at the foot of the bar. He pulled the trigger. The device throbbed with possibility. Could've made some fantastic holes with that. Could've spent a whole day experimenting with walls and doors and fruit. Gordon shook his head, clicking his tongue, knelt on the floor and drilled a clean, perfect hole through it. He made a series of holes, in a rough oval shape. He unplugged the drill and reached for the second tool, the one with forty different attachments. He sighed over the sanders, screwdrivers and polishers, but was stuck in the circumstances with the narrow-bladed saw. He poked the saw through one of the holes he'd made and began to cut the floor away. It was hard with the crossbeams but when he'd finished there was a gap in the floorboards easily big enough to drop through. He drilled and cut away the ceiling of the room below, kicked through the clinging petals of plaster, and looked down into cool darkness. The fire roared louder as it found a fresh source of oxygen and a sucking breeze blew over his head.

C'mon hen, he said, and tucked Sheena's feet and calves through the gap. Going round to her head end, he pushed to make her slide through the hole, but her thighs were coming in at the wrong angle. She wasn't bending at the trunk. Coughing now like an asthmatic, Gordon pushed his arms in under Sheena's bum and tried to lift. Still her legs wouldn't straighten. The lights went out, the music died, and the only illumination was the flames. Gordon lifted again and gave a sideways shove to the body. Sheena's thighs dropped clear of the edge of the hole. Gordon pushed gently from the shoulders, and her body began to slide, until gravity snatched her through the sawn-off floorboards and dropped her, with an impact which snapped burnt-through rafters over the dancefloor, on to whatever surface lay below.

Gordon looked down through the hole. He couldn't see or hear anything. It was troubling. If her body had hit the floor wrongly, it wouldn't be in the right place to break his fall.

It was getting hard to breathe. Gordon let his feet dangle over the edge and pushed himself off. In the moments of falling he guessed many times when the ground would begin. His feet thudded into yielding flesh, his knees folded and he toppled. He'd come down on the back of Sheena's thighs. It wasn't the softest of landings, but better than bare floorboards. The girl didn't move or make a sound. He got up. There was a faint light shining through the hole in the ceiling from the fire upstairs. They were in a wood-panelled function room, with a small low stage and chairs stacked to one side. Gordon squatted down and shook Sheena by the shoulder.

Hey, he said. I don't know the way out of here. He put his head close to her face. The giant was lying on her front. There was a blood-smeared cut on her forehead. Gordon listened at her mouth. She was still breathing. He felt her breath on his ear. He shook her again.

His eyes were getting used to the light, and the light was getting brighter. He could see red gleaming through cracks in the ceiling. On the opposite side of the room from the stage, there was a door. Gordon ran over to it and turned the handle. The door was unlocked. He opened it. You beauty. A short stretch of unburned corridor, with a couple of emergency lights glowing, and further on what looked like a set of steps leading down. Bit of a flicker of something hot up ahead, but couldn't be as bad as what was upstairs. He was out and away.

He glanced back at the girl, lying where she'd fallen through the ceiling. He clapped his hands together. He shouted at her to wake up. She didn't move. That was what the drugs and the music did to you, sure enough, and what had it been like with the boy Kenneth, trying to get him up in the morning after his late nights out. That generation had no sense of urgency. And with the bonfire out of control: irresponsible.

Lie there if you like, he called. It's your lookout.

He moved off along the corridor and down the stairs. He'd trodden a few steps when a scrabbling, booming sound rose up the stairwell, like a dumper truck tipping stones. He could feel heat on his face, and when he reached the first landing, he could see there were flames ahead. Another flight of stairs took him to a hallway where the ceiling had partially collapsed. The floor was covered in lumps of plaster and ash. Broken lengths of roofbeam, inadequately secured by Victorian builders and weakened by generations of feasting, rallying and dancing, sagged from the ceiling, splintered ends burning with an abundance of fresh yellow fire, ready to droop and make a wick of Gordon's scalp.

He'd always loved fire. Fire was the perfect child. There was no bad fire, there was fire or there was no fire, and if you made fire, it took a moment, and you stood back and watched while it made itself perfect in its own fashion. It destroyed anything without the wit to get out of its way, and stayed perfect, whatever it destroyed. It didn't need help. If you fed it, it grew, still perfect but bigger, and if you stopped feeding it, it died, without complaint. Only this fire, now, even though he'd made it, frightened him. It was the consequence he should never have had to meet, the great-great-grandchild of the fire he'd made, a generation of fire gone bad, feeding by itself for itself and careless of feeding on its first father.

There'd been no days before without fear, but this wasn't the old fear, the fear of the fascists, traitors, poofs, Pakis, cunts, policemen, assassins, priests, tax-gatherers, children, foreigners, women, false friends, mockers, jokers, wives, smart-arses and spies who crowded the places where Gordon was forced to live, all the ones who were out to rob, cheat and humiliate him, the ones he could comfort himself with the hating of, the ones who wanted to keep him from the prizes he deserved. This was the new fear, the one that up till now had lived inside him, and had no name or shape, and was all the more terrible for it. Now he saw it in the offspring of his fire, a thing without mercy he couldn't have the relief of hating because it was perfect, it was only there to consume, and you could hate it or love it, it didn't matter, it didn't feel, it burned on all the same.

To run the gauntlet without death by fire what was needed was a shield, some thick, insulating object Gordon could carry over his head for protection while he charged down the corridor.

He went back to the darkness of the function room, now filling with smoke, and knelt by Sheena. Over the stormsong of the fire upstairs he could hear the ceiling creak.

Still sleeping it off, eh, he said, and started coughing. He put the back of his hand against the girl's mouth. There was a little breath. He shook her. No response. He flipped her over so she was face up, took hold of her wrists and dragged her out of the room and along the corridor. Even with the floor supporting her arse and legs the weight was incredible. He pulled her downstairs, knocking the back of her head against the edge of the steps a few times, and laid her out at the threshold of the burning hallway. His heart was trying to bounce out through his ribs, his armpits were sodden with sweat, and each time he tried to draw in air the back of his throat and his nose stung like they'd been flayed. He coughed, piercing, whole body coughs, and each cough gathered all the strands of his back muscles into one rope of pain, and yanked it.

Sheena moaned and moved.

Don't you go waking up now, said Gordon. God, the self-ishness of the lassie, and him an old man.

The distance down the hallway was about thirty yards. Gordon lined Sheena up so her head was facing the fire. He squatted down with his back to her and reached for her upper arms. They were too big for his hands to span. He had to hook them. He puffed a bit like the weightlifters did, coughed, and hoisted the body up so that Sheena's upper body lay on his shoulders, with her shoulders covering the back of his head and her head hanging down in front of him. He looked straight ahead. A tunnel of fire, like for police dogs and stunt cyclists, who had it easy, 'cause you never saw a dog carrying one of the cyclists on his back when it was jumping through the hoops, did you?

Gordon drew in a long, slow, deep breath. He screamed, jerked himself and the immensity of Sheena upright, and hob-bled forward under the burning beams. Twice her shoulder was scraped by a trailing brand, but Gordon was unharmed. His momentum carried him through a doorway at the far end of the hallway, down a carpeted ramp and on to the floor at the feet of two masked-up firemen.

That's a big lassie, said one of the firemen. She must weigh a ton.

The old boy's a hero, said the other. See the way he came tanking out of that collapsing structure? Like Carl fucking Lewis with a rocket up his arse. Sir! Take it easy, sir, we'll get you some help. You're a hero.

They stretchered Gordon out through the Waterland foyer into the clean cold air and the rain of the night. They laid him down on a field of hoses in a half-circle of fire engines, told him the paramedics would be arriving shortly and called for the keyholder, who had sworn there was no-one in the building.

Gordon stared into the sky and blinked as the rain, glittering blue in the fire engine lights, fell on his face. He heard footsteps scraping the tarmac close by and a wing of black fabric flapped and went taut over him. His brother's narrow deepset eyes appeared under the umbrella.

Bruce.

Gordon. How you feeling?

Fine.

I don't think so.

Lost my gun. Thought you were suspended.

They're short-handed tonight. I'm here incognito. I'm the generic detective.

Seen Charlie Sturrock? He was supposed to bring baking-tatties for the bonfire.

Once we've charged the keyholder with setting a fire, we'll check out the tattie situation, don't worry.

It was my fire, said Gordon.

Don't say that.

Ask him about Catherine wheels.

Don't say it was your fire. It was Charlie's fire, OK? Bruce put a cigarette in his mouth, and took it out. The girl's got nasty burns on her back, probable skull and leg fractures and a bad case of smoke inhalation. She's going to be fine. So that makes you an official hero. That's the good news. The bad news is that Kenneth's been remanded in custody over that incident with the boys. He was a bit bolshie in the cells, and he fell and cut himself. I can't see him getting bail.

You do what you think's best, said Gordon.

Don't like to see my own nephew banged up, of course.

Gordon laughed. Bruce joined in. You should have seen his face when I came in twirling the nightstick, he said. So for kicks, I say: Assume the position! And he goes down on the floor and curls up, hands over his head. I say: Not the fetal position! But he wouldn't get up. Just kept banging against my toecap with his ribs.

He'll learn.

Of course he will. Make a man of him. Or something. What can you do when the army's given up the job?

It was my fire.

Gordon! Bruce leaned over his brother's face. I told you not to say that. Listen, some more bad news. Mary's been taken into the Royal Ed. We didn't have a choice. After we took Kenneth away the second time she turned up at the station in her karate pyjamas, striking martial arts poses at the desk sergeant. She wouldn't be told.

Mm, said Gordon.

Sure they'll let her out soon enough. You don't want to be cooking your own meals.

Aye, said Gordon. What about Smithie?

He's dead, Gordon.

Oh aye. The two brothers said nothing for a few moments. Bruce lit his cigarette. The flame of the detective's lighter appeared for a fraction of a second before Gordon went blind. The world turned black.

Gordon, he heard Bruce saying. What's the matter?

I've gone blind.

You've got your hands over your eyes. Bruce pulled Gordon's fingers away and the world reappeared. Bruce flicked the lighter again. Blind.

Hn, grunted Bruce, making Gordon see again. He waved the lighter a few times in Gordon's face and watched with interest as his brother slapped his hands violently over his eyes, then twisted his head away from the flame.

It was my fire, said Gordon. It turned on me. It was fucking horrible.

Gordon, Gordon, said Bruce, waving the lighter to and fro across his brother's face, noting that, when the flame was very close, he not only covered his eyes, but began to whimper. Gordon, are you afraid of fire? That's not good. Only animals are afraid of fire. Can you hear me? I said only animals are afraid of fire.